ExTraS

Liminal Books

Between the Lines Publishing
1769 Lexington Ave N, Ste 286
Roseville MN 55113
btwnthelines.com

First Published: April 2025

ISBN (Paperback): 978-1-965059-42-5

ISBN (eBook): 978-1-965059-43-2

Library of Congress Control Number: 2025933766

Liminal Books is an imprint of Between the Lines Publishing. The Liminal Books name and logo are trademarks of Between the Lines Publishing.

The publisher is not responsible for websites (or their content) that are not owned by the publisher.

Printed in the United States

EXTRAS

Dan Yokum

To all those who struggle to understand our world,
and to Henry who showed us the way

Jade

Most humans cannot recall when they were baptized in their infancy. However, our group was different, and some members did claim to remember their own event: the colorful lights flowing down from above, then wrapping warmly around them before entering the human bodies. My first memory of a baptism was that of my two-day-old brother when I was four. I don't know how many attended, but in later years when I was old enough to count higher, usually at least twenty-five and sometimes fifty or more participated. The ceremonies always began on what was called the outside plaza. It was about half-acre in size and made mostly of stone, with wide flat pieces on the earth and chunky cubes hacked out of granite boulders surrounding it. It mimicked much larger sites found in the Andes or perhaps Mexico.

On the day of my brother's baptism, our group slowly entered the plaza as a uniform line and formed a circle in the center. The only one of us holding something was my mother who had my tiny brother in her arms. At first, we chanted sounds in some incomprehensible language: moans, clicks, screeches, and atonal cadences. Then my

1

mother stepped into the center, held her baby out in front of her as an offering, and said in English, "We are ready for you now."

The next moment is what fixed itself in my memory. I had seen it all before. However, this time, because it was for my brother, its sights, sounds, feelings—even smells—burrowed deep and nestled inside me forever, sometimes vividly remembered, other times mostly forgotten, yet always still there. The bands of vertical light, long and thin, came into focus, and swayed and twisted above and around us. They were transparent and mostly yellow but with twinges of every shade and color imaginable. A distinct hum accompanied the light bands, its volume varying with a slightly visible coordinated expansion and contraction of the bands. Sobs, sighs, and quiet laughter from our group mingled with the hum. The smell was like the middle of a luscious flower garden and the overall feeling was one of joy and contentment.

It was the first time the term, Extra-normal, became an established part of my lexicon. I had heard the words before but never needed or wanted to attach them to an event, object, or being. As the ceremony progressed and the attendant phenomena transpired, my father whispered, "This is Extra-normal, Jade." I asked him what the words meant, and he waved his arms around him, drawing in the entire experience, and replied, "All this is normal for us, but for others, it might be an Extra they can't yet understand." Since I was still a child and, so far, free from the depths of judgment and comparison, the description had little meaning. My main takeaway was that Extra-normal meant a glorious secret, one not to be shared with others outside our group. At least not yet.

One of the light bands shrunk from the height of a building to that of my mother and dropped down in front of her. It wavered and pulsed a few moments, then slowly, gently, wrapped itself around my brother like a blanket, and merged with his pale naked body. The light caught my mother's hands and included them in the wrap, but she didn't seem to mind. She turned toward my father and me, caught my gaze, and with her face smiling and wet, slightly bowed.

Our circle re-formed into a line and walked to a large quiet pond at the edge of the plaza. A walkway at the shore led to a tiny island on which sat a building we called the temple. The temple design drew inspiration from many sources, the result being a structure I can only describe as not from the human world. It appeared small on the outside yet was always large enough to fit all of us who attended a ceremony, whether it be ten or fifty people. The walls were made of stone, cut into neat bricks that always presented a bluish tint. Vines of all types crawled up the stone and hid the lower parts of the walls. The only door was constructed from rough-hewn wooden sections, joined in such a way that it appeared to be hacked from a single enormous tree. A large seven-pointed star held the space above the door and a row of crescent moons followed the top of walls underneath the roof overhang. The roof itself was built as foot-thick layers that became increasingly smaller until, at its pinnacle, it became an actual point. On top of the point and slightly pierced by it, sat a silver sphere the size of a soccer ball. It held a specific purpose, I'm sure, but I never knew exactly what it was.

We all entered the temple and stood around a small stone platform in the middle of the space. A fluffy, thick pillow rested on the platform and my mother laid my brother on it. My father picked me up and moved next to the platform so that my face was close to my brother's. His eyes were slightly open, and he looked so beautiful and sweet that I reached out to touch him. My mother smiled and nodded and took one of her hands off my brother and laid it on top of mine. My father did the same. The others put hands on nearby shoulders or arms so that we were all connected.

My mother sang a few words I couldn't understand and followed with more in English. "You are with us now in this human body. We are separate, yet are now and will always be, one. Welcome."

A glow hovered within and around our group. It might have been caused by the sun breaking through the clouds and shining through the one enormous window at the back of the temple. Except that I remember the multi-colored harmony of that glow as being so much more.

Later, after we returned home, I caught my father alone looking out our own picture window. I asked him, "Dad, where do the lights come from? Do they have another home?"

He gave me a warm smile but didn't answer. At the time, his silence didn't bother me because I was so young. Years later, I often wished he'd just answered the question right then.

By the time I was seven, our group had grown to about seventy-five people. Most of the growth was because many of the couples had kids, although new members from the outside also added to it. Established families generally lived in simple wooden cabins with two to four bedrooms depending on the family's size. Ours had three bedrooms, and because I didn't spend enough time outside our gates to notice and compare with how we lived, I always felt I had plenty of space. The outsides of the cabins looked mostly the same: stained wooden siding, large windows, slate roofs, and three-season porches, but the insides were often more creative and individual. Ours was always an ongoing project because my parents loved making things—anything—with their hands, and treated the walls, ceilings, and floors as display areas for their artwork.

Until we were in our teens, we had little contact with the world that existed outside our few hundred acres, but our library contained thousands of books designed to teach us what that world was about. I was an early reader and by six, had already plowed through all the little kids' picture books, and began reading books with chapters and more text. I wasn't drawn to anything labeled as fantasy because, for me, fantasy was the vast reality beyond the fence along our property line. The thoughts and actions of Judy Bolton or the Hardy Boys pulled me into wild and different ways one might exist in the outer world. Ramona Quimby took me directly into her story so that I could observe first-hand the early ragged journey of a human life. Using these books as a starting point, I branched into studies of human biology, psychology, history, language, philosophy, and religion. Eventually, even the non-human subjects like math, physics, and astronomy became of interest, not so much because of the subjects themselves, but because I was fascinated with how the human mind interpreted and used the knowledge, at any particular point in time, and throughout the entire path of human history.

The Elders encouraged us to explore our individual strengths and weaknesses, and to accept and embrace them. Inevitably, due to our personal configurations, we each developed with subtle or major differences, causing some—like myself— to read fluently or understand complex math at an early age, others to develop fantastic physical abilities, and a few to embody extreme levels of creativity. After all, we were all in human bodies, which, if given a certain degree of direction, mixed with freedom and security, will always develop in unique and exciting ways.

Although we weren't aware of the extent of it until we were much older, or at least I wasn't, we were in training right from the start for a mission, a greater cause. The problem was, the purpose of the mission was not always consistent throughout ours and similar communities. The reason for this, I came to believe, was that, although so many aspects of our upbringing contained reminders that we were separate beings yet also still one, once in the human body—and especially once that body has more contact with the outside world—the concept of *separate* always struggles the hardest to be the controlling doctrine.

Adam

Adam believed the house was deserted, he'd heard Old Elwood had been taken away and put into some kind of care home, but a dull light leaked through the dirty windows, reflecting onto the thick outside scrub. He couldn't resist, he had to see what was inside. He pushed through the overgrowth to a side window, looked in, and there he was, Old Elwood, sitting in a metal straight-back chair, a single bulb hanging from the ceiling pouring shadow and light onto his wrinkled face, his hand raised up holding a pistol with the barrel pressed to his temple.

Adam yelled, "Hey!" and Elwood turned his head and got a split-second glance before Adam tore around to the front of the house. He leaped onto the porch, banged his boots on the creaky, rotten deck, and ran at the door. Elwood screamed, "Don't open it!" but Adam had already turned the knob, and pushed, and that was when the blast nearly deafened him.

A few hours earlier, Adam Kastner and his older brother, Garrett, had been casually meandering through the woods on a path that passed behind a cottage their parents had rented for the first month of the summer. The thick brush and towering pines blocked much of the light—making for a scary after-dark walk if you didn't get back home on time—but for now the sun still hung high, giving enough glow to brighten the way. A few times when the wall of trees briefly parted, a dramatic view of the ocean even opened. For most of the trip they chatted away about sports, movies, or a new idea one of them had about the nature of the world, but when the path brought them close behind a few of the other houses, they hushed up, crouched down, and scurried past, like they were trespassing.

Their destination was the summer home of Christina Luft and her parents and siblings. Adam and Garret had come up with a plan—mostly Adam but Garrett had agreed to go along with it— to spend the evening with Christina and her friend, Carrie, to get to know them and maybe establish new friendships to ease the long vacation boredom. But Adam found himself wishing for, planning for, something beyond friendship, and in typical fashion, whether Garrett wanted to hear about it or not, he couldn't stop himself from sharing the details.

"You know what, Garrett," he said, "I think I'm in love."

"With Christina? Really?"

"Well no. Not Christina. She's obviously crazy about you. I'm talking about Carrie."

"Oh, yeah. Her," he said dismissively.

"Hey, c'mon. I'm seventeen and I think I could be in love. Isn't that normal behavior?"

Garrett didn't respond. He kept walking, lost in one of his philosophical meanderings, and Adam poked him and said, "Okay, tell me where you're going in there."

"You used the word *normal* to describe a human behavior," Garrett said. "Now there's a centuries-old myth."

They arrived at the Luft house, and for the next few hours, sat with Christina and Carrie on the front porch overlooking the foggy ocean. Their conversation—accompanied by the soft tones of wind, the waves on the rocks, and the faraway moan of a lighthouse horn—covered music, movies, books, celebrities, and anything else that came up. Adam did his usual routine, changing the subject when a topic grew stale, popping in a few jokes, and always keeping an observer's attention on the others: the tone of their responses, their body language, where they kept their gaze. Christina was all over Garrett, no surprise there. And Carrie? Just like Christina, she followed every movement of Garrett's perfect body, every expression on his quiet, beautiful face. It was painfully obvious, once again, that the star of this show was not Adam. And, once again, Garrett acted like he either didn't notice, or if he did, didn't care. He was sweet, kind, and pleasant, yet—Adam was positive—on a deeper level, on one that might have mattered, his brother was not at all interested.

Adam finally excused himself, said he had to get up early to go fishing, and hustled down the porch steps. The last trace of daylight had left, taking with it the comfort and ease he might have enjoyed on the short trip back to the cottage. The Luft house was five lots away from the Kastner rental cottage and he had two ways to get home: up a long, dark driveway leading away from the water and onto the deserted road, one dim streetlight trying to break the foggy blackness, deathly quiet except for the lighthouse foghorn and unknown creatures scrambling around in the brush; or back on the path through the backyards, with the same sounds, the same small nighttime terrors, but the darkness broken up a little more by any lights left on in the houses. He chose the path.

He hurried off, happy to be away from the awkward gathering, and focused on the light from the next house twinkling through the trees.

He inhaled the soft night air and thanked the slice of moon for its occasional glow showing through the mist. The first two houses and the trail between them were an easy trot, but the next one, not so much.

That route went right by Old Elwood's house, the next one over from the rental cottage, a few hundred feet of woods between them. The other times Adam had gone past he'd put his head down and run because the house was always dark and deserted. And creepy.

He had never met Old Elwood, only heard a few references to him, mostly about how strange he was. Elwood. Old Elwood. Elwood Clamshaw. The name alone was on the far side of unusual. The older locals called him eccentric, the younger ones freely tossed out the labels: weird, bizarre, or scary. Maybe because Adam was an outsider, only there for part of the summer, they didn't elaborate, never giving much of a story to go with the adjectives.

When Adam crashed through the door and into the deafening blast, his instincts forced him into a quick drop toward the floor, and he landed on top of Old Elwood who was shockingly not dead.

Elwood screamed, "Get away from me!" and shook Adam off like he was a smelly dirty blanket.

Adam pushed himself up and scooted backward to the open door. "What the hell? What did you do?"

Elwood rolled onto his hands and knees and slowly forced his way up to standing. He raised his head to look at something above him and Adam followed his gaze to a large old-fashioned shotgun, dangling from a cord attached to the ceiling. Another cord, tied to the trigger, wound its way through a few eye-hooks attached to the door and ended in a loop on the inside doorknob.

Elwood let out a small chuckle. "Well, at least I know the whole damn thing is going to work."

Adam tried to take it all in, tried to understand. This man standing in front of him, skinny as a pencil, looked like he had never in his obviously long life had a solid meal, and everything about him, his sunken eyes, pushed-back chin, bony arms and hands, screamed of an approaching death. Yet, like a little kid caught stealing cookies from the jar before dinner, Old Elwood fought back a grin and a laugh, as if he thought the whole situation was a big joke.

The pistol Adam had seen Elwood point at his head, lay on the floor, and he scooped it up, examined it for a moment, and shook it at him. "This isn't even real. It's plastic. What were you trying to do here?"

Elwood slowly and methodically righted the chair and sat down. "You're Adam Kastner, aren't you?"

"How do you know who I am?"

Elwood hesitated, looked Adam up and down. "I make it my business to know who everybody is. Especially when I see them walking through my yard."

"Are you trying to kill yourself?"

"No, no. I'm trying to figure out a way for somebody else to do it."

"With a plastic gun?"

"The shotgun's real. You want to have a go at it?"

Adam again backed toward the door. "But why?"

Elwood's creaky voice softened. "Hey there. You don't have to leave." He put on a slight smirk. "Unless it's past your bedtime and your Mommy wants you home. Go on. Hurry home to Mommy."

"Huh? What's wrong with you?"

"Sorry, sometimes I try to be funny and I'm not. You see, my time's up. It's time to go. Move on. This ancient body has fulfilled its mission and run its course. And now I need my Dr. Kevorkian treatment."

Adam stepped forward, curious. "Why don't you just do it yourself?"

Elwood pointed to the wall. "See that folding chair there? How about getting it and sitting here next to me and I'll tell you a few things. You interested?"

Adam brought the chair over and sat in front of Elwood. The old man continued, "See, if you look around this house, the crooked scraped-up floors, the ceiling plaster falling, the cracked windows, the leaky pipes, it's just like me: old and falling apart. Now, if I had any young muscle left like you have, I could tear this place down and start over. No big deal, no great loss. Except that I can't do it myself, somebody else has to. But anybody I would want to ask couldn't do it either unless they were tricked into it."

"That doesn't make any sense. Why not?"

Elwood dropped his voice to a raspy whisper, "Could you do it? Right now? Knowing that it's a gigantic favor to an old ailing miserable man? Right now? Could you?"

Adam took a few moments. "Uh—no—I don't know."

"And why not?"

Adam didn't answer. Elwood continued his whisper. "I can't say for sure why you couldn't but maybe it's the same reason I or many of my acquaintances couldn't. Perhaps you're just like us, you're, well, something not normal. Extra-normal, some would call it, and intentionally ending the life of another human is not possible for you, either."

Adam rolled his eyes and shook his head. "Extra-normal. Interesting. And now what? You're going to tell me what Extra-normal is?"

Elwood caught the skepticism. "And now what? You're going to roll your eyes and listen to what I say only because you think it's funny hearing a weird old man saying crazy things?" Elwood stared at him, silently, and when Adam tried to stand, the voice changed to a deep, rich, hypnotic tone that penetrated the core of Adam's gut. He lost outer focus and stayed seated, almost paralyzed, as the words burrowed fast and clean, through the layers of his snarky teenage cynicism.

Elwood continued, "Listen with a careful and open mind as I tell you my story. Who I am and what I am."

For the next half-hour, Elwood rambled on, using words and phrases like: overlays, beings merging, embodiment, untethered spirits, and the one used the most: Walk-ins. Adam's attention never wavered, catching every word without a verbal response, until Elwood said, "Sometimes, the human doesn't realize the Walk-in has come on board."

The words drove a burning current into the deepest crevices of Adam's body. He twisted and tingled and shook his head. "Can you repeat that last sentence, please?" Elwood obliged and Adam stood, put his hands on his hips, stared, and said with a touch of anger, "Now why would anybody think it's okay to just hop on board some poor sucker and mess with them like that? It reminds me of what I learned in Bio last year. About symbiosis. And parasites.

Elwood also stood and laid his hands on Adam's shoulders, the dull light hitting his arms, making them appear translucent. He looked into Adam's eyes and froze him in place.

"Ah, yes my dear boy. Why? Why? You've got it now, the trillion-dollar question roiling around in that young brain of yours. You see, those of us who call ourselves Extras, who strut around with pride and joy and endless self-patting about how helpful we are, in the end, are we truly symbiotic? Or are we nothing more than parasitic? One of the oldest questions ever asked, that one."

What remained of Elwood's spell had shattered and Adam lunged at the door and opened it. As he stormed off the porch and around the house, Elwood shouted, "Feel free to come back anytime. I'd love to chat more with you."

Adam ran through the woods, losing the path, then finding it again, and burst into the backyard of the cottage. He stopped at a large granite boulder in the middle of the small lawn and sat down next to it, propping his back on the rough gritty surface. His parents were inside, probably reading or listening to public radio—no TV because they were all on vacation from most of the binary world, although his Dad had brought a laptop—and Adam wanted to catch Garrett outside before they merged back into the tiny cabin space.

The mist had cleared, and the stars glittered and danced above him. A slight breeze brought in the ocean's salty smells of seaweed and captured fish. A sound Adam couldn't identify, rustling and scratching, traveled up with the smells. A seal maybe? He didn't bother getting up to look.

Footsteps shuffled up the dirt and gravel driveway, and this time, he stood and hurried over. A figure slid out of the dark.

"That you, Garrett?"

"Yeah, what are you doing out here?"

"Sorry I took off. I got bored with the disinterest."

Garrett came up close. "So, you left me behind."

"Are you pissed? Man, those two were all over you. I thought you'd be happy."

"No, you didn't. That was messed up."

"What do you mean?"

"You know what I mean. You knew I wasn't into them like that."

Adam hesitated before responding. Fog rolled in and the stars vanished, leaving Garrett as only a vague outline in the blackness. Adam said, "But you won't ever say it. You always act like it's not there. So, what am I supposed to think? I mean, just say it: *this is who I am.* No more confusion. We're seven years into a whole new century. Nobody cares anymore."

Garrett moved closer and whispered, "I'm deeply involved in college sports and could possibly be pro baseball material. I've become a big deal in a macho male world. And it's close-minded in the way you're thinking about it but also in a lot of other ways. With all due respect, Adam, you don't know, you couldn't possibly know what anybody cares about in the life I'm in."

Garrett went into the cottage, and Adam stayed outside for another hour, immersed in his thoughts. He didn't get a chance to tell Garrett about his encounter with Old Elwood. Had it even happened? Had he made it up? He knew he had a wild imagination; everyone had always told him that. But Old Elwood? He could go back down the path and look in the window again. But for once, he didn't dare.

Jade

An outsider examining the rules for the young ones might have believed we had few or none. However, the ones we did have were always followed and the consequences for breaking them were consistent and immediate. One of the most important ones addressed our relationship with the differences between each of us. The rules promoted these differences, and as long as we followed certain guidelines, fostered respect for them. I was not one of the physical ones. I could throw and catch a ball or run through the woods at a high speed without tumbling and breaking, but the body I was born into had only an average skill set in that regard. My strength was my curious and analytical mind. In the outside world, others might have labeled me a nerd, a bookworm, a geek, or I possibly could have been a placeholder on a psychologist's spectrum. Yet, in my safe little world, the Elders encouraged and empowered my direction, as they did for all the young ones.

Sometimes the youngers did tease or belittle someone for their differences. When observed by an Elder or reported by a younger, a first step was always a simple intervention in which all who were involved met and shared their true feelings. Because of our common inner nature, this process nearly always resulted in a satisfactory outcome for everyone. Occasionally, a next step became necessary that involved some type of Elder ceremony centered around an energetic transfer, but until I was much older, I knew little about it because it was never necessary for me.

There were five communes similar to ours throughout the country and many more in different parts of the world. Occasionally individuals, couples, or even whole families transferred from one to the other. This could happen for a number of reasons: perhaps somebody was drawn to a hot summer or a frigid winter, or they needed proximity to relatives outside their community. One day, around the time I turned ten, a girl named Melinda Breeze and her mother arrived and went through the welcoming process. My father told me they had come because Melinda's father had died, but there was more to the story that I didn't learn about until I was well into adulthood. I had always gotten along well with the youngers and regarded all of them as my friends. However, when Melinda arrived, I knew within a day, that my dearest, closest companion, who I didn't even know was out there, had finally arrived. Like me, she loved her books, her study, and her library, but she was also a nature being who rolled around in the grass and dirt and allowed wild animals to eat out of her hand. And our setting would be a perfect spot for her, comfortable and safe so she could heal and reassemble after the trauma of her father's death.

As we got to know each other, we established that we were in some way sisters, and then decided we could act as twins. She was less than a month older than me, the same size and weight, and we had many of the same mannerisms: the way we moved and spoke and a similar laugh. However, many of our physical characteristics were different. She had dark brown eyes, black curly hair, and dark skin, and referred to herself as Black. My hair is straight and reddish brown, my skin, when I keep out of the sun, usually a light beige, and my eyes—like my name—a jade green. Also, our faces were different. Melinda's oval face, with a straight smile and balanced features, would be described in the outside world as classic beauty. Mine, with eyes a little too large, a slightly crooked mouth and smile, and well into my adult years, a face full of freckles, would be considered cute yet quirky. However, I was not aware of the importance of any of this—and to a certain degree, she wasn't either—until many years later when we both stepped into that outside world and the trajectory of our lives changed so much.

At first, I found Melinda's mother, Josephine Breeze, a bit intimidating because she always had a sense of order about her. Although she was a small, thin woman, she seemed to be double my size, like a fierce mama lion. She observed—with eyes like the most attentive hawk or ears like the sharpest wolf—every move I would make and word I would say. This was especially true when I played with Melinda, and I believed it was because she had to be protective of her daughter, new to our home and sad about her father dying. About a month into our friendship, Melinda and I were sitting in her living room, taking turns reading aloud from a book, and I felt her mother's presence so strong that I began to squirm. I didn't look up, afraid to, and made up a reason to politely leave. Just before I spoke my intention, Melinda stood and went to the bathroom.

Josephine rushed over, bent down, and whispered in my ear, "I'm sorry I'm being so nosy."

"I whispered back, "I love your daughter. She's my best friend and I would never do anything to hurt her."

Josephine put her arms around me and hugged me until I melted like ice on a hot afternoon. Melinda came out, flashed the touch of a grin, and sat down like nothing was going on. After that day, Josephine became my third parent.

When I was with Melinda, I always loosened up, because her joy was so strong that it bubbled out of her and spilled onto me. She was like that with everyone, but when we were alone, especially out in the natural wonderland, her lovely spirit reigned free in such a way that sometimes I felt honored I was the one who received the best of it. If she scooped leaves off the ground and threw them at me for fun, I could identify them—and I quickly learned she also often could—but she would see magic in them, in their color, symmetry, and movement. She led us to make forts out of sticks and rocks so we could pretend we were opossums, groundhogs, or foxes and the forts were our homes. A few times we even got our parents to let us sleep in them, without sleeping bags, so we could mimic the real experience.

A few years after our friendship started, we both began to experience the big adolescent change, along with all the muddled thought processes and exploratory meanderings about who we were and where our bodies—going forward—were destined to direct us. One day I told Melinda I believed I was heterosexual, but if I wasn't, she would need to be my lover. She giggled and replied, "Well if one of us goes that way, we both will have to." Before long, we did decide we were both heterosexual, yet in many ways, even then, she had become the true love of my life because she understood—and continues to understand—who I was, and she cared about me in ways never equaled by any other being.

By the time we were in our mid-teens, we began to grasp the enormity of our situation, the immense wonder of being on this earth, in these bodies, and with the other commune members who were like us. The continual overlay of energetic magic coursing through each of us had often brought with it a swirl of sensations and emotions, nearly always exciting, yet in a quiet and peaceful way so that it always felt safe. But when Melinda and I both turned sixteen, the elders encouraged us to venture outward and try new experiences beyond our gate. The protocol directed us to begin an immersion process in preparation for the expected college experience coming a few years later. The Elders gave us a list of possibilities ranging from actually enrolling in an outside public high school to joining an organization like the 4H club. Melinda and I chose to start with a dance class at a health and fitness club and we began right away.

Oh, what fun it was. For the first class, Melinda's mother drove us about an hour away to a small city, did some errands, and picked us up after. Neither of us were natural dancers but we were so comfortable in our bodies that we didn't care. At first, I was a little hesitant to throw myself into it, but Melinda was the opposite, and a quick look at her wild movements got me fully engaged. The rhythms of the music bounced off the walls and through our bodies, and the energy from the twenty or so other classmates, as it swirled around us, nearly knocked us over. After the class we were so tired we could barely stand. It was quite an introduction to the outside world.

For our next assignment, we took part-time jobs, Melinda as a server in an ice cream shop, and I in a used clothing store. Both businesses were on the main street of the closest town to us, an incorporated village called Anderson of about two thousand people. We had gone through Anderson many times with our parents and even gone into both stores, so the jobs seemed like a good fit. Neither of us questioned how easy it was for us to get the jobs and we were given little instruction about how to conduct ourselves, out in this bigger world. However, Melinda's mother and my parents did debrief us whenever we returned.

I had gotten my driver's license and drove us into our first day of work in my parent's car. I parked in a small lot, we happily walked down the main street and split up to go to our separate jobs. I followed the directions of my supervisor, sorted donated clothing into different categories, stocked shelves, and learned how to handle the customers' cash, checks, and credit cards. I finished a few minutes early and walked to the ice-cream shop. Melinda stood behind a counter, and after only a few hours of instruction, was already serving customers. She scooped out three different flavors from a glass cabinet, put them into bowls, and rang up the orders, the whole time with a calm, pleasant demeanor.

Melinda spotted me, nodded to an empty table, and I sat close to two boys and a girl about our age, eating and watching her every movement. Something about their mannerisms and attitudes disturbed my sense of fun and well-being and I tuned into their whispered comments. They put their heads close together and one of boys whispered, "She's pretty hot for a…" I couldn't hear the last word, but I knew what it likely was. The girl followed up with a nasty snicker.

My world studies gave me more than enough information about what aspect of Melinda they were referring to, but now this was a real-life slur, a direct insult to my friend because of her dark-skinned body. In our commune, we had members of different ethnicities and races and we were encouraged to study the backgrounds of our own and each other's physical bodies, one of the purposes being to allow us to come to the conclusion that our human bodies were not that different from each other. And, just like making fun of individual differences wasn't tolerated, neither was any sort of teasing about ethnic and racial differences. Melinda's mother's ancestry traced to Central Africa and her father's to India. Mine is a mix of Eastern European and French. It was one of those aspects of who we were that was of importance, but only a part of how we viewed each other.

But the twenty-second interaction with those kids in the ice cream shop put a sizable dent in my attitude. I had no idea how to respond and I didn't tell Melinda until many days later. When I finally shared the awful event, she responded with, "How did it make you feel?" And this person who I had always been, this gentle, non-violent, sweet as honey girl, replied, "I wanted to slap them hard in the face. All three of them." Melinda laughed but I could tell from the look in her eyes that the whole event made her so sad.

Our final jobs involved a family of three, a father and two children, who came for an extended stay and roomed in a large barn-like building with private suites we referred to as the bunkhouse. Our work with the children gave us our first major real-life exposure to what it meant to be an Extra in the outside world. The long-term inhabitants of our community were all Extras from birth, or so I thought. The folks passing through the bunkhouse were usually something else. We called them Walk-ins and they all had come there for some kind of help. Again, my endless studies of every aspect of the human experience would be helpful, except now I would be studying a different version, a combination of the Normal humans and an unfamiliar type of Extras. The experience would expose me to much more than studying ever could because my new role demanded that I learn how to step far beyond myself and make a difference in the life of somebody else.

The family had just arrived from somewhere in North Carolina and an Elder gave Melinda and me a quick overview of their situation. The sister, Jocilyn, was fourteen and the brother, Paul, was twelve, their mother, who was a Walk-in, had recently died, and their father, who the Elders described as a partial Walk-in—whatever that meant—had been referred to our community for help and healing. Our first assignment consisted of giving the two kids a tour of the land, and keeping them company for the day as their father received his first treatment. We headed into the woods intending to show the kids our animal forts which we hadn't visited in over a year. Melinda led the way and kept up a steady conversation about what we were seeing, the kids, in a near daze, stayed quiet, and I observed from behind.

When we reached our first fort, Melinda whispered to me, "Don't observe. Participate." She followed with a gentle tap on my chest. Whoooah. That was a surprise. I knew exactly what she meant. I knew it in every fiber of my body. She flashed me a tiny smile, and a look that said, *I'm sorry*. I frowned, trying to pretend I was angry at her criticism but she knew I was faking it. Our ability to communicate with each other, the way in which it always seemed to grow more complex, more nuanced, more specific, was always a source of amusement for us. How much fun it was for two kids to communicate so deeply with only a minimum of actual speech, even adding in some playful teasing on top of a serious conversation.

The combination of the deep woods and our energy must have done something because the girl, Jocilyn, moved next to Melinda, put her arm around her waist, and set her head on her shoulder. I crawled into the fort and the boy, Paul, followed and sat next to me without speaking. Melinda and Jocilyn followed. We huddled close together and Melinda said we could become animals if we wanted to. We decided on opossums because they are so cute in a funny-looking way, and we took turns describing what each other looked like.

We stayed silent for a while, then Melinda said, "I lost my father a few years ago. It's so difficult."

And, wow again. In a significant way, I was different from these three. My studies had given me enough information so that I could give dates and detailed descriptions of many of the most traumatic events that had ever happened on our planet. For years I'd speculated about why humans suffered so much and why, although much of it was inevitable, they still endlessly multiplied the pain through their own selfish actions. I had so much knowledge, but it was all in my head because I had never experienced a severe upset personally, and wasn't able to understand it in those parts of my being where it mattered most. Yet, at that moment I would have done about anything to help ease the suffering of these three lovely beings. I would gladly have swapped their pain with my happiness. Later on, I came to the conclusion that at some point, when I fully entered the outer world, I would experience my own major traumatic event. When it happened, I planned on welcoming it, accepting it, and growing with it. It was almost like I was wishing for it and we all know the human idiom, *be careful what you wish for*. I certainly knew it and even kept a record in my head of a whole list of them, yet the full meaning of this one managed to slip right past me.

Adam

Early the next morning, Adam opened his eyes, blinked, shook his head, and tuned into the soft snoring coming from across the room. If given the opportunity, Garrett had no problem sleeping in, but Adam had never been able to make it much past seven. The clock by his bed read six-fifteen and he slipped out of the room and into the living room. His mother, also an early riser, lay sprawled out on a couch, reading a new novel, one of many she'd bought at the bookstore before they had left for their vacation.

"Morning, Ingrid." Adam had recently begun addressing his parents by their first names, Ingrid and Clifford. "What are your plans for the day?"

She looked up and smiled. "This is it right here. You're seeing it. So how was your night with the Luft girls?"

Ingrid didn't know Adam had left earlier than Garrett. "They're nice enough."

"That's it?"

Adam went into the tiny kitchen, rummaged through a grocery bag that hadn't been unpacked yet, and pulled out a box of cereal. He got a

25

bowl out of a knotty pine cabinet and a spoon from a creaky wooden drawer. He added a little milk and sat at an antique table with a stained wooden top. He remembered details from the night before when he had dreamed about another house.

"There's coffee if you want," Ingrid said.

Does she even know about Garrett? Does Clifford know? That's just not right.

A little later, their parents went out for something, and Adam and Garrett stayed back and tried to entertain themselves with some of their Mom's books and magazines. Adam slouched on the couch and skimmed through the first few pages of a novel and Garrett leafed through a copy of a New Yorker magazine. They stayed silent, not unusual for them, and then Garrett said, "Hey Adam."

"What?"

"I want to tell you what I was thinking about. Because you and I are different in some key ways and maybe it's time I try to explain it to you in more detail."

"That would be nice. I mean, whatever you tell me I will always support you."

"I do appreciate it but I'm pretty sure what you think is going on is not what is actually happening."

I don't understand."

"You think I'm gay, therefore I'm not interested in physical relationships with women, or girls, or females, or whatever. And the assumption is that then, I like anything male. But the fact is, at this stage of my life, I don't care about any of it. There's too much other stuff going on in my life to focus on any of that right now."

"Oh. What do you mean?"

"You're the exact opposite and that's all you think about and it's hard for you to understand how I wouldn't be the same way."

A touch of defensiveness crept in. "It's not all I think about."

Garrett sat up and said, "Adam, stop. Listen to me carefully. You're one way right now and I'm another and there is nothing wrong with either of us being the way we are. We're both fine exactly as we are. Do you understand what I'm saying?"

Adam thought for a moment. "Yeah, you know what? Yes. I think I do. I guess the issue for me is that, with all your super good looks and everybody always ogling you like you're Brad Pitt or Tom Cruise, it's hard for me to imagine, well…"

"It is hard for you to imagine, and to be honest, it's becoming downright annoying, not because you don't understand but because nobody understands."

Adam shook his head. "You're annoyed because you're good-looking?" Garrett didn't answer. A minute later, Adam said, "Hey. Can I ask you something? You can tell me to shut up if you want."

Garrett laughed. Nodded. "Yep, the big question. And the answer is, yes, I've tried a few things to determine my orientation. But I'm sure you already know that." His tone shifted to serious. "What are you really asking here?"

"I don't know. It's just that there's something different about you in general. More so lately."

Like before, Garrett didn't answer. For a moment, his face seemed to transform, his stare deep and piercing with an intensity that made Adam squirm. He quickly flipped back with a sweet grin. "So, what about you in this last year I was away at school? What did you do in that arena"

"No guys and…"

"Well, I figured that. Any girls?"

Adam shook his head. "Only in my dreams."

"It'll happen soon enough. For real."

Adam looked down at the floor. "Yeah, maybe if I looked like you."

Garrett sat up and examined Adam. Again, there was something scary about it. "You know, it's not always easy for us younger folks to see what we actually look like. I mean, I look at myself in the mirror and see this clichéd, handsome, manly, male thing: the strong chin, the big white-teeth smile, the square face. And I have all the muscle stuff going on. But it's kind of boring. It's just not that interesting. And I look at you and you've got that weird wild curly hair, high cheekbones, some freckles, those big blue eyes. And yeah, some people think you're too skinny. But you have an original look. It's unique. You know, if it were possible, I'd switch with you in a second. I would stay mostly the same, maybe stay into sports if my body could do it, and still be interested in how the world works, but I'd ditch the container I'm in if I could.

Adam listened, hanging on to every increasingly strange word. Like Adam, Garrett also had an amped up imagination, and he often expressed it in unusual descriptions of the world. Adam remembered a time when he had referred to himself as a "creature inhabiting himself," as if his body were nothing more than a suit of clothes he'd put on. Adam had thought it was amusing at the time but something about his tone now, and the specific language and imagery it invoked was different. It was like Garrett was sleepwalking and the words coming out of his mouth weren't his.

He continued, "You know, last night I lay there thinking about how, when I claimed my body, my whole physical-mental thing, it might have been the wrong one. Like the whole combo of who I am might have worked better if I'd been matched up with somebody more like you."

"Hey, stop a second. Stop, please! What are you talking about?"

"Oh sorry," Garrett said. He shook his head as if he was shaking himself out of this other place he'd drifted into, unsticking himself and bringing himself back to his usual environment. "It's just a way I've been thinking lately. Or, not lately. For a long time. That must have sounded really weird."

Really weird was putting it mildly.

Adam stammered and his whole body shook. He almost couldn't get the words out. "You don't know where I went when I left the Luft's last night. I didn't tell you."

"What do you mean?"

"Uh…I, uh, I went into Old Elwood's house. I talked to him."

Garrett's voice rose. "I thought he was gone. What did he say?"

"He told me a whole lot of really odd things. And he wants somebody to kill him. He…"

"Oh my God."

Garrett stood and went to the door. "Stay here. Just don't follow me. I'll be right back."

"No way," Adam said. "I'm coming, too."

They ran down the path, now brightly lit by the overhead sun blasting through the cloudless sky and reached Old Elwood's rotten porch in minutes. Adam stood in front of the door, blocking it, remembering what had happened the night before.

"What are you doing?" Garrett said. "Just go in."

Adam pulled him close and whispered a ten second version of the shotgun blast. "Let's see if there's a back door."

They ran around the house, found the back door, and pushed their way into an ancient kitchen, with a cracked porcelain sink embedded into a linoleum-topped counter, a torn tile floor with the boards underneath showing through, and a dirty white metal table.

They yelled for Elwood, searched all the rooms in the house, upstairs and down, then pulled open a trap door in the center of the kitchen floor that led into a shallow basement. Adam climbed in and had to crouch on a musty dirt floor to move around in the tight space. The only light came from the trap door opening but he pushed his way through the spiders and mold and kicked his foot out continuously to verify that there were no dead bodies—or live ones—hanging out in the damp soil.

When he came back up, Garrett was sitting on the couch, looking around at the room. "You said something about a shotgun. Where is it?"

The shotgun, the rope that held up the shotgun, and the toy plastic pistol, were no longer there. He raced up the stairs again, looked more carefully at the rooms, and came back down to the first floor and searched those rooms.

"What are you doing?" Garrett asked.

"It's like he was never here. But he was. I know he was."

He sat on the couch and put his head in his hands. "Garrett, he was here or, or…Oh my God, what is going on?"

Garrett stood, took hold of Adam's shaking hands, and led him out the front door. "Adam stop, calm down," he said. "You need to listen to me carefully. I believe you that he was here. Everything you remember did happen. You didn't just imagine it or make it up. But you can't tell anybody about any of this. Not anybody. And if there's some way you can forget it, that would be the best thing of all. Now let's get out of here."

They hurried back toward their cottage, Garrett in the lead and Adam tight behind, his focus on nothing else but keeping up. At one point, his feet felt as if they were slogging through a thick mud, like a bad dream where your body doesn't do what you need it to do to avoid some terrible outcome. Like he would fall way behind, and another reality would trap him and it would be the end of him. He was about to yell when, right before they entered their yard, Garrett took a slight detour to the water.

They sat on the beach and stared out at the vast expanse. Fishing boats and a few small islands dotted the calm water and pillar-like clouds hung in the sky. The soft warm breeze created a sedative effect, and Adam lay on his back on a patch of sand and put his arm over his face. His body began to relax but his thoughts still spun all over the place.

He sat up and said, "How do you know whatever this is about Old Elwood?"

"Adam, please. We've been coming here for years. I've met him before. And the locals always gossip about him."

"This has nothing to do with our talk about sexual orientation, does it." He said it as a statement.

"No, of course not. And you have to let the entire thing go. I'm not going to talk about it anymore."

Garrett stood and went back to the cottage. Adam stayed on the shore and watched a piece of driftwood float toward him. He laid down again, closed his eyes and fell into a hazy sleep. He entered a dream and continued to watch the driftwood as it came close enough to the shore and moved in and out with the waves, never reaching the safety of the solid land. A fishing boat passed near enough that he could hear the voices of the people on board. He sat up and wasn't sure if he was still dreaming. No, he wasn't. But something felt different, something had been removed from him.

He went up to the cottage and hung out with Garrett and his parents for the rest of the day, playing games, going to a fresh water swimming hole, stopping for ice cream at a quaint little stand, and helping everyone put together an amazing dinner with baked pie for dessert.

The next day, Garrett said he was leaving and would see them all again in a few weeks, back at their home in a suburb of Albany, New

York, named Oakwood. Adam couldn't remember if it had always been the plan, but it didn't seem important, so he didn't ask. He remembered bits of his conversation about Garrett but they didn't seem important, either. And any part of his experience with Old Elwood Clamshaw had left him. Somebody or something had dragged it all into the trashcan and emptied it.

Jade

From an early age, I understood that change is an inherent part of the human experience. Change happens to all people, plants, and animals, to anything and everything. The general concept is not unique to earth inhabitants. It is, in some form, part of the entire reality of our infinite universe in all spaces and all dimensions. Humans, however, have a unique relationship with change, and when it comes in the form of an unwelcome disturbance, have attached the word *trauma* to it. To some degree, I experienced this as soon as I was born into a human body, and more so a few years later as the aspects of my mind that are human developed the ability to intellectualize. Yet, no matter how much I studied the world in the way I was directed to learn, my understanding always had the taint of an observational distance.

It's different for me now. In so many ways, I am no longer the person I was before, the nice, geeky girl who by nature loved everybody and everything. The difference is deep enough that, when I make a statement about the uniqueness of human trauma, I can also make the claim—even boast about it if I wish to stoop that low—that I truly know what the hell I'm talking about. From where I now exist in my internal self, if someone shares a rough and bloody story, and I cliché back to them that, "I feel your pain," I am no longer speaking in gooey metaphors.

Shortly after I turned eighteen, I began my college experience. My schooling within the commune was always self-directed and essentially a type of home-schooling. However, in keeping with our tradition of presenting a stable image, free of controversy to the outside world, we always had teachers who followed our progress, and we were encouraged to take our state and federal exams. In the outside world, I would have been a model student and might have enrolled in college at a much younger age. As was the case with nearly all of the Extra kids, I had a distinct mental advantage, likely could have pursued any major or path which appealed to me and been accepted to most colleges or universities. I followed my parents' advice and attended one of the state schools only a few hours away. I did so for reasons I believed I understood, but later learned that I was only skirting around the frame of our biggest picture. I moved into a dorm room with another girl about my age, packed my schedule with classes, and floated through the first year.

I had fun. I now had access to an enormous library where I would go to study, but I rarely studied for my classes because I didn't need to and instead delved mostly into collections of post-doctoral papers. I also learned how to socialize by carefully observing and then practicing the subtleties of young adult interaction. I went to a few parties and even drank a bit—which I confess I did like—but found the hallucinogenic tinge of any cannabis product troubling—which, since I am an Extra, was not surprising.

My distance from Melinda presented the most difficult aspect of the first year. We decided to go to separate schools for no other reason than we agreed it would be an interesting experiment. We would keep records of our adventures and observe and record our own human reactions. Then, when we came home for holidays and the summer, we would have fun comparing our experiences. Also, we were only going to be a few hundred miles from each other, and we would both have vehicles so we could always visit if we wanted or needed to. But, like always in the world of humans, the easy times cannot go on forever.

On a night in late October of my second college year, I had my first experience with what I now refer to as deep trauma. It began as a typical night out with a group of girls, dressed in different costumes, going to an off-campus student house for a wild Halloween party. I had briefly been to the house once before during the day to meet somebody but didn't think much of it. Now, as I passed through the spiked metal gate, and up the stone walk and creaky wooden steps to the massive ancient doors, the Victorian windows and roof turret glowing with ghost shadows, I laughed at my touch of fear. For the first time in my human life, I understood how there could be a purpose to the whole strange yearly celebration. This party in particular had a theme that had circulated to all who were invited. In order to attend, we needed to dress as someone or something, from a movie or book, that instilled fear in us, either as the perpetrator or the receiver of the fear. So perhaps, I concluded, this was a healthy way for humans to face their terrors and work through them.

The day before the party, a girl from another college named Jennifer met with a group of us, twenty or so, in a dorm room and brought a few shopping bags filled with clothes and accessories to help us decide on costumes for our characters. There were the inevitable witches, vampires, bloody zombies, a few attempts at skeletons, and many ghosts. The process stumped me because I had no fear of any of those things, and in fact, they all seemed somewhat ridiculous. When the costume girl, Jennifer, caught my hesitation, she asked me about what

I'd read in my childhood, what books I loved and what I didn't so much. I held back the fact that I'd read literally thousands of books and often watched movies inspired by many of the more influential works of fiction. But my memory brought me first to a children's book and then the movie version or it—both of which filled me with renewed dread as I told Jennifer the title.

"Matilda, hmmm. I don't know that one. But let me see here."

She used her phone to find photos from the movie and said, "Well this one is a winner. You look exactly like a grownup version of her." Other than my hair, which I'd been styling with bangs, I wasn't sure about that. But it was a simple costume, mostly recognizable by the bright red ribbon tied in a bow on the top of my head.

The night was going to be warm for late October and I wore a cute dress with a tight jacket over it, white bobby socks, canvas sneakers, and the red bow in my hair. I hitched a ride and the only item I brought along was my phone, which I kept in my jacket pocket. When I walked through the front doors, into a dimly lit hallway, a guy in a Frankenstein costume directed me to a large living room with a roaring fire dancing around in an old brick fireplace. He pointed to the fire and said, "The devil himself is here somewhere and is anxious to feed the flames. So, behave yourself."

Thirty or so costume characters floated around the room and an equal number jammed the hallways, kitchen, and a few bedrooms. I nudged my way into one of the bedrooms and came face-to-face with another version of Matilda. She had the same hair ribbon and nearly the same clothes. She had already been drinking and gave me a sloppy hug. "My twin," she said as she pushed past me. "There's another one here somewhere so I guess we're triplets."

Three Matildas walking around. My earlier understanding of why I was there, that it would somehow cause me to face a specific fear that

I barely had anyway, seem stupid. So what if I was dressed like this character from a troubling kid's book? What did that do? What was supposed to happen? I found a few of the girls I had come with, decided to catch a buzz, and poured myself a big glass of wine. I downed the first one, and halfway through the second glass, somebody introduced me to a guy named Richard who seemed, at first, to have a male interest in me.

He looked me up and down and walked around behind me. "Matilda, right? I bet I know what you're afraid of."

Richard seemed like a nice guy and I liked the way he looked, with his somewhat round face, brown eyes, and wavy brown hair. He wore a black suit, a white shirt, a black tie, and a black fedora style hat. Probably Mafia or an FBI agent from a long time ago. He was exactly my height, five nine, so when we talked, we could look directly at each other. But even though I had a slight wine buzz, I could tell right off that he was hiding something that made him really nervous. It piqued my interest and I kept up the conversation.

He lived in a dorm on campus but had spent enough time in this big old house that he knew his way around. He asked me if I wanted him to give me a tour and I agreed. We went upstairs, then into the attic and up a ladder into the turret I'd seen from the outside. We looked in closets, a back staircase, and down a dumb-waiter chute.

Richard's phone beeped with a text message, and he gave it a glance but didn't enter a response. "So much spam, it's ridiculous." We went back to the kitchen on the first floor and he said, "I've saved the best part for last."

A door opened revealing a dimly lit staircase to the basement. The same girl I'd seen earlier, the other Matilda, staggered up, still drunk, clutching a railing with both hands.

"You need help?" Richard asked.

"Richard White. No, I got this."

It was the only time in the evening I heard his last name. We waited until she was at the top and she stepped out, gave me another tight hug and said, "Have fun down there, twin sister. Those guys are hysterical."

I had set my half-full glass of wine somewhere and wanted more. Richard told me there was plenty where we were going. We went down the stairs into a large space with a cracked concrete floor with dirt showing through in some parts, large stone outer walls, and a crumbly brick wall at the far end. Bare incandescent bulbs hanging from the wooden ceiling illuminated a few wooden shelves, a crooked metal table on which sat many open wine, whiskey and vodka bottles, and two young men also dressed in black suits and ties.

Definitely Mafia hit men. One of them wore a simple white plastic mask sort of like Batman's Joker. The other one had no mask, only a strikingly handsome face— tanned, perfect, captivating, disarming, a big smile—and he said, "Want something to drink, my sweet Matilda?"

"Uh, sure, how about some more wine."

"Hey Richard, how about pouring her a glass and we can show her around."

Richard handed me a red plastic cup only half-full. I wanted a full glass but didn't say anything. Mr. Beautiful told me to follow him, Masked Man stayed silent, and Richard—White? I'd already forgotten his last name—stayed at the back. I took a few big gulps from the cup, downing half of the contents, and set it down.

An old wooden door led us through the brick wall, down a thin hallway with doors to more rooms, and into a smaller windowless space. Richard closed another wooden door behind him and the awareness that I was now in this room with three unknown male creatures brought with it a wave of panic. I turned to leave and Mr.

Beautiful grabbed my arm in a vicious grip. I tried to pull free but couldn't because my body was slipping away, not functioning.

I managed to get the words out, "What are you going to do to me?"

Masked Man said his first words. "You're probably thinking of rape. But why would we want to rape somebody as ugly as you." He opened a small wooden door to a dark space inside one of the walls.

I caught a glimpse of Richard's face. Fear. He edged toward the door.

"Don't even think of it, Richard," Mr. Beautiful said. "You're part of this whether you like it or not. And for you, my dear ugly Matilda, into the Chokey you go."

The drug in my wine had done its terrible magic, shutting down my body's ability to move or speak, or later scream, but leaving my mind free to fully experience everything that came next. They folded me up, knees to my chest, and slid me into the tiny black darkness so that my back was pressed against a hard, wet wall. They closed the wooden door, I thought I heard a latch of some type slide across, and then…silence.

No noise in there, just me, Jade Furlong, and my accelerating terror. I knew I had an aversion to tight dark spaces, that some part of my human configuration loathed the idea of being trapped somewhere, anywhere, but I had no idea it would be this bad. I had never experienced anything like it, only observed my reaction to Matilda, in the book of the same name and then the movie, being forced because of her bad behavior into a similar confinement—called the Chokey— by her school principal. I thought it was a horrible punishment that nobody on earth would deserve. But why was I there? And they drugged me and called me *Ugly*. What the hell did that mean? At first, I thought they would come let me out after a minute or so because the other Matilda, my twin on the staircase, had acted like the whole scene down there was funny and entertaining. Did they also drug her? No, she was only drunk. So, if they went through the effort to drug me, they must have planned something different. Something different! Panic stopped by for a nasty visit.

The frigid moisture from the floor and the wall I was against seeped through my clothing and began to freeze me. My back hurt, my legs hurt, my butt hurt, and I felt like an icicle about to shatter. Then the spiders came. In general, I didn't mind spiders, I actually liked them, but not there, not then. They skittered across my face and into my hair and one went into my mouth and down my throat.

I determined later on that I spent nearly six hours in the space. Either because of the nature of the drug, the nature of my total being, or some combo of both, I never passed out or even went into a shock trance. The closest I could get to distraction was to contemplate what it meant that two young men, one classically handsome and one unknown, had referred to me as *ugly*. My upbringing, which I now appreciated so much, had never allowed such labels to have meaning. My mind/body was the one my Extra had picked to merge with and therefore, however I looked or how my mind worked or what my body could or couldn't do, was always fine. *Ugly* might mean a rough incident—like being trapped in this space which was certainly ugly—or land or a city destroyed by war or weather. Something like that. But never a person's appearance. However…

The longer it went on, the more, *ugly*, became the perfect descriptor. After about five hours of non-stop hysteria, the drug began to wear off and I realized I'd added to the dampness underneath me. I moved my legs as much as I could, lifted my butt up about an inch, and the other smell wafted up. Then I threw up, not a lot but enough to add to the mixture. My arm functioned again and I smashed my forearm into the door. It didn't open so I smashed it a few more times until the pain made me stop. I tried to scream but couldn't get my vocal chords to work well enough. I would have to figure out a way to twist around so I could use my legs to smash my way out. It hurt so much to move, everything hurt so much, but it was the only way. A few screams made it out, not loud enough for anybody to hear, but enough to drive home how broken I was. When I got my back against the far wall, I began to kick the door, that little barrier between me and freedom, so hard that it finally opened.

I scooted out and tried to stand. I shook and cried, but somewhere, somehow my damaged self still had some common sense. I examined the door and saw that it had never been locked, it had no lock and was only held closed by the ancient wood, swelling tight with moldy moisture against the opening. The drug had prevented me from escaping hours earlier. I didn't know where my phone was and figured the captors had taken it. I wanted the phone, I wanted to take pictures, to collect evidence and I stumbled back into the room at the bottom of the stairs where I first met Richard's colluders and spotted it on the table. Next to it, sat my red plastic cup, still holding the dregs of my drugged-up wine. Oh yes. That was coming with me, also. The phone was dead—which made little sense since I had charged it before I'd left for the party—so I pulled myself up the basement stairs, through the kitchen, and out the back door of the house of horrors.

My thin coat did little to protect me from the crisp damp breeze but I was already so cold and in so much physical pain that I barely noticed it. I was more concerned with the fact that I had to get back to the dorm and into a shower before the sun came up, early traffic started, and somebody saw me. Or smelled me. Feces, urine, vomit, most likely blood mixed in—that time of the month was just about there—but, thankfully, no male body fluids. However, somewhere in the mix, churning around, ready to make its appearance, was a brand-new human experience, a different type of additive: a heaping steaming plate of male induced humiliation.

I snuck into my dorm, went directly into the showers, and found a slab of soap. I first stood under the hot water with my clothes on, then without, trying to scrub the experience off of every part of me. I tried to wash the clothes, but it took too much strength. I sat on the shower floor and curled up under the water. I almost fell asleep.

I had no towel or clean clothes so I pulled the wet dress over me, hurried to my room, and found it empty, my roommate somewhere else. I packed all the wet clothes, the remnants of Matilda, into a garbage bag, put on a thick sweater, a coat, and two pairs of long underwear, and crawled into bed. As I drifted into a hellish half-sleep, the one thought I clung to was that the red plastic cup was now safely hidden under my bed. I didn't get out of bed again for what seemed like days, weeks, eternity.

If I step back and recall my musings related to this event, even now so many years later, it still sickens me. And when a spontaneous recall happens, which will likely be a permanent fixture of my life, showing up unbidden and unexpected, whenever it feels like it, a part of me will always want to scream, to cry, to kill, to vomit again. They bruised my body—for months after, my arm and back ached and burned—but worse, they smashed my psyche, and in a matter of days, I began to experience changes to my being, including obsessive questions about who I was, what I cared about, and how I wished to act in the world.

Yet after the event, some of the specifics of my changes were significantly different than what most others would experience, and by *others*, I am referring to humans—Normals— without the Extra additives. For example, one of the most powerful aspects of my rewiring had to do with how my mind-body connection shifted. As an Extra, I did not have the access to the human trauma shield some label *dissociative disorder*, where the mind disconnects or dissociates from the body and the experience. For me, the opposite occurred. At a slow but steady pace, the event slammed my consciousness so far into my human self that I became a different being. I was no longer the other, the outsider, the observer, the content and peaceful Extra. I became so fully, so deeply human that I lost all that. At the same time, I couldn't forget the event, block it out, or hide in the safety of my brain's shielding abilities, because my being just didn't function that way. For a long time, I carried with me every nuance, every sensory note of the entire awfulness. For a long time, I lived within a slice of the human experience that is horrendous.

Even so, at first, I told nobody. Not my parents and not even Melinda. Had Melinda and I gone to the same college, I likely would have told her everything immediately after the event. Or she would have taken one look at me and figured it out. And, in this instance, she likely would have scoffed at our commune's rules and done an emergency exploration into my thoughts because, more than anybody, she would understand how to lead me out of them. But she wasn't with me, and from the time we went our separate ways, I should have been honest with myself about how our separation had affected me. Melinda was by nature much better than me at negotiating the complex personal interactions of the human world. And here I had been, by myself for the last year-and-a-half, trying to compensate, trying to fit in, and doing stupid things to make it happen.

In many ways I had been living a stereotypical college life: partying too much, sleeping in a few strange beds, skipping classes when I felt like it. I told myself it was all necessary so I could understand this new world around me, that it was part of my role as an observing Extra to immerse myself. And, I suppose in some ways this was true, it was part of my mission. But I didn't need to be so stupid about it. Gentler ways could have been available to learn what I needed to learn. And why had nobody from my commune advised me of the risks out there?

About a week after the event, thoughts began to emerge that reminded me of disconnected sparks or random patterns, or perhaps a poor sketch of a planned painting. These disturbances went on for about three days and then coalesced into something chilling and disturbing — a theory about what had happened to me. Shortly, it became a concept, not only about the event but about a possible lead-up, a whole swirling backstory to the event, specific to me because I am an Extra being from an Extra commune. I sat with the entire gamut for a day and watched — no, I didn't watch, I went blind — as a rage beyond anything I could ever imagine swallowed me whole.

Was it expected of us? Was it expected of me that something so terrible would happen to me? Was it an initiation, my cross-over welcome into this plane of being fully human? I couldn't take it so far that I believed they — and by *they* I meant my parents and all the other Elders — already knew the specifics or even the general nature of the actual event, although I came pretty damn close. But they had to know that something of epic horror would likely happen to me.

And then what? Was I supposed to glom onto that warped line about *what doesn't kill you makes you stronger*? Stronger how? Was I stronger because I wanted to smash so many people including myself? Because I now had a group of people, half the human race, that I could look at and call my enemy? I had spent much of my young years studying the big historic events, the big traumas, in this country I call my own and in so many other cultures throughout human history, and of course, I knew my personal experience was small compared to the mass slaughters, enslavements, or minimalizing, one human group has endlessly done to another. But the intent, the hatred, the viciousness I experienced was one more breeding ground from which all the human nastiness begins.

On the third week anniversary of my event, I decided to go home to what I had for most of my human life believed was the sweetest spot on our planet. The small part of me who was still an observer, who continued to carry a hint of awareness, recognized that the Jade Furlong who had last visited a few months earlier was not the same one who was about to come blasting through the palace gates and turn her parents' world upside down. But I didn't care much because, more than anything, I needed answers. And I needed somebody to blame.

I packed my car with a few things and began the drive. I hadn't phoned, texted, or emailed that I was coming but I was certain my parents would know something was up. In varying degrees, depending on the person, that's how these things work for us. And I knew that the second they saw me, it wouldn't take anything mystical beyond the magic of a normal parental connection for them to determine that I was a damn mess. I imagined standing in front of them, commanding myself not to fall apart just yet, and calmly leading them into our living room. And when my younger brother—whose Extra layer I once witnessed enter his new-born body and who for his entire life that connection had bound us so tightly together—would come out of his room, I would firmly ask him to leave. Then I would share the generalities of the event, and my parents would move too close to me, try to comfort me, and pass me some of their healing energy. As I played out the scenario, I realized I wanted none of it, I was not ready for it, and maybe never would be. I also realized that, because of the fundamental nature of our entire commune, I would be dragging them into a predicament from which there would be no easy way out.

The responsible follow-up action after an experience like mine is to report it to the police, and now that my emotional direction had begun its shift, it was exactly what I wanted to do. The problem was, an unwritten yet obvious aspect of our Extra-normal community had always centered around the concept of *hiding in plain sight*. Our little commune outside of Anderson, the tiny town in south-central New York, was surrounded by other much larger and more exciting communities, some still growing, some on their way down, and some nothing more than ghost memories still hovering on the now barren land. This was why we were there, why our piece of land had been chosen so many years before. Quirky communes were the norm in our region, and if we could present to the outside world a boring façade, and hide the fact that ours was far more outrageous than any of the others, then this was the perfect location.

If I reported my experience, I was an Extra drawing attention to my community. If I didn't, I was a human who was allowing sick people to continue their awful behavior on others. I knew the dilemma would create a terrible quandary for my parents, especially because the whole point of our small group was, in some still evolving way, to send help out to the sprawling outer world. And I would say to my parents, "Guess what, Mom and Dad? Here's your opportunity to do some good for humanity. I even might have some evidence" And, of the three perps, only two of them participated while the third one nervously watched. So, just like a shitty cop movie, I had no doubt that this third one would turn on the other two participants.

My parents would say they needed to talk to some of the other Elders to create a plan of action. They would beg me to stay with them, at least for a few days. And they would arrange a healing ceremony right away. Then they would struggle with their dilemma, and just like me, would question everything about our greater cause. And if their wordless thoughts, specific ones, accidentally spilled over to me, which can easily happen to us in these situations, I didn't think I could stand it. I had known for a long time that my parents believed I was not only Extra-normal but also Extra-special. Like I had some greater destiny, some more noble path I was preparing for. And whatever it took, whatever happened along the way was part of my special prep. My God, if I were to catch any of that crap coming from them, well…

I turned around, headed back to campus, and as I drove, began to formulate a plan to set in motion as quickly as possible. One thing I knew was that the sideliner at the event, Richard something, lived on campus, which at the State University, meant he would be one of about three thousand. At first, I couldn't remember his last name, but then, like a gift from the ether, White, right after Richard, settled neatly in my brain.

That evening, I hustled across the campus to his dorm, face forward, my entire self, taut with purpose. I went through the front doors and into a lobby and asked anybody who came by if they knew Richard White and what room he was in. It didn't take long to get an answer. A minute later, I knocked on his door, and when I heard somebody say, "Come in," I burst through the opening. He was alone, lying on his bed, listening to music with a pair of headphones. My entrance, my presence, surprised him, and he tore off the headphones and leaped off the bed. I moved in close so that I was a foot from him and blocked him from trying to escape. His round eyes grew larger and his mouth fell open. We stared eye to eye but he was ten or twenty pounds heavier. Yet he dripped with fear, and from my years of studying human history, I knew that, in a battle between rage and fear, rage always wins.

I slammed the palms of my hands into his upper chest, my fingers striking his throat, and knocked him back onto his bed. It was the first time in my human life I had ever struck somebody and it was as if something else had taken over my actions. He scooted back on the bed and pushed up against the wall so I knew I had him cornered.

I towered over him, my stance wide, hands on hips, and spoke with such calm that, for a moment, as if I were two people, I felt a slice of my own fear of this commanding speaker. But only for a moment. I pulled a scrap of paper and a pen from my pocket and dropped both in front of him.

"This is what you're going to do now. On this paper, you will write both your friends' names, addresses, phone numbers, and e-mails. And you will never tell them about this visit."

He sat up with a touch of defiance. "No way."

"I have the red plastic cup still with some drug-filled liquid in it. With yours and my fingerprints and DNA on it. I also took photos.

"Your phone was dead. We ran it down."

I had already prepared my response. I tapped my coat pocket. "But it's on now and I just recorded your confession."

He moved to try to stand. I loomed closer over him. "If you try to get up, the door behind me is open and I will scream. Now listen carefully. You have three choices: write the info; refuse to write the info and my next stop is the police station; or you can try to kill me."

My words added a new element of fear. I could feel his panic deep into my own bones. As I gave him a moment to reflect on his options, information stored in his brain lit up in front of me like shiny text on a movie screen. In normal circumstances, I would have hidden my lapse of control, but I instantly settled on the idea that, if I continued to speak first, it might disturb him so much it would seal the deal between us. And it did.

I said, "Okay, Richard White from Ashford who went away to a four-year school and left his two buddies behind at the Community College, it's time to get writing."

He wrote down one of the names, Masked Man Lance Ewing, and with his shaky hand barely able to hold the pen, started on the second name.

I jumped in. "The next name is Mr. Beautiful, Billy Squires, he lives at 610 Grant Street in Ashford, and you don't remember his cell number." He backed away again, his face hot with terror, and he dropped the paper and pen. I scooped them up, propped myself next to a dresser, and wrote down everything I could get from him.

I threw the pen at him and he covered his face with his hands. I said. "I'm thinking we need to add a new more exciting element to this whole plan. You're going to call your buddies and ask them to come visit again. You're going to tell them it was so much fun the last time that you want to do a repeat. You'll juice it up, make up a sick story they will dream about."

"I'm not going to do that," he squeaked.

I said, "Then the other option is going to kick in right now. Police. Fingerprints. DNA sample. Recorded confession. That's what will happen if you don't call Lance Ewing and Billy Squires. I'll be checking up on you, watching everything you do. Same thing with your buddies."

I slowly backed through the doorway, my eyes glued to him, turned and ran down the hall, down the stairs, and back onto the green campus lawns. I tore across sidewalks, around trees, around and behind stately stone and brick campus buildings, down a few parking lots with signs that said "Permit Only," and finally slowed at a woodsier area near the edge of the campus. I fell on the ground, rolled onto my stomach, and tried to tighten all my muscles so my body wouldn't shake. I sat up and saw a hawk with its fierce beak and talons dive down, spear a baby rabbit trying to hide in the bushes, and soar away with its next meal. I saw hundreds of cats teasing their live captive mice, just like the catnip versions in their owners' living rooms. I saw the terror in Richard White's eyes as if it were my own. I rolled further into taller grass and brush until it sheltered me. I curled up and fell apart.

Adam

After Garrett left the ocean cottage, Adam didn't see him again until the end of the summer. He had spent all of July and the first half of August at a baseball training camp connected to his school, and when it ended, spent a week at home in Oakwood before going back to school for classes. Garrett was pumped up, wildly enthusiastic about a possible draft into the baseball minor leagues, and at first, Adam didn't know what to make of him. He seemed to have lost all his weird speech patterns and mannerisms and had no interest in discussing anything remotely philosophical. But after a day, Adam adjusted and was vaguely aware of a sense of some relief because he could more easily ignore the snippets of memory related to the events at the cottage that occasionally popped into his head. If Garrett could present himself in a shallow and superficial manner, Adam had no problem hopping on board. They threw baseballs in the backyard, watched thoughtless movies, and drank beer or occasionally raided their parents' liquor cabinet.

The day Garrett was scheduled to leave, they sat in the backyard, slouching on metal lounge chairs, drinking some kind of smoothie their mother had made, and Adam said, "It's been a lot of fun hanging out with you this week. Things are a lot easier when you can act like a couple of dumbasses. Not take anything seriously."

The shift was instant. Garrett sat up and swiveled so he faced Adam. His face tightened and his eyes seemed to drill into Adam. "You don't remember anything, do you? Try to keep it that way."

Adam glared back. "What are you talking about?"

An hour later, Garrett packed his car, hugged his parents, and when he hugged Adam, he whispered, "Don't worry, man. Everything's going to be okay. Just flow with whatever comes next."

Adam watched, quiet and dazed, as Garrett's car grew smaller and disappeared around the corner.

For the next nine months, Adam only saw Garrett when he came home briefly during the winter and spring breaks. He redirected his focus to finishing his senior year of high school, getting into one of the three colleges at the top of his list, and most importantly, navigating his first romantic relationship. The romance was a typically up-and-down, emotionally draining first love, and consumed a large enough portion of Adam's thoughts and interests that he almost didn't notice Garrett's absence. But, at the end of the school year, when he and his girlfriend mutually agreed to go their separate ways, it was almost like an instant re-emergence of packed-away memories.

It was a given that the Kastners would again rent their ocean cottage and Adam would spend at least a week or two there, as would Garrett. Yet, now that Adam's attention was freed up, he noticed changes in his parents' behavior and also, began to wonder where Garrett had been all year. A few weeks before they were scheduled to go to the ocean, he overheard his parents in a hushed yet slightly heated discussion and concluded that the vacation was now off the table for the year. He couldn't hear the next part but he knew it had something to do with Garrett.

A week later, as he was going to bed, he heard them talking again, this time faintly through his bedroom wall. He pressed his ear against the wall and heard the entire conversation. Clifford said he was getting updates on Garrett and tried to reassure Ingrid that everything was still okay.

"But what about his school?" she asked.

"He may have to take a leave of absence."

"Hope Community. It doesn't give me much hope."

Hope Community. Why was she talking about it? Adam had heard the name somewhere, but it didn't mean anything to him. He booted up his computer, navigated to Yahoo, and did a search. He found a one-page Hope Community website with a few photos, an address and phone number, and a vague description of the purpose and social structure of the organization. The group was located about an hour from Albany in the southern Adirondack Mountains, not far from Adam's house. But why would Garrett have anything to do with them when he was at a school in New Jersey? Adam's curiosity soared. He wondered how he would broach the subject with his parents and decided he wouldn't, at least not until later in the summer.

He wrote a short email to Garrett, asking how he was doing and whether he was going to come home at all during the summer. He also mentioned that he'd finally been accepted at Emerson College in Boston starting the coming fall. He didn't receive a reply and tried again a few weeks later. This time he got a quick return.

"Can you meet me in Albany today? If so, I'll give you a time and address. Please don't tell I and C. Love G."

Adam responded, "Sure. Give me info."

A few hours later, Adam drove to the edge of downtown Albany, beneath an overpass supporting a busy highway, and came to a waterfront park on the edge of the Hudson River. He parked his car in a nearly empty lot, scanned the park, and spotted Garrett by the river a hundred feet or so away, standing with his hands behind his back, staring into the slow-moving but powerful water.

He came up behind Garrett, "Garrett?"

He turned and gave Adam a tight hug. "Man, it's so good to see you."

"Why are you here? Why didn't you come home? Or stay at school?"

"It's a long story." He started to walk.

"Hey, stop," Adam said. "Can't we just, like, sit somewhere and talk?"

Garrett halted. "I can't tell you much because…"

"Yes, you can. I'm worried about you. Mom and Dad are worried about you. I heard them arguing and Dad said he was checking up on you."

Garrett pointed to the water. "We can go to that dock over there."

The dock was perched high enough above the river that they could sit on it and dangle their feet over the side without getting them wet. Dark clouds hid most of the late-morning sun and enough of a breeze wafted by to deliver a faint chill. The elevated highway behind them roared with cars and buses, but other than a few boats in the distance, the water was deserted.

"This is quite a river, you know," Garrett said. "On the one end are wild mountains and at the other, our biggest city and the vast ocean."

The comment was typically Garrett and added a touch of normalcy that Adam appreciated. "Yeah, I've read a lot about its history."

Garrett ended the reprieve. "So how is Dad checking up on me?"

"I have no idea. And then Mom said something about Hope Community. What's it all about? There's not much information online about it."

"I've been working with them. They're helping me figure some things out."

"About what?"

"About me."

Adam nearly whispered, "This again." He raised his voice, tensed. "I want to go there. Like right now."

"What are you talking about?"

"To Hope Community. I read about it. It's not far from here. It's where you've been staying, right?"

"You can't go there."

"Why not?"

"Because it's still under construction. They're expanding. Making a whole big place."

"So where do you go to meet with them?"

"Uh…"

"Garrett, listen to me. I'm really worried about you and I'm going to figure out what you're involved in whether you tell me or not. I'm going to find out everything there is to find out about this Hope Community. I mean, this whole thing sounds so weird. Like some kind of secret cult."

Garrett shifted his gaze. He stared at Adam until he turned his head and stared back. Garret said, "You don't remember, do you?"

"Remember what?"

"From last summer. What happened last summer. When we were at the cottage."

Adam looked at the water and saw pieces of imagery dance and dazzle in the current. Memories lay on the surface, almost there, but not able to fully form before they were sucked downstream. The sun even broke through the gloom and helped to illuminate and intensify the frames. He wanted to turn away but couldn't. It was never complete but still enough of a replay that it reactivated a memory of his meeting with Old Elwood.

He turned to Garrett, furious. "Are you doing this? Doing this to me?"

"No. You're doing it to yourself."

"So, what? Now I'm the crazy one? Fuck you, Garrett!"

Adam hopped up, ran off the dock and back toward the parking lot. As he approached his car, powerful arms grabbed him from behind and pulled him tight against a massive body. "Let go of me," he said. But he didn't struggle.

Garrett's firm voice said, "We're going for a walk. I want you to meet somebody."

Adam didn't resist. He stayed next to his brother, matching his rapid pace, and a few minutes later they stood in front of a non-descript slightly rundown four-story white-brick building in a neighborhood filled with similar buildings and metal-sided warehouses. Garrett opened a glass front door, grabbed onto Adam's arm, and led him down an empty hallway with windowless, dark-brown veneer doors on either side. Their feet hitting the tiled floors created a tapping rhythmic sound and overhead lighting embedded in the ceiling tiles cast a pale haze.

Somewhere in the middle of the hallway, Garrett stopped, opened a door, and led Adam through an empty office. At the other end, he knocked on another faceless door and Adam heard a voice say, "Come on in."

A man and a woman, maybe in their late thirties or early forties, sat on cushions on a dingy carpeted floor. They were dressed nearly identically in stretchy pants and loose tops and were barefoot, like they were doing yoga or meditating. The room had one large window that gave a glimpse of a view of the river, one couch—no other furniture— and a few pieces of artwork on the walls Adam didn't notice at first.

"Hey Garrett, nice to see you." the woman said. "Is this your brother?"

"Yes, this is Adam. Adam, this is Max, Max Schultz," he motioned to the man, then to the woman, "and Olivia Santini."

They both said, "Hi Adam," and Max said, "Would you like to sit with us here or would the couch be more comfortable?"

Adam and Garrett were both dressed in jeans, tee shirts, and running shoes. Garrett kicked off his shoes and sat on one of the cushions and Adam did the same.

Max had straight blond hair and a round face that, with his twinkly gray eyes and wide smile, gave him a cheery expression. Memorable. He addressed Adam. "First off, sorry for the sterile surroundings. We're only here for a little while longer. Now, Garrett mentioned you might stop by and that you were interested in what he's been up to with us."

"Uh, yeah. We were always close, and we've been out of touch more than I'd like so, yeah, I just wanted to make sure he's okay."

"That's so sweet," Olivia said. "He's lucky to have a brother like you."

"I truly am," Garrett added.

She had bleached her hair nearly white, her light blue eyes had thick penciled-in outlines, and her skin was so pale it seemed transparent. A thought swished through his head that was both unnerving and entertaining. She was Old Elwood's daughter, or maybe even his granddaughter. But somehow, in some way he couldn't begin to understand, he thought she was beautiful. He caught a part of a strange mandala-shaped tattoo on the underside of her arm, in strong contrast to her skin, and it added to the attraction.

Garrett acted like he was comfortable, at ease with these people. Yet he also truly valued their opinion and wanted Adam to like them. It was fine. Adam would go along with it.

"Garrett came to a lecture I gave at his college," Max said, "and met with me afterward. We got to talking and realized we have a lot in common. I gave him some advice, he returned the favor, and we kept in touch."

"Advice like how we're supposed to function in these strange bodies we inhabit?" Adam couldn't believe what he'd just said. Was that a scowl Garrett gave him? He didn't think he sounded snarky.

Max continued, "Well, yes. There are a lot of ways to phrase it and your way certainly works. Many people, many humans, are born content and stay content throughout their lives. And others are restless and always eager to make changes in their circumstances. Then there is a group of people who often feel like something is amiss, something is not correct with who they are. They might feel that their gender is incorrect or they live in a cultural climate where expressing their sexual preference is forbidden. Or it might be a situation where they feel as if their mind, body, soul, and spirit do not sync correctly together."

"So, you believe each person has a soul and spirit."

"We believe there are a few different types of what you might call a spirit."

Adam turned to Garrett. "Is that what you believe? That your mind/body/soul/spirit is out of synch?"

"Something like that."

Adam did his best to sound genuine. "Okay, that's good. I'm glad you're getting help with it."

"How about you, Adam?" Olivia asked. "Do you ever feel like any of this could be happening to you? Like your brother?"

"Uh, well, uh…" He stopped for a few moments. "Not that I'm aware of. No. I would say no."

But he did. Max's words gave a quick and accurate definition of a feeling Adam had had for… as long as he could remember.

Olivia said, "We describe what Garrett is feeling as a Misconfiguration because the different parts of a human come together from a few sources and don't always integrate in the most beneficial way. We've developed—and are still fine-tuning—a whole healing system we call Reconfiguration, to correct whatever parts are out of sync with each other."

Adam asked, "So some of the parts you're referring to are the soul and spirit, right?"

"That's pretty close. Yes. We believe it's more complex than that but it's a good place to start."

Adam looked away and a painting on one of the walls caught his attention. It was done in oils and showed a strange temple next to a lake with mountains in the background. In the sky and the air over the lake, vertical bands of multicolored light hovered and shimmered. At first, he found it enthralling and then disturbing. He wanted to leave but he didn't want to create a scene or upset Garrett.

"What's involved with Reconfiguration?" he asked.

Max took over. His voice was like silk, soft and soothing. "It's a wonderful process but it does take time and commitment. How about you hang with us for a little bit and we can give you a sample of the beginnings of the journey. If nothing else, you'll get an idea of what we're doing with your brother and it will put your mind at ease about his personal path."

"Sure, yeah, fine. What do I do next?"

"We'll go into another room, a little more comforting than this one, and do a short session with you."

Max and Olivia stood, and Garrett stayed seated. Olivia extended her hand to Adam. He began to panic, now desperate to leave, but he'd lost any ability to do so. They were at the door and he turned to Garrett, still sitting. "You're not coming with us?"

His eyes were closed, and he sat cross-legged with his hands in his lap. "I'll be here when you're done."

They led Adam into the hallway, past a few doors, and into a dimly lit, windowless room that smelled like a calm pine forest. They put him in a plush lounge chair and sat on short wooden stools on either side of him. What followed was a series of taps and rubs from both sides, on his forehead, his arms, and his chest, and then a sense of oblivion. He was still conscious but somehow not, still in his body but also not. He felt anxious yet the anxiety was more interesting and acceptable than fearful. Was it like being in a sensory deprivation tank? He'd never had the experience but had read about it, so maybe. Except he was sharing it with two other beings. His eyes were closed but he could see them and they looked like bodies of light. Like the bands of light in the painting on the wall of the first room.

A voice said. "We're here with Adam and ask for assistance in our procedure."

He thought he'd fallen asleep, but he couldn't have because he was now sitting next to Garrett on the cushions in the other room. The two of them were alone.

When Adam spoke, it was like tones through a layer of gauze "Wasn't somebody else here with us?"

"No, we're alone."

"Where are we?"

"Someplace I come to hang out sometimes."

His voice became stronger. "How did we get here?"

"We walked from the water."

"The river. And my car is nearby. My keys!" He dug frantically into his pocket and pulled them out. "I thought I might have lost them."

"I should get going," Garrett said. "I'll walk you back to your car."

As they walked, Adam thought he'd forgotten something, like what often happens when waking up from a dream, when with every minute that passes, the memory of what it was about slips away a little more until it is gone. When they reached his car he asked, "Do you need a ride somewhere?"

"No, I'm fine. Are you going home?"

"Uh, I guess so."

The last conversation was not part of the disappearing dream. Adam remembered every word. And it stayed with him for a long time.

"Well, it was nice hanging out with you," Garrett said. "I'll be in touch soon. And remember, keep this meeting between us because Mom and Dad worry about everything way too much these days and they don't need to. I'm fine, Adam. I'm better than ever."

Jade

After another month, the constant presence of the awfulness slightly diminished, giving me room for other sensations. What came next was one of the biggest surprises of my life. I began to experience a new awareness I can only describe as the exact opposite of the early terrors, as if an outside force, some form of energetic medicine, had entered me, and its purpose was to push back against the negativity. At first, I welcomed it as the return of the familiar pervasive quality of well-being that was a defining aspect of somebody from our commune. This quality—gentle, calm, and peaceful—was always there for us, acting as the backbone of our social harmony. I could breathe again, exist again, be positive and okay again. Or so I thought. My explanation for the return followed logic stating that, unlike a normal human's response to trauma, to bury it in dissociation or compartmentalization, an Extra-normal—or, I should say, an Extra in a human body—will have an inherent natural ability to always find their way back to their underlying, stable self. It was a good theory but it didn't last long.

Over the next week, I began to notice small things in increasingly outrageous ways. I tracked a tiny spider making its way across a sunlit windowsill until its glorious hair-like legs attached to the vertical window frame, in and out of the solar glow, magically ascending to some new place. The love I felt for that spider, for the windowsill it was on, for the sun that illuminated the entire experience, electrified my being. I saw a car angle back and forth into a parking space and four humans climb out, shut the doors, and step onto the sidewalk. I wanted to know their names and every detail of their infinitely complex lives. I wanted to know all this because they were sacred, and I loved them and cared so deeply for them. And when my gaze fell on the car, I wanted to take it completely apart and figure out how to put it back together. Right there in the street because I knew I could.

It was all so joyous, so exciting, so much fun. In its peak moments, I felt connected to every aspect of reality, and therefore, I might be able to understand the entire universe. As a lifetime bookworm who had studied everything imaginable, the temptation was irresistible.

After a few days of these kinds of experiences, I began to think they were related to the reasons why growing up in our community, we were gently advised to approach any form of mind-expanding substances with extreme caution. Not because they were bad or evil—and, in fact, certain substances were thought to be helpful to the Normals and even to the Walk-ins—but because they could disrupt the well-being inherent in our Extra makeup. In short, I began to think that I was experiencing what it was like to ingest psychedelic drugs. Except, where the drug wears off after four, eight, or twelve hours, my experience had become an ongoing condition.

By chance—or perhaps by design—I overheard a few classmates discussing a party they were about to attend that night, in a private home with a limited number of attendees, and with a drug I'd heard about, ecstasy, that was scheduled to fuel the whole event. I had watched videos of enormous raves but never gone to a live one, so I went to my dorm room, plugged in headphones, found a clip, and tried to observe where my being traveled. Oh, yes! Oh, yes! The perfect music, the perfect vibe.

I tagged along, told my companions I'd already downed my substance—which I most certainly hadn't—found a center spot packed with hot writhing bodies, and let myself go wild.

I had fun for an hour or so and then it became awful. I started to feel nauseous, shaky, and the worst part, convinced that something really bad was about to happen. Without thinking it through, I left and found myself, once again, on a lonely late-night panicky escape run. I told myself that I'd be all right because this time I wasn't covered in shit, piss, blood, and vomit. But by the time I got back to my room there was no consolation left. I crawled into bed with my clothes on and thought I was going to die.

This latest experience gave the trauma one more tool to drag me away from any illusion I had about control, of myself or any aspect of the world around me. One more reason to mourn the departure of my state of well-being. Forever? I had no idea.

My lust for peak experiences toned down and the rage gradually returned, although in a different form. It became subtler, more integrated, more calculated, as did a powerful dose of cynicism traveling alongside it. Love? Did I feel love? Not so much anymore. As these impulses emerged, they also merged so that, in many ways, I actually did become a new person. I became somebody who wanted things for reasons opposite of "doing good in the world." I learned exactly what these things were and knew I could get them whenever I wanted. And nobody could stop me. Did I continue to entertain the idea that this was all some type of plan dreamed up by the Elders in my community to help me fully understand the outside human world, the world of this body that I continued to inhabit? Who the fuck cared. I sure didn't.

My calculated quiet seething mind settled on a specific subset of humans. According to my earlier studies, only one subset on the planet is nearly as large as the one I and all females belong to. The fractionally smaller group is the one I placed my anger on. As I walked around the campus, went to classes, ate in the cafeterias, went to the occasional theater or sporting event, I began to microscopically observe the interactions between males and females. I especially liked studying first time introductions between genders. With single college-aged kids, and many who are in the stage of "I'm looking for a change," introductions are often about possibilities for something new and exciting. In my past self, I would have been equally interested in introductions between single gays or lesbians, however, now I was searching for information I could apply to my own sexual orientation, that would further my own specific quest.

In my new more human state, I had begun to obsess over the *ugly Matilda* comments delivered by my captors even more than the actual confinement. Perhaps this was my own version of psychological shielding because it made no sense that I would care as much as I did. Or perhaps even one or two nasty comments from those in positions of power about a person's appearance really can have a deep and damaging effect. One Saturday, instead of studying for a class exam, I spent the day online looking at photos and videos of movie stars whose appearances resembled mine and who were considered to be *sexy* or *hot*. I studied their speech, mannerisms, clothes, and makeup. That afternoon, I drove to a clothing store and bought a new short dress, tight leggings, and a nice jacket to keep me warm in the November chill. I went back to my dorm room, dressed myself, made up my face with just the right amount of makeup, and dabbed on a quiet yet captivating perfume in a few places. At the end of my session, I looked myself over in a full-length mirror and was amazed. This person looking back at me defined a specific type of hot and sexy, not for everybody, but when you liked her you really liked her. Yet who was this person? I quickly turned away because, knowing what she was up to, I could barely stand to see her. She embodied ugliness of a different sort.

A few of my dorm mates had planned a trip to a frat party and I saw a perfect opportunity. It was only the second evening event I'd been to since my lockup and the terror circled and bit into me a few times. But my determination overrode the fear. I had set rules for myself: no alcohol, not even a sip, no drugs of any sort, and a watchful eye on every human detail. On this night I was the one in charge and nobody else was going to change that. We arrived around nine at another enormous century-old mansion that had been rehabbed and updated, this time as a frat sanctuary for young men. The outside looked immaculate and well-cared for, with freshly painted clapboard walls in one color and the complex architectural details accented in three more hues. We went inside the building and the vastness of the interior, not yet half-full with partiers, had a way of swallowing us into its purpose and plan for the night. Or was it only my plan? The interior had given up on prissy appearances. The once-lustrous hardwood floors had been scraped and muddied to a dull gray, and where the lighting allowed, the walls and ceilings, especially in the angles of where they met, hosted a thick blend of dust, dirt, and cobwebs. My only impression of the furniture was that, when the year ended, it would—or should—all go into the dumpster.

Within an hour, kids packed the entire downstairs. By then, I had bought into a stereotype, made a judgment, and grouped everyone there together as all the same genre. To the entire group, I assigned labels like shallow, immature, uninteresting. Specifically, for the males, I used: arrogant, hyper-masculine, insensitive, rude, and mean. I knew exactly what I was doing, I still had enough insight to observe my own behavior, but the reason I gave myself for being so judgy was that I was scared. Scared of these people. Scared of trying out my plan on any of them. And it was true. The terror had resurfaced and I couldn't get *ugly* out of my brain. But I also couldn't give up and validate the descriptor, validate what those beautiful lockup creeps called me. I began to notice, first one, then two, then a few more, young males hanging in groups, not talking, uncomfortable, probably lonely. One of them would be my mark. I had to start somewhere.

He stood about twenty feet away in another mixed group. I looked his way, no flirty eyes or smile, neither warmth nor iciness, and turned back to my group. I thought he'd seen me but wasn't positive so I looked again. This time our eyes met and I nodded hello and put on the hint of a smile. I turned away again. A few minutes later, I made a run to the bathroom and walked near him. He turned to me, forced a smile and a hello, and I stopped. I didn't even need to do any obnoxious mind-reading to know what he was all about. Shy, nervous, and scared. This one had no bro energy, he was too far the other way, and I was about to keep walking when he stuck out his hand and said, "My name's Tommy. What's yours?"

Ah yes. I detected a bit of an edge. And with his soft face, big honey-brown eyes, and cute hair, he had just the right look. I played the role to the max. I became sweet, kind, and attentive, with the perfect amount of animated humor and intelligence. I quickly figured out what he was looking for and became that person.

Around midnight, I took him back to my room and began my game. I got him all worked up, then stopped, then started again. One more time, when I refused to do more than let him give me a few chaste kisses, he stood and said, "Hey Jade. I'm going to go."

I'd thought I was in control of him but he easily flipped it the other way. "Why?"

His tone was polite. "I'm sorry but I guess you're just not right for me."

"Why, because I'm ugly?"

He shook his head and rolled his eyes. "Ugly? Hardly. The only thing ugly is this weird game you're playing."

"So, you really don't think I'm ugly?"

"What the fuck is wrong with you, anyway?" He opened the door and as he walked through, said, "I've got enough of my own problems. You're the last thing I need in my life right now." He slammed the door behind him.

My roommate was gone for the weekend so I was stuck alone in my tiny dorm room for the rest of the night, trying to extract some meaning from my stupid waste-of-time attempt to make myself feel better. At first, I actually did feel a touch better about myself, because some random guy told me my physical body wasn't ugly. But, so what? I mean, why would I ever be so fragile that it should make a difference to anything? I kept replaying in my head all the bad interactions I'd had in the last month with the male gender, decided I needed a break from all of them, maybe forever, and finally fell asleep.

As I drifted back to daylight the next morning, my first thought was that I had now experienced in a small form one way the human species fuels its endless suffering. The oppressed can become the oppressor—or often wishes to but doesn't succeed—who then oppresses, and like a house of mirrors, it goes on and on for eternity. Intellectually I had understood the pattern from the time I first dove into the history books and now I had played first-hand with its underlying constructs. I sat with this new awareness for a while and then tried to tune into my internal rage-o-meter, wondering if this big insight—humanity lesson number three-hundred-eight-seven, or something thereabouts—might have tamed it down a touch. Oh sure, it certainly did. But only for a day or two.

The last month had been too intense to prioritize following up on my threats to Richard White. And he certainly didn't contact me. I decided he was my next mark although I was now less clear about what that meant. But I did need to follow up with the whole matter and somehow get my earlier threats relayed to the other two lockup characters, Lance and Billy. The next day, I walked across the campus to Richard's dorm, found his room, and banged my fist on the door.

The door opened and a strange face and voice said, "Yeah? Can I help you?"

"I'm looking for Richard White. Is he in there?"

"Wow, no. He left school about a month ago."

"What?"

"Yeah, he just took off, dropped out. He wouldn't tell me why. Something bad must have happened."

I rushed out and sprinted back to my room. What the hell, what the hell! I ran through any possible scenario I could think of and they all ended with the other two going forward with no consequences, not now or ever. I had the phone number of one of them, Lance Ewing, and considered calling him. Or going in person to Ashford, his hometown. Or doing the most responsible action which was going to the police. All options were bad so I decided to give myself another few days and then do something.

The next day, I left the campus in my car and drove to another nearby town to a discount clothing store to buy a new thick coat. The icy chill of the approaching winter was creeping in around the edges, letting us know what was on the horizon, and I wanted to be prepared. As long as I had decent warm clothing, I had always loved winter and the crisp breeze and gray clouds hinting at an early snow were a welcoming sign. As I drove, I had the heat on but cracked the window so the cool clean air could invigorate me, and I considered revisiting my younger days and buying a new pair of cross-country skis.

In an instant, the mood changed, as if somebody out there had flipped a switch to off. The wrongness of my situation roared over me like a grey landslide. I looked in my mirror and saw a car I'd noticed earlier. It had to be following me. Or maybe not. Maybe the last month had finally done me in and reality had become an endless paranoid hallucination. I pulled into a large parking lot in front of a strip mall and parked near the clothing store. The car behind me also pulled in and parked a few lanes away. A man stepped out and my intention was to run to him and ask him why he was following me but the shaky panic thing took over and I couldn't do it.

Until he passed my window and I saw who it was and my rage came back in all its glory. I pushed open the car door and yelled to him to stop. I stood a foot from his beautiful face which now, because of who he was, looked only monstrous. "Billy Squires, right? Or Lance Ewing. I get you mixed up."

"Who the hell are you?"

He tried to walk around me but I stepped in front of him. "I have the cup with the drug and wine. And I have a recorded confession from Richard."

"I have no idea what you're talking about."

And once again, I dove in to where I didn't belong, directly into his mind, telling myself I had no other option. This guy was Billy Squires and he knew exactly who I was. He also knew exactly what I was doing.

He cracked a tiny smile and said without words, *Get out of my head, Jade. You don't belong here.*

Once again, he had me, except this time it was so much worse. No amount of rage was going to get the best of him. It was all I could do to keep from puking right there. All the epithets I might have placed upon him a few seconds earlier had now become meaningless. Even the terms kidnapper, torturer, anything, didn't begin to describe the nightmare of who and what this person was.

I had grown up with the term, Walk-in, which referred to an Extra who had entered into an already-developed human. My ancestors were Walk-ins and had been part of the communal movement centered around the early baptisms that had tried to create a less complex and more predictable human format for the Extras to enter. But the communal movement had its own share of challenges and the practice of walking in only grew more common. In general, Walk-ins were not much different from the Extras from birth. However, in the last few decades, a phenomenon had developed where fully-grown humans turned the tables and summoned in the Extras for their own purposes, oftentimes to the detriment of the other humans around them. In other words, they received powers without the accompanying compassion and wisdom and used those powers for their own personal gain. We called those beings Stealers and they did not like beings like myself who came from a commune and whose Extra aspect was summoned at birth. And this man, who had tortured me and now stood in front of me, was a Stealer of the worst sort.

As I ran from him, I began to grasp the enormity of the situation. The awful event I had experienced was not a random happening and its purpose was in no way designed to assist me in my growth. Those two men, Lance and Billy, had targeted me because I was an Extra-normal from birth who had a reputation outside the walls of our compound as somebody who, once she came of age, might become powerful in a way I did not yet understand. Their act had nothing to do with growth and wisdom, it was meant to destroy me. And the scariest part came when I realized I was only a small slice of the whole scenario.

My car could barely contain me on my ride home. I saw the defeated face of the innocent boy from the frat house and begged him to forgive me. Like replaying a painful movie, I imagined that I rushed back to Richard White's dorm room, took his shaking hand, pulled him off his bed, hugged him, and told him I was sorry. And I vowed to find him in the real world, to make sure he was okay. I also again decided to make a trip home and tell my parents everything. They needed to know and they would understand that this was not a matter for the local police. It went far beyond that.

I left the next weekend. It was now the end of October and most of the leaves had finished their journeys and fallen off the trees. The evergreens now took over the show, preparing for the inevitable white blanket that would cover them in another month or two. I didn't give my parents an advanced warning, drove through the gates of our community, parked my car, and walked into our house. The house was empty for an hour and I sat on a couch and breathed quietly to calm myself. When my parents arrived, they laughed and hugged me and showed me their love, but they knew something was wrong. Perhaps they had known before I'd arrived. It was even possible for them to have gone into my persona and found out specifics, but like other members of our community, they would never do that. And they didn't need to anyway because I was ready to share.

I was relieved my brother was not there, that he was with a friend somewhere. He was fifteen and still a gentle soul and I couldn't bear to be the one who took the first nasty piece out of his safe world.

My parents sat on either side of me and I started. "I'm not going to tell you the details of the actual event because they are not necessary but I will share my reactions for you to evaluate."

For the next few hours, I said what I could, what was most important. They cried, they sighed, and they climbed deep inside my pain. Then the buzz began, and a field of love, release, and relief encapsulated me like a miracle drug, and drained away some of the violence, the horror, and the memories. It brought a gentle quiet I hadn't experienced for so long and I slumped on the couch and felt my entire body, my heart, my breath, and my mind, slow down, at least a little bit. My doubts about this community, my doubts about being an Extra, my doubts about everything faded. However, the buzz also brought a companion along in the form of a question that to this day I still cannot answer: should I have returned immediately after my trauma to this safe space, or did I take the correct path and muddle through the ensuing insanity? Among humans, the road not taken often seems like it would have been a better option, second-guessing and all that, however, I am not entirely human, am I? What a conundrum. And then, my mother added some words, a summary of sorts, that elevated the past month to a whole new level.

"You are in a unique position now, Jade, and you get to decide, to make a human decision about what you will do next. One of the most important aspects to consider is that, when you leave here, when you mingle again with the outside world, your human qualities will re-emerge in strength. Your biases, fears, pleasures, and attractions will return in strength. That's just how it works. And you will continually experience the overwhelming human desire to control the events around you, even though you know it is fundamentally impossible. You know all this and I'm only reminding you. However, you are an excellent observer, one of the best who has ever been among us. And you can continue on the outside with all the drama of who this Jade being has become, and start to do amazing, helpful actions. But only if you believe you are ready. Or perhaps you don't ever wish to go that route. Again, this is your decision."

"And the Walk-ins? This Billy Squires character? Ultimately, we're all Walk-ins. So why do I hate him so much, and before I returned here, hated all humans, which I guess includes all of us here?"

My father gently took my hand and said, "You know the answer to that."

"If I go back out, he'll find me and try to damage me."

"He won't. It will be taken care of. But you do have to be very careful, always watchful."

"Taken care of," I said. "It sounds so horrible. Do I want to know what it means?"

"We will find him and try to do a conversion healing. But again, you already know all that."

My mother said, "Changes are happening out in the world, and we need observers."

"I also need to see Melinda in person right away. If I was a target, she surely will be also."

Even here in the safe place, the home of love, acceptance, compassion, and any other good stuff, my outside experience found a way to creep in. They saw I was getting worked up again and my mother said, "We can take away the memories for a while. Your Extra overlay does not allow your brain to do it automatically, but we can do it. You should consider it."

The speed and certainty of my response surprised them. "Absolutely not. I'm done with all the erasing processes."

"Well, at least I can do this." She leaned over and put her hand on my heart, and a final layer of tension still balled up in all my muscles drained away. My breathing slowed and the thumping in my heart, that had become the norm for me, stopped. Just like that. Her action reminded me of how easy it was to be a child growing up here. The outer world talks about the privileges one group of humans has fought to get, nearly always at the expense of other humans. I had never thought of it this way but the truth is, nothing could top the privilege I had growing up the way I did. Maybe my parents were right. Maybe I did have something to offer.

I left through the gate and made it about ten miles when the first odd thing happened. I thought of Melinda and instantly knew she was aware I was on my way to see her. It was strange because we had never before attempted to communicate in that way. And then, a half-hour later, I passed through a small town, stopped at a traffic light, and spotted somebody who looked like Billy Squires. All my noble and wholesome intentions vanished. It wasn't him but the appearance triggered a nasty thought accompanied by an even more horrendous vision. I wanted to tie up and kill the motherfucker and I saw outside the windshield a short video clip of myself locking him in a coffin and burying him alive.

Adam

Adam had come to a more secluded part of the quad to sit outside and to write. It should have been a perfect mix—two activities he loved, being outside and writing—but once again he couldn't concentrate. Another of his passions, finding an unobtrusive spot and watching the actions of others, always won out. When he was younger, he loved being around people, talking, telling stories, entertaining, keeping conversations going. However, after the difficulties of the last three years, he often kept his distance and only observed. And now, two weeks into his first semester at the four-year college he had transferred to, this type of distracting activity seemed to be present everywhere.

For the first hour, only a few other students passed by and he made a good start on a short story assignment he was working on for a creative writing class. The class was so popular that entrance was determined by a lottery. Among other things, Phelps college was famous for its creative writing and journalism majors, and he had drawn one of the lucky numbers, a relief because, for many reasons, he had already set sail on his academic voyage and chosen journalism as his major. Parts of his history, his life, needed serious investigation and he was not going to give up, he would never give up, until he fully understood certain events and the people behind them. Next, he planned to write in great detail about what he learned. He planned to out a few characters, to ruin their awful lives, and make them take responsibility for what they had done and were continuing to do to many vulnerable people.

He looked up from his laptop as two young women approached the general area where he was sitting. They laid out blankets and a picnic basket and set up a meal with plates, bowls of something, and glasses filled with soda or wine, he couldn't tell which. He considered going over, introducing himself, and trying to strike up a conversation, until he saw that they were also in his creative writing class. And one of them had a look about her that he found interesting, or if he was honest with himself, nearly irresistible.

For some reason, she unsettled him. It was something about her unique appearance: her thin face, which even at her age, still hadn't lost a distinct cover of freckles, her long straight brown hair with a hint of auburn, her slightly uneven front teeth that she fearlessly showed when she smiled. And the way she smiled, which was often, seemed almost like a challenge. *See, I'm not perfect*, it said. *I have physical imperfections, and I don't care.* She appeared as if she never wore makeup or at least none that decorated instead of only enhanced her look. He spotted her in the first class, and for the next three classes, had carefully positioned himself so he could watch her, without her being aware of it. Her name, Jade, was perfect and so beautiful. She did have green eyes, jade colored eyes, although, from as close as he'd been to her, they sometimes looked gray. She wore glasses with slightly tinted lenses so it was hard to tell for sure.

Maybe she knew he was watching her. During the second class he had an overwhelming feeling that, even though she didn't once look up from her group, she knew he was there and knew he had been observing her. Like she was the observed who was also an observer herself, and she knew exactly what he was up to and didn't appreciate it. Or maybe she did like it. Either way, he couldn't stop himself, so one way or another, he had to find out.

He scanned his memory for the name of the other one. Melissa? Marinda? Melinda, that was it. He would walk over and introduce himself. He had always liked that part of meeting new people because it allowed him to make a good first impression.

He put his laptop in his daypack, strapped it on, and walked by the two. He stopped and said, "Jade? Melinda, right? I'm in a few of your classes. I'm Adam."

Melinda looked up with a smile. "Yes, we know."

He liked that they knew his name. A good sign? Jade stared at him with an unreadable expression.

He was about to continue walking when Jade said, "Are you hungry? We have plenty of food. A few others were going to come and didn't show."

"Oh yeah, sure. Thanks."

He sat across from them and their positions on the blanket created a triangle with the basket of food in the middle. A few maple trees shaded them enough to make the bright afternoon sun tolerable. He liked being able to shift his gaze from one to the other or both at the same time. He liked being able to absorb Jade's appearance without being obvious.

Jade took a paper plate and a plastic fork from the basket and set them in front of Adam. She pointed to the other items on the blanket and said, "We have potato salad, hummus, and some good crackers. We got it all from that little deli just off campus. Eat as much as you want."

She pulled a bottle out of the basket. "And we have some wine if you're interested." This time she smiled. "But you have to be of age."

"I am that for sure. Old enough for that bottle and," he looked away, across the quad, and said in a near whisper, "who knows what else?"

He looked back and caught the quizzical expressions on their faces. He tried for a matter-of-fact tone. "I'm a transfer from a two-year school and I didn't start college at all until I was nineteen."

"Oh, that's so cool," Melinda said. "Jade just transferred here, too, for her final year. But we've known each other for a long time. We kind of grew up together."

"Oh. Where are you from?" Adam asked.

Melinda answered. "A small town in south-central New York called Anderson. You've probably never heard of it."

"I think I have. I'm from the Albany area."

Melinda talked more than Jade. She obviously liked conversation and presented herself fluidly and easily. Something about her made him think of Garrett but he wasn't sure why. They didn't look alike, she had shoulder-length black curly hair, dark skin, and dark brown eyes, and Garrett was blonde-haired and blue-eyed, but something was going on there. Maybe her mannerisms or the tone of her voice. He didn't have a quick answer and let go of the thought.

He asked them both about the short story writing assignment, how far they had gotten, what their plots were, and neither one answered. "Sorry," he said. "If you'd asked me the same question, I wouldn't have wanted to answer, either. But I bet you're both skilled at observing the world around you and can come up with some good ideas."

"Why would you think that?" Jade asked, monotoned.

"Uh, I don't know. I just thought, maybe."

Melinda said, "Well, we're all trying to improve our writing skills or we wouldn't have taken the class, would we? So, it's safe to assume that we all try to pay attention to the world around us. Right, Jade?"

"Sure." She poured herself another glass of wine.

A bit later, Adam helped the two pack up the leftovers and get ready to leave. When Melinda stood and stepped ahead, he understood another piece of the connection. It had to do with strength and symmetry, or as many would describe it, perfect beauty. In that way she was exactly like Garrett, and to take it one step further, Adam was positive that, again like Garrett, none of it was all that important to her.

When they reached a point on the campus where they would split up, Jade said to Adam, "Since you're of age and it's Friday, do you want to meet up tonight at the Crow's Nest? You know, that little bar on River Street. Music starts around nine and you'll meet a lot of people."

"Yeah, sure. Thanks for the invite."

Adam left the campus and ambled down a side street lined with coffee shops, delis, clothing stores, a computer repair shop, a few bars, and anything else that would interest students. He returned to his room in an off-campus student house he shared with five other guys. So far, the house was okay but he had already begun looking for a different, more private situation for the next semester. He had said he would meet at the bar later but wasn't sure he would follow through. Would it be an unnecessary distraction, a waste of time? Would it lead him back to the rough places, mental and physical, he'd spent so much time in over the last three years? He was here at school and finally had a serious direction, a goal, and he didn't want to screw it up.

Then there were the two women. Melinda was certainly nice enough. He had no problem with her, but Jade was a different story. She was a strange one. Her essence was bleak, so bleak, and she barely tried to hide it. But he was the same, wasn't he? Just like her. Maybe, for some warped reason, that was why he was so attracted to her.

He arrived at the Crow's Nest at nine-thirty and the music was about to start. He showed his driver's license at the door, paid a five-dollar cover charge, went directly to the bar, and ordered a cheap beer. It would be the first of two because that was all he would allow himself these days. He disliked the feeling of too much, the feeling of being out of control, and the awful hangovers the next day. But what he hated the most was losing his ability to watch what was going on around him, to study it with clarity and purpose.

Melinda and Jade hadn't arrived yet and the club was still only half-full. He sat on a bar stool facing out and scanned the entire space. The bar top ran the full length of the room and the stage snuggled in a far corner. Four musicians, two male and two female, scurried around setting up amplifiers, a PA system, microphones, and a small drum set. He hadn't bothered to check on the band beforehand, what type of music they played, or where they were from, and now tried to guess from their look and the instruments they were setting up, what they would be like. One of the women pulled a small accordion out of a pack and laid it on a chair, and then a fiddle out of a case and began to tune it. A bass guitar materialized in the hands of the other woman. And he saw a large upright bass propped sideways on the floor. The drums and guitars belonged to the two guys, and they all had microphones. Hipster Americana, playing a few originals, and covers ranging from current music to songs they'd heard as kids on their parents' tape decks. He decided he would hang for a half-hour or so, and unless the music grabbed him and held him, he would then leave.

The band finished their setup and sound check and began a song. The volume was manageable, the song unusual and kind of fun, and he decided he would stay with them for a while. Just as he resigned himself to being stood up, a group of five people pushed through the door. Melinda led the way and Jade came in last. He made eye contact with Melinda and her group followed her over to him for a round of introductions. She hugged him gently and followed her friends closer to the music. Jade held back, moved in close to Adam, and gave him an unexpectedly strong hug that almost made him flinch. He returned the pressure and fell into the field of her scent. Whatever it was she had on pulled the anxiety he had tucked away right out of him. He also smelled a hint of some type of herbal toothpaste, and underneath that, a few too many glasses of wine.

She presented a much looser vibe than she'd had earlier that afternoon, and if she was wanting to party with him, well, he was ready. She pulled one of the stools closer to him and sat. He said, "Can I buy you something?"

"OK, but I buy the next round."

The next round. Probably he would be having more than what he'd planned.

At first, Jade asked the questions and Adam answered. He shared where he was from—which she already knew from their earlier meeting—what his family was like, what music he liked, what he like to read, what he hoped to do when he finished school, and on and on. He knew he was holding back volumes. Such as: *do you have any siblings? Yeah, an older brother who I haven't seen in months and might be missing.* But he stuck it out, muddled through it with an endearing amount of humor and humility because, by then, he would have done about anything to flip the script and be the one to ask the questions.

They paused and sipped their drinks and Adam said, "Tell me what it was like to grow up in Anderson, New York."

"Well, all I can say is it was quiet, safe, friendly, and boring. But I liked it there because I was also boring. I liked to read and study and all that kind of fun stuff."

"Did you travel at all? You know, go visit other places?"

"Sometimes, yes. We have friends in a few places. We went to Chicago and DC to visit them, and to New York City quite often. So that's about it. Not much to tell you."

She was hiding most of her life. Just like him. He downed his second beer and began to feel a buzz, and with it, a small loosening of the flood gates that held back the torrents of his inner struggles. She wasn't going to get off that easy.

He asked, "And what's your plan when you leave here? If you could have it go any way you want, how would your future play out?"

"I'm in the writing class but don't see myself as a writer so much, especially fiction. I guess if I continued with writing, I would want to do articles for good magazines. Or maybe be an editor. Something like that. I also have a long-standing interest in history and am going to apply to a few graduate programs and see what happens." She looked toward the stage and said, "Hey, look, they're all dancing."

They watched the group, a few swirling and twisting, their hands and arms drawing patterns in the air, and others with their feet anchored, bobbing up and down. Melinda stood at the side with her body in a gentle sway and her mouth moving to the words of a popular song the band was covering.

"Look at her," Jade said. "She's so gorgeous."

A moment later, Adam moved close to her ear and said, "You're gorgeous, too."

She backed away and stared at him with that cold, humorless look he'd seen earlier. "Now, I just said Melinda is gorgeous because I've known her for many years and know that her entire being is gorgeous, not just how she looks. But you don't know me at all so when you tell me I'm that, you can only be referencing my superficial exterior. Would you not find such a comment kind of shallow and maybe even insulting?"

"Hey, hey, stop. I was just trying to be nice."

"Or maybe you just want something from me."

"No, I don't."

"I know the look. The checking her out thing. Observing from afar. You're one of those types."

This got to him. "Really? If I'm that type then I'm quite sure you are also."

She slid off her stool and hurried toward the bathrooms. As his eyes followed her, he caught another look at Melinda. She nodded at him, walked over, and sat on the empty stool.

"Everything okay over here?"

"Uh, not really. What is wrong with her? I was just trying to be nice. She said you were gorgeous and I told her she was too. And she lost it and said I was shallow and insulting."

Melinda gently took his hand and looked directly at him. Her eyes moistened, her mouth pursed, and her head slightly shook. "The last two years have been so hard for her, so difficult. She's been working through some major issues."

"Yeah, well you know what? So have I. My brother, who I was very close to, took up with a weird group of characters, a damn cult, and he stopped speaking to me or my parents. And, and..."

She squeezed his hand a little more. "It's so difficult existing in these human bodies, isn't it? Trying to negotiate the ups and downs of being human. It takes so much effort and sometimes it's absolutely exhausting. But we do the best we can to make it work."

His face froze and a dreamy detached feeling settled over him like a thick blanket. Those words again. Those words he'd forgotten. Who had said those words? Garrett spoke the language and likely lived within it on his long adventures in the fantasy of cult land. Another memory hovered below the surface, like a random chord the band was trying to play, stifled and wet, working to reveal itself, to take form and find its place in the music. Somebody else, something else that had happened. It taunted him and refused to come into focus.

"I have to go," he said. "Please tell Jade I'm sorry about what I said."

When Melinda hugged him, he imagined he felt electricity from her hands into his back and from her cheek into his. He only imagined it. It wasn't real.

"I'm sorry, too," she whispered.

He lay in bed in his spare little room, thankful it was at least private, and tossed around in the warm sheets. He had forgotten to open the window to let in the cooler night air and unclog his stuffiness. He opened it, lay back down, and a slight early fall breeze touched his face and sent him away to the other side. He stayed asleep for a few hours and woke with a sense of energy rushing through him, carrying with it all those hidden memories from his past. Old Elwood. That was the name. And the short meeting with those strange phrases. The ones Garrett used and now this Melinda person was using. He remembered running back to Elwood's ancient house and scurrying around trying to find traces of his earlier visit. Garrett had assured him it was all real, had actually happened. All real? What did that even mean anymore?

He had one question he desperately needed answered but he didn't want to track down Jade for it because she was way too strange. He would avoid her as much as possible and try Melinda instead, who was likely every bit as strange but knew better how to hide it.

A few days later, as he walked toward the campus, down the same street where the Crow's Nest was, he spotted Melinda going into a coffee shop. He was not much of a coffee drinker because it made him too hyper and messed with his sleep, and he'd never been in this or any of the other coffee shops in the town. Since his night in the Crow's Nest, he had tried to let go of any urgency he'd had about wanting to talk more to Melinda, or anybody else, about his memories, but it had become a near obsession and was not about to go away. The urge, the thrill even, of a potential discovery, a connection to follow which would add to an understanding of who his brother was, what he'd become, and now, where he had disappeared to, was too powerful to ignore.

The cute little shop had funky stained wooden tables and chairs, glass-fronted cabinets filled with pastries, and a counter piled high with the latest caffeine creating gadgets. As he ordered an iced green tea mix, he caught a glimpse of Melinda, sitting in a far corner and opening her laptop. He didn't look over and ruin his attempt to disguise the fact that he'd only come in to see her, that it was not a coincidence he was there.

He picked up his tea and turned his head, and she was looking at him. She smiled and motioned him over. He sat across from her and did his best to give her a neutral pleasant look.

"It's nice to see you again," he said.

"You too. I like working here because you're around others, but once your head is down and you're obviously lost in your work, everybody gives you space."

"Unlike what I'm doing?" He grinned as he said it.

"No, no. I'm not nearly ready to dive in yet."

"Hey, I wanted to ask you something and I hope it's not too weird."

The amused look on her bright face seemed genuine. "Weird is always fine with me. What's up?"

"Uh, I was wondering if you've ever heard of a guy, an old guy, who went by the name of Old Elwood."

At first, she didn't answer. Her face clouded and her eyebrows scrunched. Then she sat up and seemed to pull herself together, like she was shaking away her unease so she could present herself in an unconcerned manner. "Well, yes, certainly. He's a character in a picture book that looks like it should be for children but is more for adults."

"Really? Wow."

"Where did you hear about him?"

Like her, he tried to keep his face neutral and his body still. "Oh, somebody I know was talking about him like he was a real person."

"That's sort of the point of the book. He shows up when you're young and tells you things he thinks you should know. Then he disappears." An additional tone, slightly defensive, entered her voice. "But why are you asking me?"

He matched her tone. "I asked you because the other night you phrased a thought, a few sentences, in such a way that reminded me of how my possibly missing brother also speaks. And the other one who speaks the same way is this storybook character who I am suddenly remembering I met once and who is very real."

She became more defensive. "It might be that you think Old Elwood is a real person when in fact he is only somebody you invented in your dreams because you had subconscious memories of him from an earlier exposure to the book. Did somebody actually tell you he was real?"

Adam looked at her and felt like he was, one more time, slipping into a large dark hole. Once again, someone had tied a rope around him and was pulling him in. What was most disturbing was that this time, the one with their hands on the rope was someone who seemed so kind and honest. Yet, here she was, spinning circles around him, and dragging him with her into some kind of major bullshit about this whole Elwood thing. And anything else that had to do with his brother.

He leaned in close and said in a fierce whisper, "The one who told me he was real was my brother, Garrett. After I met the old man, I told my brother and he assured me I wasn't dreaming. But maybe I'm all mixed up. Maybe I don't remember any of it correctly. However, in order to figure out what's real and what's not, I do believe I need to see this book. Maybe you could tell me where I can get a copy."

She looked down at the table. "It's been out of print for a long time."

He picked up his paper cup filled with tea, left the shop, and slowly walked up the street toward the campus. He was in no rush to get there now and the thought of sitting in classes all day seemed like a slow torture. He wished he was more into drugs or alcohol because he wanted something to turn off his racing thoughts before they dragged that long uncoiling snake of anxiety too far inside him.

Instead of going to his next class, he went to the library, found a quiet space with a comfortable armchair, pulled out his laptop, and opened the short story he was working on for his class. He reread parts he'd already written, tweaked the grammar, punctuation, and spelling in a few places, and started writing where he'd left off the last time. Except, he couldn't focus, he didn't want to focus, and the whole idea of writing a short story for a class now seemed unimportant and irrelevant.

What surfaced as most pressing was to try to figure out who these two young women were and get details about where they were from, beyond only the name of some small town in central New York. They were hiding something about their background, he was sure of it. They might even have some connection to his brother, some information about him. They probably didn't know who Garrett Kastner was, but they might know quite a bit about where he'd been living for the last three years.

He opened a blank Word document and began a list of everything he knew about Garrett's current life. He was only a few minutes into it when two ideas popped into his head. The first one centered around the deeper focus of his studies at school. He would ask the teacher of the creative writing class if he could bypass any assignments involving fiction and swap them for non-fiction, his selling point being that he wanted to write a few magazine type articles focused on investigating something or someone. And he would push the fact that he was willing to do serious research on any subject he chose. The second thought related to the first. He had two trips he needed to make. The first one would be once again to the Hope Community to track down his brother. The second would be to Anderson, New York, the home of these two strange young women who spoke in such odd yet familiar ways.

Jade

Even before Melinda came back to the apartment, I knew something was off. I could taste it, smell it, feel it in the subtle shake going through my legs. And then I saw a strange movie clip like thing in my head of what had just happened with her. These types of events had been showing up for a few years for both of us, and we didn't bother shutting them down. But those gifts often extended outward, and when we were back in our home, we carefully monitored them. Adam was so spot on when he accused me of being an observer—yes, I am that, it's a key part of who I've always been—but I and most of the Extras had always made a conscious effort to never take it to the next level. The phrases I carried around with me, that guided my behavior in such matters, rattled on about how connection means kindness, caring, and empathy. But never an invasion into the depths of another being, especially without their knowledge. Or something like that. Yet the purest intentions behind all those lines that were supposed to give direction and inspiration, with the buzzwords encouraging faith and goodness, not only eluded me but also annoyed me. Because in those days, my observations were often not fueled by a desire for empathic connection but by a desire to survive. And this was one of those times. The scariest part for me, at that moment, was that I was certain the actions of this character, Adam, were motivated by the same sentiment.

The creaky wooden front door to our cozy two-bedroom apartment opened, and Melinda had barely entered the room when I said, "You saw him. What did he say?"

"Hey, stop it. Don't do that."

"I'm not doing anything. It was one of those body things with the movie playing in my head. The danger thing and then the visuals."

Melinda paced around, disturbed. I hated it so much when she got like that, which was almost never, because I fed off of it, devoured it. I sat, and for once, made an effort to take charge. "Hey, let's just sit down, relax, and ground ourselves. Then you can share and we'll make a plan."

We sat, closed our eyes, and breathed together. Or she seemed to. I did little more than observe the nuances of the fear and anger flowing through my pathways. It occurred to me that I'd been at Phelps College for only three weeks, in that funny little town and funny little apartment, with my closest friend, and it already wasn't going well. At all. Because of me. Because I was still such a mess.

"Maybe I need to leave here. Maybe I'm not ready for this. I could go back home for a year or so."

"Jade, knock it off. Nobody is leaving here, especially you."

Ahh, the relief of having her back. "You all right now?"

"Sure, how about you?"

"Oh sure. Why not? Now, my first question. Is this guy, Adam, a Walk-in? Like a messed-up Walk-in? Maybe even a Stealer?"

"I couldn't tell. He's mentioned his brother a few times now and he believes he's connected to a cult. And now his brother is missing. But get this. This is so weird. He asked me if I'd ever heard of somebody named Old Elwood. And he said he'd met him, and his brother told him Elwood was real."

"Wow. Yeah. At the very least, his brother's a Walk-in."

"We need to be careful going forward how we act around him. And what we say to him. He believes we know things." She softened her tone, allowing her kind and caring self to resurface and set the example I needed to follow. "But we can also try harder to be nice to him."

I didn't answer. I stood still as her last words surrounded me. It was a pivotal moment, a reminder, a re-connection with who I used to be. I would never again be the same person I was those few years before, but I could allow the essence of that person to reawaken inside me. I saw my younger brother, I saw my father and mother, I saw our house, I saw our sacred land and community, I saw my dear Melinda standing in front of me. I whispered, "No, Melinda. *I* need to try harder. I need to stop this. This way I am, this way I've been. I need to not go into weird tirades just because some guy named Adam Kastner, who certainly is dealing with his own deep shit, tells me I'm gorgeous. It's not safe and it's not helpful."

Melinda got a hint of her humor back. "But you really are gorgeous."

"I'm something, that's for sure."

Adam

Adam's meeting with his creative writing instructor went better than expected. He gave such a convincing explanation of what he wanted to do and why he wanted to do it that the instructor encouraged him to withdraw from the class and transition into an advanced journalism class. He left her office feeling good about the move and proud of his negotiating skills. It was a powerful reminder that the most effective way to lure folks into any plan he might have was to be respectful, polite, and attentive, then mix it together with a whole lot of easygoing enthusiasm.

He had second thoughts about going to Anderson. The two-hour drive each way would mean he would have to skip a full day of classes. And weekends were out in case Melinda and Jade decided to make a quick trip home. Whatever he did needed to be something they wouldn't know about, and that approach alone stirred up guilt. Suddenly this kid out of nowhere wanted to go poking around in their hometown trying to get information like they were some kind of criminals. Which they weren't. Yeah, it was pretty warped. Except, a connection with his brother existed, it had to. And when he thought

93

about it that way, he would do anything to find out what the connection was all about.

Before he went any further, he needed to do more research. His apartment internet connection was slow and annoying, so he brought his laptop to the college library, and for privacy, sat in a far corner behind some bookshelves. He opened two browser windows, one for Google and the other for Yahoo, and put in a few search requests. "Cults" and "Anderson, NY" produced no results so he tried "Communes in Central New York." A list came up but all the entries referenced Ithaca which was a much larger city about twenty miles north of Anderson. Included were Eco-village, a world-famous planned communal housing development that he'd heard of, the Twelve Tribes community, a religious group he was also familiar with, and some earlier communities that had disbanded. He then entered "Hope Community," the group Garrett was connected to, followed by "New York State," "Ithaca," and "Anderson." The entries with Ithaca and Anderson produced no results and the one with New York State had predictable information about Hope's growing location in the southern Adirondack Mountains. Their website always featured new information, but he usually visited it at least once a week and didn't bother with it then.

He was about to give up when he remembered a list that he'd found a year before of communal organizations throughout the United States and the world. He entered into the browser, "intentional communities in the United States," and found the list. Again, the city of Ithaca had listings with detailed descriptions of communities past and present. But this time, Anderson also had one called The Land Trust. Like its name, its description was short and unexciting: "a small community dedicated to preserving the land." But at least it was something. And it did have a street address.

He had another idea, this one more exciting, but also likely to carry with it an even larger basket of guilt. The due date for the short story assignment was that day and the teacher had told the students they could submit their stories as attachments to her email, handing them in digitally if they anticipated any difficulty making hard copies, and she would then print them and store the digital copies in the college folder assigned to her. What an easy hack. He was good at it, actually great at it, but since he'd grown out of his early and mid-teens and his moral compass had expanded, he no longer took part in the practice. He poked around some, found the folder, and found Jade's submission. Melinda's story was not there yet.

The assignment suggested the story be between three and five thousand words and the Word document showed four thousand nine hundred and ninety-eight words. He read the first few paragraphs and determined it was about a young girl needing to leave the safety of her home and find a new life. The story gave no time period or location, and the girl was traveling on foot with just a pack, so the events could be happening anywhere. Adam had always been a voracious reader and quickly identified an atmosphere reminiscent of Homer's *Odyssey*. But it was subtle. And brilliant, until the story's vibe shifted to another author and book, Steinbeck's *Grapes of Wrath*. It was almost as if Steinbeck had taken over writing the story. Still brilliant or just weird? Adam also tuned into the girl's descriptions of what she saw as she walked along. At times her words felt like they were lifted directly from a botany or zoology textbook.

The ending crept up and delivered a knockout blow that, once again, pushed Adam's world back into the dreamy, disconnected space of Old Elwood, Garrett, and the Hope people. Oh, the feeling. In some strange way, he was beginning to get used to it. He read the last two sentences, then read them again, hovering on each word. Jade had lifted the sequence, word for word, from a book Garrett had given him many years earlier. The book was a short graphic novel about a ten-year-old boy whose parents, after a dystopian event, abandoned him in a large, foreign city. Adam hadn't seen the book in years and had no idea what had happened to it. But he remembered the line: "We are castaways, traveling throughout the rough and tangled world. Yet, when we find our people, we remember our purpose and why we're here." He thought another short sentence in the book had followed: "We're here to help." But he wasn't sure.

The next morning, he told a few of his roommates he needed to make a quick trip to his home near Albany. He packed a few things, just in case, and hopped in his car. But when he drove off, he headed in a different direction. He struggled to keep his attention on the road, to keep his wandering thoughts in check. He blasted the radio or popped in a few CD's, and sang along. His phone's maps app occasionally chimed in with a new turn, but he missed one and drove a few miles the wrong way. When he realized what he'd done, he pulled onto the shoulder, and before he turned around, closed his eyes for a moment and forced himself to calm down.

He had to pass through Anderson to get to the road the Land Trust was on. The town was small but had a short active main street with a used clothing store, an antique store, a bookstore, an ice cream shop, and a couple restaurants and bars. In a few more miles, he turned onto a smaller road, and a mile later, the maps app voice announced his arrival at the destination.

He pulled into a small parking area, got out of his car, and surveyed everything around him. A wide gate constructed of metal pipe and wire mesh stood open next to him and a dirt lane led away into a thick stand of evergreens. On either side of the gate, an eight-foot fence, constructed of wood poles and more wire mesh, separated the road he'd driven on from the woods. The ground had been cleared of any underbrush, and he could see far into the woods. Yet, no structures or other evidence of human inhabitants were visible. And no sign marked the entrance to the lane, not even a No Trespassing sign. On the other side of the road was a simple mailbox marked only with a PO number, and behind it, stretching out a few hundred yards was a field with an assortment of vegetable crops growing. A few figures moved slowly in the distance, crouched over and working the earth. If he hadn't had his phone app, he never would have found this place. To anybody driving by and not knowing exactly where to look, it was invisible.

He contemplated what might happen if he walked, uninvited, down the dirt lane. Everything looked so clean and pure, wild yet obviously cared for. A gentle breeze touched his back like hands nudging him. Sure, why not take a walk? He turned back to his car, thinking he would lock it, and spotted a figure coming through the field across the road.

The person moved slowly, aimed directly toward him, but with no apparent intention to try to stop him. He waited, and a minute later, a boy, maybe fifteen or sixteen, with a hint of a gentle smile, walked across the road. Adam tried to hide his shake. The boy gripped the straps of two canvas bags, one in each hand, with the top greenery of some kind of produce spilling out of the bags. He looked like a male version of her, so much like Jade.

"Hey there," the boy said. "Can I help you with anything?"

"Uh yeah. I'd heard something about this place and I was trying to get information about it because it sounded so interesting. Do you ever do tours."

The boy gave a small laugh. "Tours, yeah, I guess we do sometimes. But to tell you the truth, we're kind of boring here. Unless you're really into organic farming, or alternative schooling, there's not much of interest." He laid the bags on the ground and stuck out his hand. "My name's Samuel but call me Sam."

Adam shook it, "I'm Adam.

"Hey, you want a bunch of carrots? We grew way too many this year."

"Oh yeah. Sure. I love good carrots."

Sam dug into one of the bags and handed a dozen or so thick orange carrots to Adam. "So, how did you hear about this place?"

Adam would get caught if he made up a story and there was no getting around what he had to confirm. "These two girls at my school, at Phelps, are from here, I think."

Sam's face lit up. "Jade and Melinda. And I'm sure you're wondering, right?"

Adam nodded.

"Well, yes. I am Jade's younger brother although sometimes we're mistaken as twins. And you're friends with them?"

He had walked into another deep hole and the only way out now was to either be honest with this kid or to get back in his car and leave. "Not really friends. We were in the same writing class together and they invited me to go to a club and hear some music. I guess I said something Jade didn't like."

Sam lost his smile and stared at Adam. Adam wanted to back away but Sam's gaze held him in place. However, when he spoke, his voice sounded soft and quiet, filled with caring and kindness, "She can be pretty rough these days and I'm sorry if it disturbed you. Her heart will always be large but her emotions are still unsettled."

Adam couldn't look away. It was as if the kid was a pure version, a safe version, of his strange sister, Jade. His entire mood shifted. He wanted more than anything for the kid to take his hand and lead him down the lane into this place he now knew existed, back in the woods somewhere. This was where he would stay. This was where he would live. Where he would be safe. Where his mind would quiet down and his questions would all be answered. It all seemed so perfect.

And then his phone rang.

It was his mother who rarely called during the week. He looked at the phone, looked back at Sam, and said, "I better get this. It's my Mom."

Sam backed away. "Oh, sure."

Ingrid's hysteria flooded out of the phone and into Adam, and Sam heard enough or felt enough to increase his distance. She spoke for less than a minute and Adam choked out, "I'm coming right home."

He hung up and sat flat down on the ground, his back against his car. He looked up at Sam, his face white, his fists clenched, and said, "My brother is dead."

Sam dropped down beside him, ready to comfort, and said, "Oh no. I'm so sorry. That's terrible."

At first, Adam's mind blanked into a void and he sat, stiff and vacant, staring unfocused. Sam positioned himself next to him, shoulders touching, and also stayed quiet. The haze slowly lifted and the new reality made its way in, edging out Adam's sense of well-being and quiet adventure from a few minutes earlier.

"My mother is home," Sam said. "I could take you to her."

Adam pushed him away and stood, and Sam also scrambled up. Adam glared at him and said, "The real reason I came here was to find out what the connection is between all of you," and he waved at the dirt entrance and the gate, "and that sick cult north of here. You know, the Hope Community. Because, just like my brother, you all use the same words, say the same shit, so you must be connected somehow." He climbed in his car, backed out onto the road, and roared away.

He drove straight to his parent's house outside Albany and never returned to Phelps College. A few weeks later, his father came and picked up all of Adam's belongings.

Jade

Six years later…

It took Melinda and me another six years of study to gather the experience and credentials for our next step. I use the singular *step* because we made our separate plans together and agreed, when we were finished, to live close to each other and preferably in the same town or city. The specifics of my path were considerably easier for me than the challenge Melinda undertook and by the time we were finished, my reverence for her brilliant mind knew no bounds. I finished my Ph.D. in World History, wrote my thesis on the topic of History of Science, and Melinda became a licensed Physician's Assistant. Had she wanted to, she surely could have become any type of medical specialist, but she chose a quicker route so we could start our next chapter at the same time.

Melinda took a position with a practice near Albany that embraced a variety of alternative modes of treatment, and rented an apartment nearby. It was perfect, exactly what she wanted, because her underlying mission, and mine also, was to spot Walk-ins in general and keep close notes on those we determined were troubled Walk-ins. Also, the specific types we were most interested in were ones we believed were connected to the nearby Hope Community.

My job, as a teacher at Clark College, also near Albany, did not impress me as much, yet it was also an ideal setup for me as an observer. I began at the level of Instructor which, at the age of twenty-seven was considered an admirable achievement in the academic world. However, the actual work I did was mostly a rehash of studies I had pursued earlier on my own. In my first semester, I taught a few basic classes and also a cross-major class, the History of Science. I loved everything about this class: the prep, the sequencing, and the freedom to present it with a small edge of Extra insight. Going forward, for the second semester, I talked my way into another cross-major creation, the History of Religion. I also planned a third class which I never presented: The History of Human Sexuality.

I planned this last one because sex between humans was a subject that I gave a lot of thought to, not so much because I desired it, but because I still had difficulty understanding it, likely because my own upbringing concerning the subject was so different from that of most of the outside world. Growing up in my at-birth commune, we treated sex as simply another part of the human experience, and at an early age, learned how living creatures of all types, including humans, re-created. The fact that sex could be pleasurable and exciting was not any more important than the excitement of creating and enjoying wonderful food, any sort of artistic creation, or growing produce in our gardens and fields. However, we also learned that sexual activity in the outside world was endlessly more complex and always controversial, and in keeping with our community's obsession to avoid outside observance of our mostly hidden group, we scrupulously followed a few outside rules specific to sexual interaction. We knew the sordid history of sexual abuse in so many religious or spiritual groups, and we strived to create a presentation where an outsider would not misinterpret our group's behavior and suggest we were doing anything along those lines that flouted the standards of the outside world.

If community members under the age of eighteen wished to experience human sexual connection, they needed to ask their parents or primary caregivers for permission. This applied to same-sex as well as male/female matchups. The approval was always granted as long as both parties stated they were willing participants, and if the match-up did involve a male and a female, the participants received detailed instructions in effective birth control. Then, within reason, participants could meet in private places whenever they wished. The set of rules made sense to all of us and we never considered rebelling against them because we understood their purpose. However, when a person turned eighteen, they were no longer allowed to match up or even continue to match up with somebody seventeen or younger. Our group knew this was ridiculous in some instances, such as if one participant was a half-year younger than the other. But by the time we were that age, eighteen, or even much younger, we had come to fully share responsibility for our home and our people, and if we did break that one rule, we did it carefully and privately.

Melinda and I were close friends with another boy who was a year older and we each had match-ups with him, but I was so wrapped up in my learning that, although I enjoyed the experiences, they weren't overly important to me. However, he and Melinda continued their liaisons until he moved to the outer world. Melinda also received from her mother some specific information concerning match-ups that I didn't receive. This was because an aspect of Melinda's Extra layer had merged with her human body in such a way that she could sometimes transmit healing energy — also referred to as Extra energy — to another person. My mother could also do this and helped me many times when

I first visited after my traumatic event. Melinda learned that it was possible to combine healing energy with the energy of sex, but she was cautioned that it was complex, and like all energy forces in our universe, if applied incorrectly or with the wrong intention, could be harmful instead of helpful. For older members of the community, as long as they fully understood the dangers, the practice was not forbidden. However, they were expected to never bring the practice into the outside world. The reasoning was obvious: humans already misused the energy of sex far more than any other energy on the planet. To add another element to it that would make it exponentially more powerful and would most likely be disastrous.

Melinda was told not to share the teachings with others, but of course she did with me. We even discussed experimenting together and decided not to. However, a few times in that first summer after my trauma, Melinda did put her hands on my head or my heart and pass a jolt of something so exquisite I always fainted into a sleepy bliss. And once, when I was alone in my apartment and had plunged so deep into the pain of my trauma that I felt like I was drowning, the jolt came out of nowhere. The next day I asked her about it and she said it just left her body without any conscious intention and came to mine. She also said this had never happened before and she believed it was because our connection was so powerful and intertwined.

Over the next few years, while finishing my Undergraduate studies and throughout my Grad School years, I did occasionally do match-ups with men or women, mostly to try to expand my knowledge of human sexuality. But as time went on, I came to genuinely like the experience, as long as it was with a kind and caring person. However, I never took it so far that we declared ourselves a couple. I realized at one point that I never thought about my match-up partners when I wasn't with them and had little interest in a long-term relationship. Yet one face, one person from my past, continually showed up, uninvited and unexpected in my churning thoughts: Adam Kastner. I always asked myself why. Why him? About two years before I finished my schooling and began teaching, I even started dreaming about him. I shared the first dream with Melinda and asked for any insights she might have, and her only response was to take my hands, put her brightly lit face close to mine, and say, "Because it's inevitable."

A few days later, I picked up a magazine in a bookstore, opened it to the table of contents, and immediately fixated on the title, *The Primitive Human Still Lives Within Us*. The author was Adam Kastner. At first, I couldn't imagine it was the same person because, like Melinda and me, he would only be twenty-seven years old, and who at age twenty-seven would get published in this particular magazine? I bought it, brought it home, and devoured it. The words spoke brilliantly, and the theme, or the concepts behind the theme, could almost have been taken from myself, from my own beliefs. I opened my laptop, googled his name, and on impulse, first clicked on images. A few different thumbnails came up and I found one suitable for enlargement. I clicked on it and there he was, Adam Kastner, with the slightly odd but thoroughly captivating face staring right back at me. A string of emotional responses, all of which were disturbing, rumbled through me. And for a minute or so, I couldn't look away.

Next, I found the beginnings of a Wikipedia entry that detailed some of Adam's activity in the last six years. He had finished his undergraduate degree through Empire State College, earned an MFA in Journalism from another school, and spent a few years traveling around the world, supporting himself by writing what he believed were interesting articles, all of which could be read on a blog titled Adam Kastner Writes. I spent the next hour or so pouring through every word of the blog itself—not the articles, not yet—and whatever warm fuzzy feelings I may have had about him slowly and steadily evaporated because, for me, because of who I am and where I came from, a lot of his opinions, orientations, investigations, and assertions were downright terrifying.

When my brother, Sam, had his brief encounter with Adam, I naturally heard about it but never came across any further information about his brother's death. And, because I so badly wanted to move on to a happier, less paranoid way of existing, I didn't go looking, either. But now, here it was, all laid out, what Adam had been told and what he had come to believe. Garrett's death had been labeled a suicide but Adam believed he had been murdered. And, because Garrett had been so involved with the Hope Community and their growing presence in central New York, Adam believed his brother's death was in some way connected to them.

The human sensation of deep chilling fear poured through me, and my loyalty, my instinct to defend and protect my people at all costs ramped up with a fury. Thankfully I had relearned the ability to step back, examine myself, and analyze what feelings were most appropriate and helpful in an unexpected situation. What surprised me was to find another small piece clinging to the greater thrust. Regardless of Adam's mistaken conclusions about my commune, the Land Trust, it was a certainty that his blog was monitored, possibly by somebody whose interests were much different than mine. In other words, I suddenly cared about Adam's safety. Six years earlier, I had spent an hour in his presence, yet for some reason, I was now concerned about him. But concern is not the correct word. Concern can mean a heightened desire for all beings to be safe, and as an evolving Extra, I strived for that. The feeling I had is called *worry* and is much more human. So, there I was, worrying about Adam Kastner, and I had no idea why.

The next day I read all the articles the blog linked to and came away with awe at Adam's writing ability. The subjects varied and many were done on assignment, but all conveyed a clear and concise meaning. I reflected back to our creative writing class and imagined what he would have thought of my strange mix of styles in the short story I wrote, and was glad I didn't show it to him. For the next few months, I continued to check back for updates on the blog entries but no new material ever appeared. Then one day, all the entries had been deleted and I never went back to the site.

I also attempted to follow the lockup trio of White, Ewing, and Squires. As time went on, internet searches became more efficient and revealing and I occasionally got some new hits. Lance Ewing had died in a car accident. I tried to extend my blessings but was still far away from an act of forgiveness of such magnitude. Richard White, who I still believed was not an Extra of any type, had married and was living in Albany. And Billy Squires? Nothing. Back when I'd told my parents about my incident with the trio, my father had said they would take care of Billy so he would no longer present a danger to me. At the time, I thought I understood what he meant—they would apprehend him, and in some way re-program him—and I believed the specific type of intervention, with the energy sources many of our group had access to, would be an act of love and kindness. At the time, I never doubted its effectiveness. But now, I experienced a wave of uncertainty and wondered where he was hiding. I was reminded that there would never be a guarantee of Melinda's or my safety—or of any other somewhat visible Extra—as we established ourselves in the outside world.

Adam

Adam and Jackson had already waited a half-hour. Jackson sat quietly with his hands in his lap, his eyes closed, not in any formal meditation thing, but more like a weird trance. Adam scrolled through his phone, rereading articles from Axios, Vox, Huff Post, and a few others and finally gave up. He could sit in his awful chair another hour, finally get in to see Mr. Big Bucks Producer, Carter Freedman, in his twelfth floor New York City office with an inevitably stellar view, give a high-speed pitch for all of two minutes, and leave with nothing. He hated this part of what he was trying to do, absolutely loathed grubbing for money, and he was beginning to regret leaving his meeting two days earlier with Sara Leeds. He'd left that one because he regarded her as competition for what he was trying to do, and believed teaming up with her would mean she would pull the project in her direction and away from what he wanted it to showcase and highlight.

The problem was, Sara Leeds had been wrapped up in UFO's and military records and flashes in the night sky for so long, Adam believed the whole documentary would swing that way. And, although he had no difficulty entertaining the possibility of Sara's work being factual, he wanted to minimize those and any other influences still regarded by the general public as too far out. As long as he had control of the tone and direction of the documentary, he was going to make sure it was grounded in a reality the majority of viewers could accept—nuanced and seemingly balanced but with a subconscious bombardment of fact snippets—so that, when the ending came and the film wrapped, most viewers would walk away absolutely appalled. It was what he hoped for, anyway.

A young man swooped in and said, "Follow me. He's ready."

The man led them into a large but sparse office with a nearly wall-sized window view of the East River. A few mostly empty bookcases lined one wall, on another wall a large abstract painting lorded over a small couch, and almost in the center of the floor was a massive desk behind which sat Carter Freedman.

Carter motioned to two chairs in front of his desk. "Morning boys. Take a seat and tell me what you're thinking."

Adam's first impression of Carter was: an average amount of wrinkles and gray hair for somebody in their mid-fifties; well-groomed but not overly done; dressed down yet neat and clean; a friendly welcoming vibe. Adam had done his research and right then was seeing a nice uncle who would be fun to hang out with. But this guy could be viciously direct when he needed to be. And whatever information was out in the world about Adam Kastner and Jackson Marshfield, Carter already had it tucked away in his head somewhere.

Adam started in with an overview, aware that Carter would have already read the one Adam had sent and only wanted to hear how he spoke. He covered what he believed was going on in the Hope Community, what research he had done a few years earlier, how the community appeared to be growing quickly, and how he had connections to a few ex-members—which was a bit of an exaggeration.

He briefly outlined how a documentary would proceed, then waited for the expected set of questions he hoped he was prepared for. And he almost was, but not entirely.

Carter's demeanor shifted. It still contained the kindly uncle, but a stern, inquisitive side appeared looking for answers. "It all sounds interesting. And I will be honest, although you are both young and inexperienced with an actual film documentary of this scope, you have an intensity that has piqued my curiosity. I naturally have questions about the specifics of your idea but what I would most like to know, and I'm asking you, Adam. Why are you so damn obsessed with the whole venture? Your personal past is not easy to access, and before I go even one baby step further, I want to know what you're really after here."

*Oh my God. Now what do I do? He's actually interested but…*Jackson poked him and nodded at him to go for it. Adam began with the story of how Garrett came to be his brother, or half-brother really, with the same father but a different mother. As Adam understood it, their father had split up from Garrett's mother, their father had then remarried Adam's mother and then had Adam, and when Adam was still a baby, Garrett came to live with them. He was Adam's new big brother and Adam quickly became attached to him. He had told the story many times over the years, but right now, as he said the words to Carter Freedman, they sounded hollow, as if the insides containing a deeper meaning were not there. He carried on about the shifts in Garrett's personality after he went to college, and after he got involved with the Hope Community people. Garrett's speech patterns changed, the way he viewed the world changed, and the whole situation amounted to many traumatic years for Adam and his parents. When he heard Garrett had died, had committed suicide, he had a hard time believing it went down the way the authorities said it did.

"And why was that?" Carter asked gently. "What caused you to believe that?"

Cornered again. He believed Garrett would never do it because he was too involved in the world and loved his life. That's what he would need to say. No way was he going to share a meeting with some fictitious man named Old Elwood who had said he was an Extra and Extras were incapable of taking their own lives. Extra. What did it even mean? And what about the other hidden place? What about Jade Furlong and her brother and that other one, Melinda?

Adam gave the hackneyed answer about Garrett's lust for life, love of his parents, etc.

"I'm sorry about your brother. To be honest, with a so much investigative ability at my disposal, I knew you had a brother but found no information about what happened to him. Now, as the saying goes, I see that you have some major skin in this game. Maybe too much. From my point of view, this could be your biggest strength or the opposite. If I go ahead with this, I will have to be assured that it's a motivator and never a distraction from the facts. From what I've read of your writing, you are generally a clear thinker, an observer of the truth."

Adam nodded along until there was a pause. He said quietly but forcefully, "I know what you mean. I understand what you're saying."

The meeting was going somewhere. Adam could barely believe it. So unexpected. Carter laid out his concept, picking up on Adam's and Jackson's hope to become involved with the community and how that might work. They even discussed how a documentary infiltration had taken place in North Korea, with a small crew using recording devices to capture events. It kept getting better and better.

After a longer pause Carter said, "Before we wrap this up, I have a few more items. The first is a question. Adam, I'd like you to share one part of your experience to date with anything to do with the community you haven't told me yet. Or maybe anyone. All good journalists will have at least a few parts of a juicy story they've kept to themselves."

Adam managed to keep his composure but his brain lit up with anxiety and doubt. Old Elwood? No, no. That would be crazy enough to blow the whole thing. What came out of him was perfect because it was real and it had happened. He went back six years earlier to his brief stay at Phelps College. He described his meeting with Jade Furlong and Melinda Breeze and some of the ways they spoke about things that were so much like his brother. He recounted his trip to Anderson, NY, to the Land Trust, and his short interaction with Jade's brother, Sam. He even personalized it, describing how he felt at each moment.

When Adam finished, Carter said, "Now that is interesting, very interesting. This state has seen all sorts of cults and communes over the years, especially in the area around Anderson. I'd never heard of that one. At some point, it might be worth it to try to get more info about it."

Jackson spoke for the first time. "Am I to understand that we may have a shot at this?"

"You are correct. We have a few more steps to go and this next item is one I insist on. I believe you know who Sara Leeds is and you might be aware that I have worked with her on a few of her projects. Now, you two are talented and ambitious but don't have enough experience to take this on yourselves. So, I would like to appoint Sara as the overseer of the project. It will still be your vision but she will make sure it always stays on track."

Sara Leeds? He had no idea she and Carter had worked together and were in communication. She must have talked to him. "I just don't want this to come across that I believe these cult people are aliens or something like that."

"No, you don't. And she wouldn't want that, either. But they do believe they have some outside influences. Extras, right? Maybe they believe in other dimensional spirits or something like that."

Adam only heard the word Extra and didn't catch the last sentence. The word brought him chills, and as it always had, made him want to run. But again, he caught himself, faced the reality of the situation, and said, "Yes, you're right. And I'm fully on board with working with Sara." He turned to Jackson. "Are you okay with it?"

"Sure. It's fine."

Adam thought they were done but Carter kept going. "This idea of other dimensions or infinite space, a lot of folks might say there's no difference between the two. Sara will get on board with it. But what is at the core of the Hope Community beliefs is a key part of this story, and call it whatever you want, it's got to be included. I'll set up a meeting with the three of you."

A week later, Adam and Jackson returned to Carter Freedman's offices, and when they arrived, the same man as before ushered them into a small windowless room containing only a table, four chairs, and a whiteboard. Sara Leeds was already in the room, pouring through a pile of papers. She stood when they came in, shook each of their hands, and sat down.

"Will Carter be joining us?" Adam asked.

"No, but he briefed me on what he would like to have happen."

Oh God, here we go. Is it time for me to leave?

She continued, "And I would like to explain a few things before we get going. So please just hang tight and hear me out." She grinned a bit. "And please don't leave until I say my piece."

Whatever...

"I understand where you're coming from, and I want to be clear about what I see as my role. Now, let's imagine we're making a huge movie and you each have your titles, and I have mine. I see myself as the Producer, or maybe Carter is the Producer and I'm his assistant. I oversee and advise but I also listen. My role is to support your vision, to believe in your vision, and hopefully sometimes offer helpful suggestions." She looked at Adam. "And what does that make you? I see you as the Director. And Jackson? You're the Chief Cameraman."

Adam liked what he was hearing, maybe even loved what he was hearing.

"Now, what I'd like to do next, if both of you are in agreement, is try to get up on this whiteboard a list of what we each know about or believe we know about the Hope Community. And I'd like to start."

She began at the whiteboard, the back of her head to Adam and Jackson, her hand moving slowly and methodically. The first two items didn't say much and were more of an obvious introduction. She hesitated before starting the third, started a thought, erased it, and started again. It was almost as if Adam could see her thoughts churning, searching for the perfect string of words. He found himself mesmerized by her process because it was similar to his own. She was forty-two, and in their line of work, she had fifteen more years of experience than him. He'd read everything he could find that she'd ever written and knew she was one of the best journalists out there when the subject sucked her in. Now, watching her, he began to like her. He liked how she was dressed in an attempt at a business suit, yet she still looked kind of a mess, and how she didn't obsess over keeping her wavy hair in control and her round face made up to perfection. Maybe she could be his nerdy older sister or something like that. She listed five items, turned back around, and he read a familiar look of frustration and concern in her scrunched dark eyes and pursed lips.

"Not much info yet," Adam said.

"Do you have more?"

"Only the personal stuff with my brother and that other outlier community."

She paced a few feet with her clenched hands behind her back. "And therein lies the problem. This group is so different from one like Rajneeshpuram in the eighties where anybody could walk in there or into the surrounding town, or the Scientologists who are always defecting and ready to spill their guts to whoever will listen. This group has got the tightest controls I've ever seen."

She stopped, closed her eyes, took a deep breath, unclenched her hands, and Adam finally got it, why she was really there, why she wanted to work with him, why Carter wanted her on board, and why he needed to let go of his reservations. "Hey Sara," he said, "Are you here right now because you're caught up in the challenge or because the Hope Community scares the crap out of you?"

She sat across from them, broke into a big toothy smile, and pointed her shaky index finger at him. "Both reasons, Adam. Both."

He was ready to talk, ready to share his whole story, about his brother, about his brother's death, and about his brief encounters with Jade and Melinda. Jackson only knew a fraction of the story and would likely find much of the fuller version weird and disturbing, but Adam no longer cared. And Sara? Any stories he had to tell would not be any stranger than much of the phenomena she'd written and spoken about over the years. They shared the same page.

He started with the specifics of how, when his mother married his father, Garrett was already born, living with their father's ex-wife, and three years later Garrett came to live with them. From the start, Adam adored his big brother and they stayed close until Adam's last year in high school.

He continued with the year when Garrett dropped out of college and connected up with the Hope Community people. He recounted how Garrett's personality bounced all over, from grounded and present, to almost boringly unexciting, and then entering near trancelike states in which he would describe himself and the world around him with a distinct and unusual choice of words, concepts, and phraseology. Something had come loose within his mind, and he began to connect with this group of strange people who he believed could help him put it back together.

Adam described in detail his meeting with Garrett on the edge of the Hudson River where it passed by Albany, and his first experience with Max Schultz and Olivia Santini. He jumped ahead to another meeting with Garrett a year later, when he'd convinced his brother to take him to the site of the new Hope Community compound in the southern Adirondack Mountains. They had met in a coffee shop in downtown Albany and Adam had driven first west, then north, through tiny back roads until they reached a dirt pull-off and a trailhead. They hiked uphill for about a half mile until they came to a knoll overlooking a valley. A large construction project directly in the center of the valley dominated the view below in such a way that the few other houses were barely noticeable.

"Amazing, isn't it?" Garret had said. "They're building an actual town down there."

It reminded Adam of a pit mine of some sort, maybe a South American copper mine. Backhoes dug foundation holes and bulldozers pushed dirt and gravel around to make roads. "It looks like there are three different sections. Can you tell me what they are?"

Garrett answered, "As far as I know, the building near the front that's nearly done is a welcome center, almost like a museum, and the area in the back where those streets are will be where people can live. Then, around it all will be areas devoted to agriculture."

"What about the large holes in the center? They look like they're being prepared for foundations for some pretty big buildings."

"I believe they will be for barns or warehouses. Something like that. Amazing, isn't it?"

Adam's next Garrett story was a short one. He had gone to a concert at the performing arts center north of Albany, and before the start, had seen a group of young people on the back lawn, twenty or so, gathered around somebody who was speaking. He went forward, mingled in, and realized the speaker was Max Shultz. As Max spoke, Olivia Santini went from person to person, handing each one a flier. She came to Adam, winked and smiled, handed him a flier, and said, "You already know what this is about. But come anyway. I believe you're ready now." The flier contained a dumbed-down version of what he understood as the Hope philosophy and listed a few events happening in the newly opened Hope Community center in the Southern Adirondacks. One of the events, which Adam never went to, was portrayed as a raucous blast of a party.

Adam's last recall covered his most difficult period. He told how Garrett had stopped responding to phone calls, voicemails, or emails from Adam or either of his parents. He had tried calling the Hope Community, using a number on their website, and when nobody answered, left many messages on their voicemail. His father supposedly did the same, but Adam wasn't sure about that. He ended with a description of his trip to Anderson, to the home of Jade Furlong and Melinda Breeze, where he stood in the commune parking lot with Jade's brother and received the news that Garrett had died.

When he finished, Sara said, "I'm so sorry, Adam. It must have been horrible." She waited a moment and continued, "I am sure you're already aware of this, but the controlling folks in the cult not only know who you are, they most certainly followed your blog when you had it up, and if they let you in, let you get close, their only reason will be that they think they can gain control over you. It's how these situations always work. But this group has taken the art of seduction to new levels. So, where to start? Right now, that's the key. Continue to go to the lectures, continue to take notes, and now might be the time to step forward and express further interest. Do you have anything to add to the plan?"

The words entered his head, and he spit them out with no thought, no pre-examination. "I need to find Jade Furlong and Melinda Breeze. Pin down who they really are and what their connection is to the Hope Community."

Once again, Sara broke into a big grin and pointed her index finger at him, this time holding it steady. "Yes. Good one." She picked up her phone and frantically began pounding in searches. "Melinda Breeze looks like she's still in med school, not sure, but Jade Furlong is a new instructor at Clark College. Looks like one of her courses is called 'History of Scientific Thought.' Good one." Adam started to speak and she said, "Wait, wait, one more thing. You said you found the name of their community on the national listing. Yeah, here it is, The Land Trust. And that's all there is. We have to find out more!"

Sara's excitement bubbled over and Adam went there with her. He looked at Jackson, who had said little throughout the meeting, and tried to interpret his slightly scowling expression. Concern? Doubt? Skepticism? He wasn't sure. Then Sara upped the whole situation with a new request.

"Adam, you spoke of how your brother always shared an interest in creative ways to view our world and referenced a few times how, as time went on, his descriptions of what it means to be human evolved and became more unique. And then you said that the one woman, Melinda, seemed to copy the same way of speaking. But I'm not quite getting it. Like a piece is missing here. Like…" She stopped, her enthusiasm quieted, and her face clouded. "I'm not getting something."

Is she saying she's missing something from what I said or from her own memory?

A hint of desperation crept into her voice. "Adam, please, if there's more, I need to know."

The option to turn back had departed. He would continue and Jackson would likely think the whole project was too far out and walk away. But Sara Leeds would do…What? He had to find out. He slowly and carefully described his entire interaction with Old Elwood. He included when he'd told Garrett about it and when they both ran back to Elwood's house and found it empty with no trace of him. He remembered every detail of the encounter as if he'd written it all down as it happened. That was weird enough, but Sara's face, glued to his, her large eyes seeming to grow even bigger every minute, and her breathing, fluctuating between the extremes of non-existent and near hyper-ventilation, was way over the edge.

When he finished, Sara put her head in her hands and said, "It's all so familiar and I don't know why."

Adam refrained from looking at Jackson, not wanting to see his reaction. Jackson said in a gravelly whisper, "I don't know what to think."

Sara pulled herself together. "And this is why you believe your brother didn't commit suicide, correct? Because an Extra something walked into him at some point. Over-laid itself onto him. And for an Extra of any type, it's not easy to kill a human and even harder for them to kill themselves. Am I right?"

Adam nodded.

Sara stood, paced around, her body twitching, wrote some more on the whiteboard and said, "It's at the core of their beliefs and we need to know everything about it.

Jackson had the same shaky body movements and Adam felt like he was about to pass out.

Sara's entire demeanor shifted back to her earlier organized and professional persona. "You know what? This is all most exciting. We're all freaking out about what this might mean to us personally and that means we're on to something. Something big. Now, let's get started."

Jade

On September 3rd, I began teaching my first classes. I had a solid grasp of the subject matter and confidence in my speaking ability, as graduate school had given me endless practice at speaking in front of others. I'd learned to enjoy it and could even be a bit comedic if the energy of the students required an uplift to keep them interested. Since I would be meeting with all new students, I decided to put those skills to work so they might wish to come back for more. I began with a corny slightly fictitious intro about who I was and where I came from, made a few barely funny jokes, and played up my nerdy bookish persona as much as I could. And I never looked at my notes once because I forgot I even had them.

After my second class of the day, the History of Science, a student approached me and asked, "Dr. Furlong, do you lecture without notes?" She was short and thick and wore her black hair in a bun on top of her head. She stared at me like she was a police officer and I was somebody she was considering arresting

Already and it was only the first day. My reactions kicked in and I answered, "Oh gosh, no. Only the first class. My memory is not nearly

121

good enough to routinely wing it. I hope I didn't come across as ill-prepared."

She continued to stare, almost like she couldn't take her eyes off me. "Oh no. I'm sorry if I have implied such a thing. It's just that you impressed me so much with your command of the subject matter and I love the words you use to convey your thoughts."

I did not like this and was not ready for where it was going. "Can you tell me your name?"

She extended her hand, and I shook it. "Erin Mason."

"And where are you from, Erin?"

"Oh, I'm from Ireland." She smiled. "But I'm doing my best to mimic the local American accent to fit in better." She switched her voice to an Irish brogue. "And when you started speaking, you sounded like you're from around this area. I got so caught up in what you were saying and the words you used that I loved listening to you."

She left the room and I shook my head and inwardly laughed at myself. I had to remind myself that my role—and Melinda's, also—was to find, evaluate, and give direction and assistance if needed, to Walk-ins of any type. I needed to accept that others would sometimes find me first. It was inevitable. I needed to remember how Melinda and I had perfected our quirky human personas and likely would rarely interact with other Extras outside our commune anyway. And when it did happen, there was usually an instant unspoken agreement of, "I won't out you if you don't out me."

However, we could feel the energy of change, the first hints of an impending eruption, a foreshadowing of how ours and many other Extras' lives were going to be reconfigured. It had always been the direction our world was headed and our best approach was to embrace it. Although we couldn't yet fully understand and articulate the specifics of the paths we chose, we had to accept where we were, right then, in one of the planetary hot spots where the force of this change would be especially profound, dramatic, and chaotic. And one way or another, we would be thrown directly into the center of it. Walk-ins of all types were about to flood our world. Even this young Irish woman named Erin might have approached me specifically because she suspected I was an Extra of some type and just wanted to chat about it.

I planned one-on-one meetings in my office with each of my students and came up with a few clues they might identify and respond to if they were Walk-ins or an Extras-at-birth from another commune. I kept the space neat but not pristine and filled two large bookcases with an assorted collection of books on the subjects of history, philosophy, religion, and many others. I even had a few about paranormal experiences. With such a wide variety, an observant Extra might wonder if their teacher was also one. I hung a few small poster reproductions of famous semi-abstract paintings, and the real giveaway, a small original watercolor I'd found in a second-hand store of a small lake with hills in the background, an odd temple-like structure in the foreground, and hovering in the blue sky, long, thin strips of yellow light with pointed ends. I framed it and hung it off to the side where only somebody who was overly curious would spot it.

Throughout the week, I had more students come through who were possibilities, but if so, were not yet ready to come forward. Then, on a Friday evening, I went to Melinda's apartment to eat dinner with her and found her door unlocked. I walked in, and she was sitting on her bed, looking out the window at the fading daylight. She mumbled a hello and didn't get up to give me her usual enthusiastic hug. I hesitated, surprised, because I had never seen her like this. I sat next to her, put my arm tightly around her, and whispered, "You're not okay. Tell me why."

She slunk down and put her head on my shoulder. "It's like death from a thousand cuts. Each one is no big deal but cumulatively they're doing me in." She moved away. "I shouldn't complain. It's not like what happened to you. Nobody locked me up or anything like that."

"Hey. Stop it. For you to say what you just said, you who never complains about anything, it is a big deal. A very big deal."

I had to control my fear because whatever was going on was most unusual. For the entire time I knew Melinda, especially after we left our community, especially after my most traumatic event, many times just the presence of her calm being kept me away from the edge of a meltdown. In that moment, I realized that I likely had depended on her way too much.

She stood and turned to me and I got a clear look at her face. "Oh my God, Melinda. What did you do?"

"It's just makeup. I was experimenting."

"Did you cut your hair too?"

Her exquisite black curly hair that always danced around her shoulders had a few big chops out of it. She dropped her voice to a whisper. "I knew it was coming. I knew I was at the edge of the cliff and one more dose of nastiness would push me over. So today was the day. This man came in a month ago with a few tick bites and a case of Lyme. I went through the medical process and then he came back today for a follow-up. He's one of those confused men, especially about women like me, and it makes him so angry that it bubbles right out of him."

"About you."

"You know, it's the same crap that happens over and over. They are so attracted to this," she pointed her index fingers at her face, "but are so repulsed by the idea of this." She waved one hand over the dark skin on her opposite arm. "The beautiful face with the dark-skinned body is more than these awful white creatures can handle. I came home and thought about it, about what I could do physically, what I would allow myself to do. My conclusion is that, because of how the human members of this planet have evolved, this Black body is not solely mine. Its ownership is shared with all the other Black female bodies and, therefore, it is not my right to make drastic changes. However, the so-called beautiful face, at least minimally, is mine to mess with if it will deflect some of this never-ending disturbing attention."

I said cautiously, "Melinda, are you sure?"

Her eyes lit with a fire I had never seen in her. She grabbed my hands, and I didn't dare look away. "Jade, I will tell you that I experienced a horrible emotion. I actually felt hatred toward you. Toward you! Because you're a white person. That can never happen. Do you understand?"

The shift was so dramatic. Because of the body I'm in, I could never fully understand the specifics of her experience and the resultant feelings. However, I certainly could grasp the force of overwhelming trauma and the raw power of its resultant anger. But I had no skill, no ability, no method, no training to do anything to help her. I could only hold her hand, say reassuring yet probably meaningless words, and stay with her and hope I didn't create more harm. I did not expect what she said next.

"I want you to pass the healing energy to me."

"Wait. What? I can't do that."

"I think you can. It will be enough so that I can at least continue to put one foot in front of the other."

She gave me a small slap on my shoulder, then bumped her forehead against mine and I slumped backward onto the couch. She commanded, "Now, sit up straight, close your eyes, and let it come through you."

A jolt of wild current entered the top of my head and flowed through my entire body. For a moment vicious lightning bolts blasted their way into every body cell, but the transformation quickly took over. It started at my feet and worked its way upward until all the pores of my tissue opened and drained away the stress and pain of human existence. I couldn't move. I didn't want to move.

Melinda's husky voice said, "Now, give it back to me."

"How much?"

"All of it."

I didn't know what that meant but my hands seemed to understand. One went to the back of her head and the other to her heart and then I don't remember what happened next. Other than: we breathed together, and I thought I was her or she was me or something like that.

Sometime later, Melinda rustled around, sat up, and said, "It's so hard for me to deal with this shit these days. I am in this body which I am happy with, which I love, yet so many out there are insanely bothered by it. And it just doesn't end. Ever. But what's really confusing me now is that, as an Extra, I can take a break from it. Just fill me up with the Extra energy meds and I'm at least a little more okay. But what about Normals who look like me and receive this same constant feedback? I mean, how the fuck can they stand it?"

I didn't know what to say. So many curses in such a short time. So unlike her.

She continued. "And the Extra thing by itself is nearly impossible to fathom because what are we, anyway? Are we some kind of privileged special beings sent here to change the world? If we are, we're doing shit-all nothing worth anything. Maybe I need to stop trying to understand it. Maybe I need to give it all up because… this whole damn mess, in this body, in this world, it's just breaking my heart."

More silence. Then she let out a hint of a laugh, stood up and said, "As long as it's the two of us, we'll never quit, will we?"

"No, we won't. We can't. I had this thought that, if you died, I would die also. Weird, huh?"

"Yes, we are certainly that. Now let's get ourselves together, grow into who we are, and figure out how to pass our privileged gifts on to others who need them more than we do."

I looked at her face with all the strange makeup and laughed. "If you still want to do the facial makeover, I can give it a try. But you have to go gradually so people around you don't notice. What you could do first is try dressing differently, I think frumpy is the correct term, so I'll take you clothes shopping. And your hair. Decide what you want to do with it and I'll make an appointment right away."

Adam

Jackson left first from the meeting with Sara Leeds. "I have to go. I have a few things to do. I'll be in touch," he said and hurried out of the room.

"You think he's okay?" Sara asked.

Adam forced himself to find a bit of levity. "Do you think *we're* okay?"

"I know this is about as intense as it gets for you, and Jackson might bale. If it happens, I can help you find somebody else. But at this point, I don't think either of us could walk away from what we're doing. Am I right?"

Adam nodded.

She made her eyes grow big again and stared into his, again with the hint of a grin. "And I thank you from the depths of my being, from this mind/body I am inhabiting, that you shared so much with me."

Adam shook his index finger at her, mimicking her, laughing. "I intend to find out exactly what kind of Extra being you are, Sara. Are you ready for that?"

She waved the back of her hand at him. "Shoo. I need to get with Carter and figure out how the money's going to work. I'll let you know by tomorrow."

He sighed. "The money. It almost seems irrelevant." He quickly added. "But it's not. I still like the money."

He exited the building, headed north up First Avenue, and stopped at an orange and green colored food-truck selling ice cream and smoothies. He bought a large smoothie—banana, strawberry, blueberry, and kiwi—and continued until he found a bench at a bus stop to sit on. He took a big pull through the straw and immediately felt dizzy. He took the plastic top off the paper cup and saw movement from little ant-like things swirling around in the thick liquid. *I'm hallucinating, But why? Maybe I'm just tired.* By the end of the meeting he had liked being with Sara, probably because she was so unusual, bizarre even, yet grounded at the same time. He wished she had come with him. *But where am I going?* He stood and began walking. He knew the answer and also knew why he was hallucinating. Whenever his mind had entertained even a flash of a thought related to any of this Extra stuff, whether it was from his brother, Sara just now, or Jade and Melinda so long ago, it had always put him into some kind of altered state. It was almost like, whatever his brother Garrett was all about, had rubbed off on him a little. And where was he going? To track down Jade Furlong as soon as possible.

He retrieved his vehicle from an indoor lot and drove out of the city, heading north toward Albany, to his parent's house in Oakwood where he was staying until he found his own apartment. After living in so many places for the last six years—endless travel, crashing on couches, holing up in tiny cheap short-term rentals all over the world— he was back with Ingrid and Clifford. Or, for the next month, back with Ingrid because Clifford had taken off on some wild adventure of his own that Ingrid wouldn't say much about and Adam knew better than to ask.

He came through the door, went into the kitchen, and found Ingrid sitting at the table, face glued to her laptop, searching for something on the web. Next to her sat a cup of coffee, nearly untouched and growing cold

"Hey, Mom, what's sucked you in so deep?"

She didn't look up. "Mom again? Not Ingrid anymore?"

He went to the sink and filled a glass with water. "Which do you prefer these days Mother Ingrid?"

"Not that."

He moved around behind her to see what she was looking at and she closed the laptop. "Mom, seriously. What are you looking at?"

She looked up at him, her expression pained. "Do you really want to know, Adam?"

Adam backed away, "Uh, Mom. You're kind of scaring me. So yes, I guess I do want to know."

"It's actually quite simple. Your father is once again away and his explanation of where makes sense on the surface but not really."

"He has to travel, Mom. It's his job. And he's done it for years." Adam sipped his water. Then, in a quiet voice, "Is he having an affair?"

She breathed out a small laugh. "Oh God, no. No, not that. It's just he's more secretive than usual. And then there's you. Just like him. The apple doesn't fall far and all that crap. I've only ever known what you've been up to after the story comes out. And this time…Can you tell me why you left the house at six this morning?"

"I met with a producer, a money guy, who says he's interested in helping fund a documentary I want to do."

"A documentary. That's a new one. With a film crew and all?"

"It looks like that's where it's headed."

She sighed, "But, of course you can't tell me what it's about."

"Not yet. Please. I just can't yet."

"So, I have to sit around and worry about you for the next six months?"

"You don't have to worry, Mom. Seriously I won't be in any danger."

She stood, went over to the coffee maker, and poured another cup. "You want some?"

"No, but I have something I want to ask you. Something I've been wondering about for a long time." Ingrid nodded. "If Garrett came to us when he was three and had lived with his mother until then, why did he never go back to see her?"

"Well, he did at first. You were just a baby so you wouldn't remember. And she had a lot of health issues and wasn't able to care for him.

"I just think it's odd that he would never talk about her. And I never met her or knew anything about her. Like, what were her health problems and what did she do and what was she like? For my whole life, nobody would ever talk about her."

Ingrid squinted and tightened her mouth. "Adam, there isn't much to say and I don't know why you're so interested in all this now." She sat back down in her chair. "I hope none of this has anything to do with this new thing you're working on. It doesn't, does it?"

"No. Not at all."

Yet now it did. Over the years, Adam made small attempts to find information about Cynthia Kastner, Garrett's birth mother, but nothing had ever come of it. He added Cynthia Kastner to his mental checklist of things to pursue.

Adam slept that night in the same bedroom he'd had growing up. When he moved out, his parents had re-decorated it, painted the walls, tore out the old carpeting, and put in new furniture, yet it was still the same room with the same level of comfort. He'd been all over the world and he still loved to come back to its safe space. They had also redone Garrett's room but nobody ever went in that one. He drifted into the beginning stages of sleep, hazily planning his next morning's trip to Clark College when his body and mind snapped awake. He switched on the light on the bedside table, sat up, and looked around. Was somebody else in there? Of course not. Why would there be? He sat for another minute and concluded that it was the stress from the earlier meeting making a harsh exit. He turned off the light, laid back down, and tried again. No luck.

He opened his laptop, googled Jade Furlong, and found a new photo of her that accompanied a short biography on the Clark College website. He blew it up on the screen just under the point where it would start to blur and pixelate. When the photo was taken, she had looked to the side of the camera, so he didn't have to stare directly into her eyes, her green—jade—eyes, the color sharper without glasses. As he remembered, she still had long, straight brown hair, with a hint of red, the smile with the slightly out-of-line front teeth, and freckles. He tried to get a true hit off the photo of what she was like now but only saw a pleasant, funny, almost theatrical character who would be a joy to spend time with. But it wouldn't be that simple. No way. The photo only captured her head, neck, and shoulders and the top of a pile of books, visible in the background. He made out the blurry title of the book at the top of the pile: *Myths and Legends in Human History*. The bottom of the photo cut off the title of the second book but he believed one of the words was *Allegories*. She was obviously high up on the intelligence spectrum and he added that to his list of her descriptors. He forced his gaze away, shut off his laptop and the light, and finally drifted into sleep.

At eight the next morning, he left the house and began his drive. Only fifty miles separated Oakwood from Clark College, and he arrived in less than an hour. He wished he knew where Jade lived because then he could have just gone to her place, knocked on her door and…then what? No, it was better to track her down on the campus with hopefully many other people around.

He parked the car in a city lot near the campus and prepared himself for what was next. The predicted hot and sunny afternoon was still hours away and the cool breeze allowed him to comfortably wear a light jacket, necessary because it had easy-to-access pockets. He put a small digital voice recorder in one of the pockets and promised himself he wouldn't turn it on unless Jade was informed and agreed to be recorded. He walked around the campus until he saw someone who looked like a professor and asked him where the History Department offices were. A few minutes later, he entered the building, spotted an office directory map on a wall, and found Jade's office. Her schedule was attached to her door and gave an office hour starting in fifteen minutes.

He left the building and walked in the opposite direction of where he thought she might be coming from. The Clark campus had a much different feel from the stately stone and brick buildings, tree-shaded walkways, and sprawling lawns at Phelps College, where he had briefly been a student and where he had first met Jade. Clark was a relatively recent addition to the New York State system and its campus was comprised of cold gray concrete or yellow brick structures, open concrete quads devoid of grass and trees, and a large central fountain area where students were expected to congregate but probably never did. He wondered why Jade chose Clark for her first position. Maybe it was all she could find or maybe she wanted to stay somewhat close to where she was from.

He circled back to Jade's building, waited a few more minutes, and went in. Her office door was ajar, and he gave a soft knock.

"Come in."

She was sitting at her desk, with a book in front of her. She stared a moment. Then, "Oh." She quickly stood. "Adam?"

"You remembered my name."

"And you remembered mine."

Her answer contained no hint of sarcasm. Although surprised, she seemed genuinely happy to see him. At first.

Her tone shifted. "Are you here for an apology? Because I am sorry that I acted so snippy with you that night six years ago in the Crow's Nest. And I'm truly saddened by the loss of your brother. You met my brother who I'm so close to and I can't imagine how it must have felt for you to lose yours."

"Thank you, yes, it was a rough time."

She motioned to a chair. "Please sit. I have some time until my next class."

She seemed so professional. Sort of like Sara Leeds, but what? Fifteen years younger? They would probably get along great.

"So, what can I help you with, Adam?"

Their eyes met and she flinched, a barely visible crack in her façade. He had some sort of effect on her just like she had on him. But it wasn't just the *I'm attracted to you and you are to me* scenario he had become so familiar with—and bored with—over the last few years. It was almost as if it had nothing to do with any of that.

The words slipped unbidden out of him. Probably the worst approach he could have had, he thought later. "We're both observing each other, trying to figure out why we make each other so uncomfortable."

Her entire presentation changed, and he remembered her eruption the night in the Crow's Nest when he had told her she was gorgeous. Unlike the last time, she didn't get angry and instead allowed him to see concern bordering on fear. "Well then, in the spirit of honesty, I'll tell you why I'm concerned. I found your website, poured over your blog which then disappeared, and read anything I could find that you've ever had published."

"Is that a compliment?"

"You are an excellent writer with a sophisticated and insightful outlook on so many aspects of our world. And here you are, after all these years, in my office wanting something from me. What is it you're working on?"

"A documentary about the Hope Community."

"A documentary meaning a film?"

"Yes."

She didn't answer. She clasped her hands together like a fisted prayer, brought them to her mouth, and closed her eyes, as if she was contemplating a great treasure or a disturbing possibility. She opened her eyes and looked at him. "And you believe that the nearly unmarked lane through an open gate outside of Anderson where I grew up leads to some answers, some big connection to Hope Community. All because you once heard my friend, Melinda Breeze, phrase certain ideas in a way similar to that of your brother who was involved with Hope. And also, because of the Old Elwood story."

"Uh. Yes."

Her tone was factual, professorial, and again, somewhat sweet. But she'd taken charge of the conversation, controlling its direction. He began to squirm.

"Adam, let me ask you. What do you think your place is in all of this? Who do you think you really are?"

"Huh?" From the moment he'd walked into her office, he'd been so focused on her that he'd barely looked at the surroundings, at her office and its contents. His eyes darted around, scanned the pile of books and those in the bookcase, passed over the different artwork on the walls, and settled on the small watercolor of the temple and the bands of yellow light, much like the one he'd seen years before in Max Shultz and Olivia Santini's gathering spot.

He pointed to it and nearly shouted, "What the hell is that painting? What is it?"

She stayed calm. "It's just something I found in a used furniture store. Now the most help I can give you at this moment is three names of people you might want to talk to. The first one, Billy Squires, is likely still a Hope member. Lance Ewing might be dead but maybe not. I believe they're Walk-ins." She raised her voice. "Is that the term you want to hear me say? Or how about Extra? Extra-normal. Walk-ins are all Extras and Extras are all Walk-ins but the two labels seem to have taken on slightly different meanings out in the bizarro world. You can munch on that one for a long while after you leave."

She lowered her voice. "And then there's Richard White. Who knows? He might be a Walk-in by now. A little late to the game but it's still always possible. Never too old and all that." She wrote the names on a slip of paper and handed it to him. Then, in a voice, so stern it could crack him like an egg, she said. "And Adam. Do not ever try to talk to Melinda Breeze. Not ever. She's off-limits. She's a true helper. There's another term for you to investigate. Helper. She's dedicated herself to actually helping people out here, not just fucking things up more than they already are. But if you can find out any info about the three characters who I just gave you, feel free to come back here and I'll come up with some more juicy stuff for your research."

He stood to leave, and she said, "Hey Adam, one more thing. Nobody makes a film documentary by themselves. Who else is involved?"

"Sara Leeds."

He wished he hadn't answered. He noted her look of amazement and hurried out of the office. When he reached his car, he put his hand in his pocket and felt the voice recorder. He'd never turned it on. He'd forgotten all about it.

Jade

As I settled into my first few weeks as a teacher, I began to ponder a whole series of deep questions about who I was and why I was there. This was likely because I was done with the rigors of Grad School with more time to myself, but still in an academic setting. My parents and the other Elders from my home had a tradition of never answering profound questions outright, believing that knowledge has the most power when it is arrived at through our own experiences. Those traditions were especially in place with the young ones configured like Melinda and me. When I thought about what it meant to be an Extra in a human body, other than talking with Melinda, I was on my own. Damn, their approach always annoyed the hell out of me. But I did get this one tidbit directly from my parents: an Extra essence without a human body can only get so far on the big cosmic journey. However, a human paired with a perfect Extra match might be able to stumble along to a distant stop where true wisdom and clarity reside.

What I most wanted was clarity about whether there was an actual purpose to my lockup experience. Like, did it have some greater meaning? Certainly, the perpetrators had, in their minds, a reason for their actions, and that reason might have been to target me specifically. But at that point, I was fumbling through vaster generalities carrying bylines like *meant to be, pre-ordained, destined,* and the like. As if this event had been staged by a higher power for my benefit, either as payback for an earlier deed—or misdeed—or as a learning opportunity. Okay, to a large degree, I was on board with all the karmic learning stuff, but not to any simple conclusion that, therefore, our universe on the grandest scale functions predictably, and that all events, trends, and actions, both human and not, can be pre-determined if one knows where to look or who to ask. I rejected the idea of an all-knowing universal overlord. However, if there is no director of the chorus, does it mean that our universe is nothing more than a constantly and randomly changing shit show, an ongoing drama of chaos and impermanence? I believed then, and continue to believe now, that this is mostly true. Yet, some thread of something—preferably positive—bonding all reality together, had to exist. And in my rapidly evolving mix of Extra-ness and Human-ness, baked, spiced, and ready to serve, I finally began to get it. Love of some sort or every sort is the only constant in this infinite, messed-up cosmos we all exist in.

Yet, if love is the universal binder, why is universal hate always lurking in the background, always bonded with its own mysterious threads? As I began to experience a love of all aspects of my reality, I also acquired a front-row seat to the hate plays still performing daily within my own being. When Adam Kastner showed up at my door, unannounced, I delved deep into places I hadn't visited in a long time. Since we were both skilled observers, when he arrived, with his entire camera-eyed character recording every detail, it got me so worked up that I responded to him like a total asshole—and was forced to watch myself doing it. He scared the hell out of me, and how did I deal with it? Dominate. I dominated so I could heave the fear right back at him, drive it deep into his bones, and make him tear out of my office, stumbling over his own doubts and insecurities. All fueled by my desperate desire to feel unafraid, to feel better. Except it did *not* make me feel better in any way. So, I did what I always did in those situations: I called Melinda and invited myself over for dinner.

As was typical, Melinda's travels through the land of profound questions were nearly similar to mine except with much less drama. She had submerged herself in her work and was already participating in a volunteer hospice care program. Her energy seemed boundless and her calm, centered demeanor captivated most people she came in contact with. Yet, when I spoke with her, which was nearly every day, she struggled in her own way, trying to move ahead with her understanding of her place in the world. She just hid it better than I ever could.

Walk-ins were showing up everywhere adding to her confusion. I could spot some of them, but she had subtle skills I hadn't yet mastered and possibly never would. We both kept notes and waited—impatiently—for the right moments to establish contact. But the whole process unsettled us. And now, Adam Kastner was back and we both believed he was a harbinger of something. Exactly what, we didn't yet know.

I entered Melinda's apartment, and when we did our hello hug, she felt especially buzzy, like I was embracing a sunflower with bees burrowed into the seeds, looking for pollen. And right off, a typically weird time spent with my closest companion morphed into something odder than ever. We sat down at her cute little four-chair table with a vase full of wildflowers in the center, poked over a simple pasta and salad meal, and I filled her in on my meeting with Adam, with an emphasis on my response and how it made me feel.

"When I'm threatened, when I sense a threat to our community, any variety of universal love—compassion, kindness, empathy, caring—instantly evaporates and…and…it's upsetting me. I mean, time is running out here and one thing I know is that I've got to get a handle on this."

I started to cry, not big sobs or water torrents, just a little bit of wet behind my glasses and I took them off and poked at the wet with the sleeve of my blouse. I put my glasses back on and looked at Melinda. She'd had her beautiful hair cut much shorter and was doing something to it that turned the curls into plainer waves, she'd made up her eyes in a way that shrunk their size, her lips were a dull pasty color, and she'd disguised her figure with loose, professional pants and a plain white shapeless blouse. By current media standards, the label, *gorgeous*, likely would no longer apply to her. Yet, when I saw the same tears in her eyes and she said, "It's okay Jade, really it is. Your honesty, your wisdom, your search, your caring, it's all so exquisite," she continued to be the most beautiful being I'd ever known. I changed the subject.

"Oh, thank you. You're always there for me." I swirled pasta onto my fork, slurped it into my mouth, and said off-handedly while chewing, "You know, even with all your modifications, you are still stunning. Is there anybody at your job who's shown an interest? I mean, in a good way?"

"Thankfully no. I mean, I'm not in the right place to pursue anything anyway. How about you?"

"Same thing." And then I said it. With no forethought, barely an idea of what I was saying, the words poured out. The words that had been playing around in the back of my mind for how long? Months? Years? I guess I just couldn't contain them anymore. "Remember when we were young and we talked about experimenting, you know, physically experimenting with each other? Do you ever think about doing it now?"

She laughed. "All the time." Her face changed to serious. "Oh, are you thinking about it? I mean, do you want to, like now? Even with my changed look?"

She also knew it was there, it had been all along. I had no doubt she felt the same. I nodded. "I know the being inside your body and that's what I'm so attracted to. If you want to."

She smiled the most enchanting smile, took my hand, and said, "It would make so much sense, wouldn't it? After all this time, it would be such a comfort." My hand began to shake. She continued, "But unfortunately, I don't think we can."

"Huh?" I could feel her tremble.

She stood and whispered, "I want to show you something. And it might be upsetting. But know that whatever happens, I still love you."

I drifted into a dazed space, not understanding where this was going.

She said, "Stand up a second." She pulled me close, and placed one of her hands between my thighs, and the other on my breast. "Now, tune into how this makes you feel, the excitement of it."

I felt like I was going to pass out. For a few minutes, she told me soft, suggestive, sexy things. She leaned in and touched her mouth to mine, and I heard a crack like a bomb going off. Somehow, I ended up on the floor on my butt with a shock-like feeling ramming through my body. A glass of water had tipped over on the table and the water dripped onto my legs, burning them. Melinda stood, extended her hand, and pulled me up. I backed away from her, shaking my head.

"And I don't think it's just me," she said.

"But it came through you."

"This time, yes. Are you okay?"

"Uh, yeah." I was so relieved. "I guess I am."

"Then I want you to do the same thing to me. But this time let's play it up a bit more."

"Are you kidding? Why?"

Her voice went soft. But firm. "Jade, listen. We've got to learn to control all this energy while we still can. Now, take my hand." I did and she looked into my eyes. "Tell me how you feel about me, how I make you feel."

Oh damn. I unloaded. I told her everything I loved about her, starting with the sound of her voice, then on to most of her body parts. I delved into the nuances of her amazing mind, her multi-faceted personality that was always so kind, and when I began on her body movements, her breath became heavy and her eyes half-closed. She told me to stop, nodded and said, "Do it."

I put my hands in the correct places and kissed her, and another bomb knocked us apart. This time we were ready and stayed upright.

"It's so disappointing," she said. "There's no pleasure in it at all."

"And this time, it came through me."

She took my hand and led me to the couch. Our unfinished meals sat on our plates growing colder. She continued to hold my hand, pushed next to me, and talked for the next few minutes. The buzz between us continued but we could handle it at the level it was at.

"We are in love," she said, "and have always been in love and always will be in love. Do you agree?" I nodded. "But because we're both enmeshed in our mission as Extras, we never felt the need to do the whole traditional human part. And now we want to. But Jade, even as Extras, there's something different about us, and if you put us together, well, we're especially odd. It's almost like what's inside us is more than our human bodies can handle, and we just saw what happens when we tried to connect them sexually. We have to figure out what's going on. Either figure out how to damp down the energy or to expand ourselves to accommodate it."

Expand ourselves. I liked that. Something large and wonderful clicked in my brain. "The latter," I said.

"The latter?"

"Yes, you said we can expand ourselves and maybe we can." It was my turn now. "Since we've known each other, we've always had a relationship, unlike most humans. Or even Extras like my parents. It's magical in the sense that it rises far above who we are individually. Do you agree?" She nodded. "We've always been supportive, we've offered suggestions but have never been judgmental or nasty or mean. Or jealous. It's as if the relationship is innocent and pure but simultaneously wise and experienced. Now, what if we visualize ourselves together growing bigger, as grand as we can be, universal even, and this energy pushes our creation, our pure love out into this planet we inhabit. It soars to the sky, then softly, gently rains down upon our earth and all who live in it."

We sat quietly for hours, playing with the concept and trying to tame the near-infinite power behind it. Eventually, we both slid down on the couch and fell asleep.

The next morning before I left, Melinda said, "If you want to explore sexual activity further, I say go for it. Male, female, any other gender configuration. And keep close mental notes on how it works with the energy charge. But unfortunately, I think you should not connect with Extras of any sort in that way, at least for the time being."

"Are you sure you won't get jealous?"

She shook her head and laughed. "Jealousy. It's such a strange component of human behavior, isn't it?"

"And you don't want to do the same?"

"Not right now. I'm way too busy. And one other thing. We don't know what Adam Kastner is or exactly what he's after but we do know that, for many reasons, he's a person of great interest. So, I think sexual contact with him should be avoided."

I gave her a playful nudge. "You are sooo jealous."

"Oh, stop."

I went back to serious. Sort of serious. "Melinda, the truth is that right now and possibly forever, you are the only one I can imagine being with in that way. And even if I wasn't, Adam Kastner would not be on my list. He's a mystery for many reasons, including why he upends me so easily. I mean, I do find him attractive and all that stuff, but I think we're too much alike and we would destroy each other."

"And he's working with Sara Leeds."

"Remember when we read all her books?"

"She's impressive. And close, so close to so much. She may be a Walk-in and doesn't know it yet."

Adam

Adam ran out of Jade's office, across the campus, and back to his car. He didn't know what to do next. He didn't want to go back to his parent's house but, at first, couldn't think of anywhere else to go. He would see what he could find about the three names Jade had given him. He also had an interest in another person, somebody he likely should have searched for already: Jade's brother, Sam Furlong. She would have lost it if he'd asked for details about Sam, especially contact information.

He drove to a Barnes and Noble bookstore, went inside and bought a decaf coffee, and perched at a back table. He opened his laptop, searched social media for Sam Furlong, and found nothing matching. Next, he searched for the three names Jade had given him. When she'd written them down and shoved them at him, she was so upset and angry. But why? The degree to which he'd blown his whole meeting with her began to sink in. Unless these names had some meaning he could uncover, it would mean he'd left with nothing of value. He should have insisted she tell him what they had to do with her, why they were so important, and what connection she thought they had to Hope

146

Community. He felt like storming back to her office but knew it would only make things worse.

He did a search, poured through social media for Cynthia Kastner and found nobody who seemed to be a correct fit. He thought she might have never taken his father's last name or had changed it when they split. Or maybe they never officially got married. He moved on to the list Jade had given him. He found an obituary for Lance Ewing and no other information to verify anything beyond that, but Billy Squires was a different story. He had a Facebook page that listed his hometown and age and he had given a "like" to the Hope Community page. However, it showed no current address or information about what he had been doing for the past few years. Adam studied the few photos Billy had of himself, even clicked on one and blew it up a little. Something about his face unsettled Adam and he closed the photo and began to scroll through Billy's friends. He found Richard White, which was somewhat of a jackpot, and scoured his page.

Richard White worked at a law firm in Albany as a paralegal and had near weekly posts of his activities with friends and family and occasional work colleagues. Richard also listed Hope Community in his "likes" and even had a few entries in his history of the lectures he'd been to at Hope. He'd actually attended the talks, not just watched them online as Adam had. Adam scrolled through the "friends" list, found one with the last name of one of the partners of the law firm, and found another "like" for the Hope Community. Was the law firm connected?

Next up, he would keep moving forward, track down Richard White, and possibly, despite Jade's warnings, even try to contact Melinda Breeze. But his encounter with Jade had shaken him up enough that he wanted to do nothing for the rest of the day. Maybe go to a park somewhere and walk around in the woods or sit by a river. He slugged down his coffee, hoping it would give him an anxiety-free boost, and headed back to his car. He sat for a minute and his next move seemed to formulate by itself. He let it percolate, let it solidify into a perfectly logical plan. He picked up his phone to give Sara Leeds an update, but dropped it back on the passenger seat, and drove off.

He had read everything ever written about the Hope Community, either by members or outsiders, which, compared to other similar growing communities, was not much. He'd also watched on YouTube an ongoing lecture series presented monthly by different community members. The subjects always followed a common and accessible theme: such as addressing appropriate and helpful ways for people to interact with each other to find a sense of harmony and well-being in their lives; or occasionally, the speaker would teach specific exercises to help viewers learn to control their actions and emotions so that they could be more effective at achieving their life's goals. He never saw anything he would consider groundbreaking or even unusual, and when watching, always focused his attention on the live audience in the room and the speech patterns and mannerisms of the speakers. Inevitably, the speakers were well-spoken, fully fluent in the nuances of their chosen subject, and exuded a powerful charisma. Neither Max Schultz nor Olivia Santini, who he'd met years earlier, ever spoke.

The events were carefully staged, Adam believed, but the audience response— rapt attention and ramped-up enthusiasm—always came across as genuine. A few months back, he had begun to freeze a few frames of the audience. He would take screenshots and then try to compare them to the audiences at other events. The process was painstaking and inaccurate but revealed that a person generally attended four or five lectures and then that was it. They never appeared again in the audience.

Hope Community was about an hour away, and as Adam drove, he reflected why he'd never gone there in person before, at least to one of the lectures. It wasn't like, even with all his travel over the last few years, he had never been around—briefly visiting his parents, sometimes living a month or more with them—to make the trip. In addition to the lectures, the community had a small public section, almost like a museum, where outsiders could read about the history and philosophy of the community, and see a short slide show. Also, because one of the foundations of the community was to research and develop the most advanced biodynamic and regenerative farming practices, they had a farm store to sell their produce. Even so, although he had a near obsession with Hope, he had never bothered to make the short trip.

He wondered why, yet if he only scratched the surface of his reasoning, he knew exactly why: the idea of being so close to those people, to that community, terrified him enough that it was always easier to simply not bother making the trip. He was about halfway there, moving along at sixty on a well-traveled two-lane highway, when turning around, and possibly even forgetting about the whole documentary idea seemed like a good option. He pulled into a small carved out dirt-covered area with a few other vehicles and turned his car off. A trail led out of the area and flashes of sunlit water shone through the trees. Likely the vehicles belonged to some folks standing in a slow-moving river, wearing rubber waist-high waders to keep them dry, casting fishing poles out into a gorgeous expanse of pure nature. Wouldn't that be a more sensible pastime?

I have to do this, I have to. I owe it to my brother, to my parents. My parents? The thought of his increasingly mysterious father and frustrated mother, once again disturbed him. A whole other section of his life that was easier not to examine. A whole other undefined reality. Reality? An increasingly tenuous concept. But hadn't it always been that way?

He got back on the road, and in what seemed like a minute later, pulled into a newly paved parking lot, half-filled with about thirty cars. At the far end of the lot stood a dark-stained wooden archway with a sign, proclaiming in letters carved into the wood and painted a soft white, Welcome to Hope Community. He left his car, didn't bother to lock it—who would ever steal here? —and slowly walked to the sign. The archway marked the beginning of a well-maintained gravel path leading into an inviting canopy of forest. The path curved, and he couldn't see what was at the end but could hear voices. He remembered being at the entrance to the commune where Jade and Melinda had grown up. In some ways this was similar, but in another important way, much different: Jade's commune tried to hide from the world and this place, although not screaming out its presence for all to see, at least had a Welcome sign.

He rounded the curve and came to a large bungalow-style building looking as if it had been built at least a hundred years earlier. Yet, he was sure it was only a few years old. It had weathered cedar shake siding, a massive wrap-around porch accessed by a short set of stairs or a curved ramp for handicap access, and large dormer windows. From the outside, it appeared to be two stories, but when he entered, a vast open space with eighteen-foot ceilings greeted him. Well-placed windows allowed in natural, tree-shaded light and calming forest views, and high above, the dormer windows added to the ambiance. Large but cozy, impressive but not oppressive.

He signed a guest book laying on a table, using a fake name, Jaime Marsh, and scanned the room. A display of some sort was placed close by and he started there. It consisted of a short timeline of the community and a world map showing where other similar communities existed. He noted that the Land Trust in Anderson was not shown. When he reached the next display, he realized that the placement of each display had been laid out in such a way that it positioned the viewer on a specific path. He could leave the path if he wanted, but the subtle arrangement of chairs and small tables containing written information discouraged the viewer from abandoning the layout of the journey. Each display had a specific theme and purpose. One described in detail their experimentation with different farming methods, one covered the way children were encouraged to learn, and one outlined volunteer and outreach work that community members did in the outside world. Adam was skeptical about this last one because he'd never come across anybody in that role.

A few other visitors were just ahead of him and one, a thin older man with a wispy white beard, had stopped and was sitting in one of the chairs. As Adam passed, the man said, "So, what do you think so far?"

"Huh? Oh yes, very interesting." Adam reached his hand into his jacket pocket and clicked on the voice recorder. "And what do you think, sir, if I might ask?"

"Oh, I've been here before. My second time. I'm humoring my wife because she's stuck on the place. She watches all the lectures and even went to one." He pointed across the room. "That's her over there about to go into the next part."

"And you don't share your wife's level of enthusiasm?"

"No, I don't. I'm a firm believer in Christ. A fundamentalist if you need a label. But over the years I've found that, when my wife strays, it's best to just follow along and she always returns to the fold." He added quietly. "At least she always has in the past."

"And what would you do if she didn't return? If you don't mind me asking."

The man looked up at Adam, stared with steely eyes. "I would do everything within my power to find out why. That's why I'm here now."

Three, then four possibilities of who this man in front of him really was cycled through him: a Hope plant who evaluated everyone walking by; a Hope plant who was there to specifically evaluate Adam Kastner when he finally visited and walked by; some version of Old Elwood which would mean he'd once again entered a dimension he couldn't begin to understand; nothing more than a sad old guy who genuinely feared he was losing his wife. Adam forced himself to choose the last one.

The man looked down at his feet. "This time I'm truly frightened," he mumbled. "These people might be connected to the devil himself."

Adam liked that. The devil. Another direction to follow, to add interest to the documentary. "Can you give me your name, sir?"

"Raymond Elmshaw."

Adam's eyes widened. Wasn't Old Elwood's last name Clamshaw?

Raymond locked his gaze on Adam, nodded, and waved his hand in a shooing motion. "Go on then, Sonny. I know it's a funny name but it's the only one I've got."

Adam could now clearly see three people ahead of him. The one he believed was Raymond Elmshaw's wife approached a large wooden door, opened it, and closed it behind her. Shortly after, the two other people, both older women, did the same. He spent only a minute or so at the last three displays, reached the door, and read a small sign that said: Please Continue. He entered a much smaller room with tiny windows letting in only a glimmer of light. Yet in the darker space, Adam could still see clearly due to an elaborate setup of floor lighting calling attention to three more displays.

He went to the closest one. It consisted of a table with four large computer screens and chairs in front of them. Headphones with a mouthpiece microphone were laid on the table at each spot. He sat and read directions on the screen: put on your headphones and say into the microphone, "I'm ready." He followed the instruction, and for the next ten minutes watched snippets from some of the talks given by community members, all of which he'd already seen. In the end, another screen prompt appeared that said, "If you would like, please comment on what you just viewed."

Adam said, "I'd like to learn more. Go deeper."

A new string of words on the screen said, "Please go to the next table."

The next table was exactly like the first except that it had only three screens and the three older women from the last room were already sitting in front of them. He considered going to the final table, with only two screens, but wasn't sure if he would be going against some kind of protocol. He decided he didn't care and was almost at the final table when a person he hadn't noticed, sitting in an unlit corner, came over to him.

The first descriptive word that popped into his head was *gorgeous*, which he found odd because, ever since he'd been reamed out by Jade Furlong, all those years ago, for referring to her as gorgeous, he'd mostly dropped the word from his vocabulary. But this woman was certainly that, in much the same quirky way Jade continued to be. As she stood in front of him, introduced herself as Nicolle, and extended her hand, he had another of his otherworldly thoughts: *if I was gay or a straight woman, would she have appeared as a male? If I was thirty years older, would she have appeared as also that much older? If I had no interest in any part of physical seduction and lived solely in the world of knowledge, would she have appeared as an ancient wizened character who knew everything about everything?*

He shook her hand. "My name is, uh, Jaime. Is this okay that I'm skipping the second table?"

"Oh sure, if you want. It all depends on what sort of information you're searching for."

He wanted to click on the recorder but didn't dare. She would certainly know. Or maybe she wouldn't care. Maybe she would expect it. He reached into his pocket and switched it on. "I've been interested in the Hope Community for a while and watched all the lectures. But I'd like to know more about any underlying belief systems community members might have in common."

"Such as…"

"Well, let's see. Like what happens to us after we die or where we were before we were born. Is there a part of us that goes on and continues to exist after death? That sort of thing."

Her face lit, like in a theater production when a character would speak and the lighting would subtly brighten their appearance. "How wonderful. Most people aren't interested in us in such a way and it's exciting that you are. Of course, not everyone anywhere, including here in our community, shares exactly the same beliefs about such matters. But most of us here have a similar view on how the world we exist in now interfaces with the world of the eternal universe."

The eternal universe. One of Garrett's phrases he'd forgotten.

She led him to one of the chairs at the third table. "Please take a seat here and put on your headphones, and get ready for an amazing experience."

He pointed to the second table. "What about the three over there?"

"Oh, I'm quite sure they're finished for the day. And I'll sit across from you just in case."

Adam sat, put on the headphones, and said, "Begin."

The video began with a middle-aged woman sitting on a rock by a gently flowing stream. Trees with rustling leaves shaded the sun and bird songs could be heard occasionally. The woman wore dark green denim slacks and a t-shirt that had, *LOVE,* written gently on it. Her look—a warm smile, soft brown eyes, undetermined ethnicity, and dark wavy hair—exuded kindness and comfort, like somebody a person like Adam would love to have as a classroom teacher. But her opening lines were unexpected and a little disappointing. She talked about peoples' inclination to want groups like Hope Community to all share nearly exact beliefs about subjects related to spirituality or religion. She emphasized that, although certain core concepts— something existed before we were born and continues to exist after we die—were accepted by most members, variations included a range of ideas.

After about five minutes, Adam found himself becoming increasingly annoyed. *This is a milquetoast ramble designed to obfuscate what is truly going on here.* He stayed with it a few minutes longer, then said, "Stop," and surprisingly, the video stopped. He stood and the young woman sitting across from him, Nicolle, also stood. They were alone now in the room. The three other women had left.

"You seem disturbed. Was that not what you wanted to see?"

He forced himself to match her calm. "Not really. I guess what I wanted to hear about from somebody inside here," he waved his hand around, "was a description of terms I keep running into out there." He pointed to the door.

Her head slightly tilted and her eyebrows moved closer together. "Oh, can you tell me more?"

Adam let it all flow out of him. "Yes. Like, what is an Extra, and what is a Walk-in and what is the difference between the two? And where do these things come from and what is their purpose? And, do they all mean to do well in the world or are some not so kind and wonderful? And, most important, are any of them here within this compound?"

"Of course. I should have known it. All excellent questions. But Jaime, unfortunately, I'm not the best person to speak to about those questions, at least not right now. I would have to ask you to come back at another time and meet with the right person. Would it be all right?"

"Uh, yeah, sure."

She handed him a business card. He hadn't seen her take it out of a pocket. Maybe she'd had it in her hand the whole time and he didn't notice. "This has my number on it. When you're ready, call and I'll set something up."

"Could I bring another person along?"

She didn't hesitate. "Oh, of course. Now look over there." She pointed to a far wall. "You can go through the door and you will be right outside near your car. Thank you for coming and I do hope you contact me." She extended her hand. "We like to hug here. Is it okay?

It lasted only a few seconds but everything about it was wonderful. He went through the door and into bright sunlight, and as he drove away, a quiet ecstasy coursed through him. But a few minutes later, his detached observer persona, salted with a touch of paranoia, kicked in. This woman's five-second hug transferred something to him and the intention was to seduce him to come back for more. An action straight out of cult seduction, past and present. Intro to Cult behavior 101. Except she had specifically tailored whatever it was she'd transferred to someone like him. It was not a cheap inter-sex come-on, it was more like, "I know who you are and what you need to feel settled and secure in the world. So, come on back—when you're ready—and hop on the inner-peace train. We'll take you where you need to go." It was so damn intense and so, so scary. But he'd opened the door and the option of running away and never coming back was now a thing of the past.

Jade

Over the next week, the Walk-ins became more visible, as if Clark College had a special program for them. They exuded a special energy and elicited a unique feeling I had not noticed before, and I attributed my new awareness to the energy exchanges I'd had with Melinda, both positive and negative. I'd tapped into an ability to embody a fuller presence if I wished, and more of the world opened up for me. In my first Monday morning class, I did my normal routine and noticed nothing unusual. During the second class, two students, one on each side of the room, seemed to devour every word I spoke, like I was handing out something they were desperate to consume. I made eye contact with both of them, and while talking about medieval medical practices in Europe, threw in a few choice lines about body-mind connection.

At the end of the class, I again mentioned office hours in case anybody needed individual guidance, and shortly after I returned to the office, I heard a knock on the door. A young man came in, introduced himself as Jacob LeBlanc—which I already knew—and took a seat. He quickly spotted the small watercolor of the lake, temple, and bands of light, pointed to it, and said, "That's what it's all about, isn't it?"

I gave a vague response. I wasn't going to jump to conclusions. "It's an interesting piece. I found it in a second-hand store."

"I've seen a few other versions around. One was done in oils and is bigger. I've also seen copies."

"What does it mean to you? What do you get from it?"

"Oh, come on Jade, uh, Professor Furlong. You know what it means to me. Same as you. We're both from the same world, so to speak. Although you strike me as an Extra-at-birth, a communal type."

At least he didn't know exactly where I was from. But he was a near-brilliant observer, and I automatically slipped into my, *trying to control the narrative* mode. "Are you from one of the communes?"

He snickered. "I wish. This latest Walk-in stuff is one step away from being way out of control. I mean, I'm hearing stories about masses of full-grown humans receiving overlays. I got mine at a young age so it could have been worse, I suppose."

"Can I ask where you're from?"

"How about I ask you where you're from."

"Jacob, I'm here to help. That's my purpose for being here, for taking this position at this college in this geographical location that's been designated as a hotspot."

"Sure, but let me ask you this. Are you really here to help or to only observe and send your findings off to some Elders somewhere who think they know what to do with the info?"

That struck a nerve. What a comment. I sat on the edge of my seat and fixed my gaze on him. But I consciously stopped myself from grabbing info from his thoughts because he seemed the type who would pick up on it. "I think we're on the same page here. You're obviously a skilled observer and maybe more and we're both trying to size each other up. So, I'm going to be bold. Do you have any connection to the Hope people? Because I don't."

"Actually, I do. But I severed ties with them because…"

He slumped down in his chair, and tapped his foot on the floor, but didn't continue.

I said, "Since you know what you are, I'm going to say the classic Extra phrase." He managed a weak smile and we spoke the same sentence together: "It's so difficult being in these human bodies." A lame password sentence anybody could learn and copy. But it was a start.

I said, "Did you ever know a guy named Garrett Kastner?"

"Hey."

"Oh God, I'm so sorry. It just popped into my head. I know his brother."

"Yeah, well I do, too. I was just a little kid and Garrett helped me out. But he was a mess and his brother, Adam, was so much worse. Look, all I want is to be able to trust somebody, you know? You don't have to tell me where you're from. I know you're from one of the closed communes and I wish I could have found my way there."

"Jacob. People like us do desperately need to trust each other. So, let's try an experiment here. I think, or at least I hope, that we're both excellent judges of character, even without all the Extra stuff. But I'm going to let you in some, and you can decide for yourself if you trust me. Is that all right?"

He sighed and gave a gentle smile. "It's all fine. I know you're safe. I can tell."

"You can come talk to me whenever you need to. And, if you don't mind, I would like any insight you might have into Hope. I have to admit, more and more I agree with you about this observer role, you know, passing on information and nothing happens."

"Well, I can tell you this. I get it second-hand but I think there are a lot of Walk-in types who are scared shitless about what they think is happening at Hope, like they're in some kind of internal war or something. And these Walk-ins think you at-Birth commune folks are a bunch of elitist do-nothings."

"Do you use the term, Stealers?"

"I don't hear it much these days. They try to blend in or something. But that might be what's going on at Hope. Or, at least at parts of Hope. They're doing all types of experimental stuff, but one group who is way out there is trying to steal the whole operation."

We agreed to meet again in a few days, we shook hands, and Jacob left. I stood at the window and stared out at the quad, at a group of passing students, the edge of another concrete building, one of the few trees gently moving in a faint breeze. My vision lost its focus as my mind fixated on one particular string of Jacob LeBlanc's words: ...*you at-Birth commune folks are a bunch of elitist do-nothings.*

Later in the day, another hand tapped on the slightly opened door and the young woman from Ireland, Erin Mason, walked into the office. This time, she was dressed in all black clothes: jeans, denim jacket, high boots, and black eye shadow. The contrast was with her hair which she'd dyed a bright red. In an earlier class, as I did one of my scans, I'd seen the hair but hadn't tuned into the rest of her appearance.

"Hi Erin. How're you doing today?"

She said with her Irish accent, "Fine, Ms. Furlong. Just fine."

"No central New York speak today?"

She laughed. "It's too much work to keep it up. And I decided I don't need to fit in. Even out here in the small towns, nobody seems to care how anybody speaks." She pointed to her clothes. "Or dresses. It's nice."

"I'm glad you feel that way."

"See, the thing is, I like to observe people and I don't want them to notice me doing it but the only ones who do notice, here anyway, seem to be other observers."

Here we go again. I had to laugh. "Who are you reporting to?"

"It's like this, Ms. Furlong. I'm from a town across the border from Northern Ireland. I know, from what you teach, that you understand in detail the political and social chaos of the area's history but, my God, you Americans know how to take such chaos to a whole new level." Her words sped up. "I'm from an Extra-at-birth commune of sorts. We integrate with the outside earlier than the ones here, and many of us have come to believe that a country's level of excessive turmoil manifests in how—in the background—their Extras handle the inevitable influx of newcomers. So, in typical fashion, the epicenter of what we think is a planetary trend is right here in this stubbornly self-important country where wonderful experiments are attempted yet generally fail due to the unbalanced selfishness of those involved." Her volume increased. "I mean, why don't you people look in the mirror for a change, study your own history and learn something and…" She stopped, shook her head, and looked away. Then much slower and quieter, "I'm sorry. We're all, well, really disturbed. I was hoping you could help me, enlighten me about what's actually going on."

For a few moments, her words left me speechless. "Erin, am I understanding this correctly? You were sent here to observe. I understand that. But why did you come to this school and then take my class? How did you know who I was?"

Her look suggested I'd just asked a stupid question. "I came to the school as a cover. Just like you're teaching here as a cover. I had no idea you would become a teacher and work here. That was just a lucky break.

My Elders knew of you, of course, because you're their connections' oldest child."

"Their...who?"

Now she was really confused. As was I. "Your parents. Damien and Therese. Everybody knows who they are. They talk to my Elders all the time."

Adam

Shortly after he left the Hope Community parking lot, Adam passed a road he believed led first north, then slightly west, and circled to the back of the community property. Most likely, it was the same road he'd taken with Garrett so many years earlier when they had sat up on a rocky knoll and looked down on the construction happening below them. He pulled over, made a U-turn, and turned onto the road. After a mile or so, he pulled over another time. He could find the knoll again, he could even hike down through the woods to the back of the Hope property, but somebody—or more likely, many bodies—would, one way or another follow every step he took.

His phone had a good signal so he set it up as a hotspot for his laptop, and for no other reason than he needed to see something, anything, he connected his laptop, opened Google Maps and the satellite view, and hovered over the property. Nothing new there: the same large bungalow welcome center, the same grid of streets and small buildings near the back, and three much larger buildings in the center. He zoomed in as far as he could and identified a few backhoes and a small dump truck which might be in a different location but were always there somewhere. He took a screenshot for a later comparison, closed the laptop, and shut his eyes.

If expansion or any secret activities were happening, they had to be underground. Wouldn't that be a smashing story if he could ever pull it off. However, the entire project seemed more daunting than ever. He couldn't hide from these people. He couldn't disguise himself or secretly bring in a camera and fool them. Any story he could get would need to involve a degree of transparency on his part that would be like if he walked into a hostile country, told them he was a spy and asked if they would allow him to do a story about them. The Hope people probably already knew everything about Adam Kastner, knew he was coming and had already planned how the entire situation should best play out. Eventually the rush of worries racing around wore themselves out, and although they were justified, most of them were enhanced by his typically overactive mind.

He remembered the voice recorder in his pocket, dug it out, and fumbled with the control switch. If it was somehow all erased, he would...It wasn't. The conversations were all still there. He listened to parts of them, was inspired by what he heard, turned his car around, and headed home.

As he drove, he prioritized what he should do next and came up with three items, each one more difficult than the previous. First, he would call Sara Leeds, to fill her in with what he'd done so far, and to get a finance update from her. Then, he would figure out how to meet with this guy, Richard White, who was on the list Jade had given him and who was a fan, at least on Facebook, of the Hope Community.

The complexity of his final task presented the biggest challenge and he would have to give it some time before he acted on it. He'd played back a few times in his head his last meeting with Jade, analyzing her behavior, and decided that, more than anything, she was desperately afraid of something. This led to memories of what it had been like, so many years before, to stand next to his car in the parking area outside Jade's commune, to watch Jade's younger brother approach from the field across the road and hand him some carrots. The whole vibe had been calm, safe, and so gentle, and he had wanted more than anything to walk down the dirt lane leading from the parking area and into the soft woods. Until his mother called and told him his brother was dead and upended his whole world. But what if his mother had not called then? What would he have found down the dirt lane? What was Jade Furlong trying to hide or protect, then and now? He needed to find out. He needed to step back and not make assumptions about who was who and what was what. He needed to meet with Jade again and find out who she truly was. Yes, she and her friend Melinda seemed to speak the same language as his brother, Garrett, but it didn't necessarily mean the Hope Community and the Anderson Land Trust were intimately connected. In fact, there was a profound difference between the two. Jade's group tried to keep people like him from bothering them, and the Hope Community said, "Welcome, Adam. Come on in. Let us show you around. Let us seduce you into coming back for more." Jade might be every bit as disturbed by the Hope Community as he was, and if so, she would be invaluable as a resource if not an ally.

Adam thankfully entered an empty house, with no parents to ask him annoying questions about where he had been and what project he was working on. He went to his room and called Sara Leeds. She answered on the second ring.

"Hey, Adam. I'm glad you called. Everything good?"

"I have a lot to tell you. I had a few adventures since our meeting. One of those *yesterday seems like an eternity ago* situations."

"Before you begin, I have some news on this end. Okay?

"Sure. Go ahead."

"First off, your videographer, Jackson, called me and quit."

"He quit? Why?"

"I don't know why. He wouldn't give a reason, just that he wanted no part of any of it and to tell you. I'm sorry, Adam. He kind of just hung up on me."

"Which means Carter's money is no longer there, right?"

"Unfortunately for the time being that would be correct."

"How about you, Sara? Where are you at with this whole thing?"

After a long silence, she said, "I can't let this go. I feel like I should but I just can't. So, talk to me. Fill me in."

Adam went over every detail of his visit with Jade, his later conclusion that he needed to meet with her again, his online searches for the three people Jade wrote down, and his experience at the Hope Community. He believed he'd left out nothing including that Sara was invited along if or when Adam returned to Hope.

"Okay, that's impressive," Sara said. "And I do appreciate your memory. It's quite remarkable. First off, on the subject of accompanying you to another Hope visit, I will have to give it some thought. And second, I do agree that you would do well to find out more about Jade and her friend, Melinda. And, if you somehow manage to wrangle a tour of their commune, I would love to tag along on that one."

"Does it mean you also have a different sense of what their group is about? That it's maybe different than the Hope community?"

Sara's voice tensed. "I'm not sure, Adam. I'm not sure what it is but something else does seem to be going on there and I'm, well, I don't know what I am exactly." She laughed. "If you know much about me, which I'm sure you do, what I just said is way out of character. But this is all very confusing. Earlier today I came across a whole lot of strange things about a small commune outside of Anderson hidden in the woods. And a few others like it, one in Virginia and one near Chicago."

"Whooah. What? Tell me."

"Do you ever go on Brackon? You know, the radical religious forum?"

"I have but not in a long time."

"I usually check it out and others like it every few weeks, and this morning I found a thread about the communes saying they were hotbeds of Satanism. Like they practice satanic rituals."

"Could you get anything about who was posting?"

"Nothing. But they were rough. Like hinting at violence."

"Well, now I have another reason to go back and talk to Jade. And I'll start following the thread. But I think my next move should be to track down this Richard White character. Do you agree?"

"Yes, and on a different note here, I'm not about to give up on Carter. I think we should meet again in person in a few days and review how we might go forward. We might have to present a completely new plan."

"Sure, we can do that."

"But Adam, it may take a while and, if you need funds to get you through, I can loan you some."

"Wow, thank you. I guess you really are sucked into this project."

"We need answers."

A few hours later, Adam received a text from his mother saying she and her father had taken a short trip and would be gone until the next day. "Enjoy the quiet house. Unless you plan on having a wild party." It was a running joke that Adam tolerated. Wild parties only existed for him in a much earlier part of his life and he knew his serious demeanor, so different from when he was young, bothered his mother.

He found a bag of French fries in the freezer, made a few grilled cheese sandwiches, and absently ate, his attention glued to his laptop search for more information on Richard White. He located Richard's work address and then tried a few different searches until he found his home address. Both were less than a half-hour from his house. He finished eating and began to formulate a plan that might work. But only if he found out a whole lot more info about this guy, including what his connection was to Jade Furlong. Should he call her? Even thinking about it made his stomach queasy. One more time, he questioned why. His annoyance finally overshadowed his fear and he called.

"Adam?" she answered. "This is an unexpected pleasure."

"Oh. Well, I'm glad of that. Are you in the middle of something? I have a few questions, but I can call back."

"No, no. In fact, I wanted to talk to you. I…look, I need to apologize for, uh, being so nasty. And I think we both have the wrong impression of each other."

"Yeah. Wow. I was thinking exactly the same thing. Like, I just assumed you're part of something that maybe you're not."

"Adam, this is the truth now. I promise you it is. No matter what I am or how I speak or what I believe I am, I am not connected to Hope Community. And Melinda also is not. And my brother and parents, none of us are connected other than in this different way we believe we are constructed. My group has always tried to keep a low profile and it's really scary that you or anybody wants to disrupt it."

"I understand. I do. Earlier today I had all these memories. Like what it felt like when I stood in the parking area with your brother, Sam, and stared down the dirt lane leading into where you grew up. I mean, before I got the phone call about my brother. I wanted so badly to go in there with Sam. More than anything, I wanted him to grab my hand and lead me through the woods. The feeling was so powerful, it felt like I was being drawn into heaven or something. Is it for real?"

She whispered, "Yes, it is."

"This is why I started remembering it. This morning I went to Hope's welcome center and took a tour through a museum-like setup they have. And then talked to somebody, this person who seemed to tailor her responses directly to what she perceived I'd want to hear. So, when I left, I had the exact opposite feeling from when I stood in your parking area."

"You went to Hope."

He shuddered, "Yes, and it was so intense, and now I don't know if I can continue with the whole thing. My video guy quit, Sara Leeds wants to continue, but the money was pulled. Maybe I should just give up on it."

Jade stayed silent for a moment. Then, "You know what? Right now, as you're telling me this, I'm having the exact opposite feeling. Like you've got to keep going. Go figure. Would you be up for meeting again?"

"Are you sure?"

"I'm sure."

"Then yes. I want to. Also, I have something more to tell you. Lance Ewing is supposedly dead, Billy Squires is hard to track down, and I have a whole lot of info on Richard White. But I need to know some things. Like where you met him, where he went to college and why you want me to meet him."

Silence. "Jade?"

She mumbled, "I'm still here."

"His Facebook page shows a lot of interest in Hope as does that of his employer. They're connected."

"I know. I've seen it."

"Then why do you want me involved?"

Her voice became a monotone. "SUNY Binghamton, eight years ago. He watched while the other two drugged me and locked me in a tiny closet for the night."

"Oh no. Why?"

She told him how Richard had suddenly left but she didn't give any of the details. "It wasn't a random event. They targeted me because of where I'm from. Before that, I had a positive reputation or something, like I was some kind of chosen one from my group, and those guys wanted to destroy me."

"But they didn't. And they won't."

"Thank you, Adam. I mean that."

He left his house in the early evening, the September sunlight starting to fade, and went for another drive. Richard White's house was in a quiet, tree-shaded middle-class neighborhood, similar to the one Adam currently lived in. A car sat in the driveway and a kid's tricycle was visible on the large front porch. Lights shone through the front windows, but as he drove slowly by, he didn't see any human movement.

He continued until he came to a small mall with stores and offices mixed together in a long two-story building. He parked, looked up Richard's Facebook page on his phone, and examined photos of him, storing the images in his memory. He left the car, casually strolled past the row of businesses—a hair salon, a FedEx office, and a small grocery store—and found the door to Cohen & Banks Law Offices. Lights shining through the front window lit up an office where somebody was standing next to a desk, talking to a seated person. He went into the grocery store, bought a small bag of pretzels, and made another pass by the law office window. The two people were still talking. The chances were slim that either one would be Richard, but he went back to his car and waited.

Five minutes later, a woman walked out, followed a minute after by a man. Adam hopped out and hurried over to the man. It was Richard White.

"Hey, excuse me. I'm sorry to bother you but are you a lawyer here?"

Richard slowed but didn't stop. "No, I'm a paralegal."

"Do you take on new clients? I came here to get something in the grocery store and saw your sign."

He stopped and turned to Adam with a slight smile. "What's the legal problem you have?"

"It's not that big of a deal. It's a divorce thing and we were going to do it all ourselves, but I think I need legal guidance."

Richard's affect shifted from *I'm in a hurry*, to *tell me more, I'm interested*. He nodded and said, "We get a lot of those and we're always here to help." He took a business card from his pocket and handed it to Adam. "It would work best if you call first thing tomorrow morning."

Adam read the card, then looked at Richard. "Richard White. You know what? I think I know you. Did you go to SUNY Binghamton like eight years ago or something?"

Richard forced a smile and said in a light voice, "I did. I don't know if I remember you."

"My name is Adam Kastner. I was pretty nerdy. Had my head in the books and kept a low profile. I didn't party much."

Richard kept his face neutral, but with his piercing eyes and a tremble in his handshake, he couldn't hide from Adam that he'd switched over to high alert.

"If you can get here first thing tomorrow morning, like at nine, I can do a meeting with you."

"Sure, I'll be here. It was nice to meet you, Richard."

When Adam returned home, he spent an hour reviewing his online presence, including his website and social media to ensure there were no clues to lead Richard to think he had any interest in the Hope Community or any other similar group. He knew he couldn't fool the Hope insiders, but he at least wanted to deter Richard until after their meeting.

The next morning, he arrived at the Cohen & Banks offices promptly at nine and was shown into Richard's small office. Richard sat behind a desk covered with stacks of folded fliers that he appeared to be sorting.

"Sorry," he said. "I can finish up with this later. Have a seat."

Adam picked up a flier and sat in a chair in front of the desk. The flier read: James Banks for New York State Senate.

"I'm working on a mailing," Richard said. "Mr. Banks is perfect for our district. If you want, you could take a few of these and pass them around."

Adam took a handful. "I'll look them over."

'Well, then. How can we help you here?"

"I guess I'd like to know how much a divorce will cost if we do it through you."

"A lot depends on what assets are involved, but I have a write-up which lays out general costs." He reached into his desk drawer and pulled out a sheet with approximate expenses neatly spelled out.

"This is helpful. I'll look it over. Our main issue, which is a little more complex, is that we've been working together on a written project, and she might bail on me and will want to get some reimbursement for her efforts."

"I saw that you're a free-lance writer."

Adam grinned. "Checking up on me. That's good. I did the same with you and your colleagues. Because of my work, I do it with everybody. But I try not to be obnoxious about it. Well, actually though, I was wondering what this Hope Community is that you and your partners liked on Facebook. The Hope Facebook page and their website don't say much."

Richard reached into his drawer. "I've got some written info here." He handed Adam a small booklet. "They're all good people. The best. They genuinely care about making the world a better place."

"And one of them is running for State Senator." Adam held up the fliers. "Sounds like a good move."

Richard changed the subject. "Interesting that you were at Binghamton. It seems like decades ago. I guess we're getting older. Who else do you remember from there? Maybe I knew a few of them."

Adam made up some names. "Well, let's see. I'm still in touch with Bruce Banefeld and he and I used to hang with a guy named Greg Peters. Also, there was this girl who was pretty cool. Her name was Jane, I think, but I can't remember her last name." He gave a general description of Jade. "But, like I said last night, I mostly kept to myself."

Richard kept up his cheery presentation, but his hand twitched a few times and his gaze hardened.

Adam continued, "But we're getting sidetracked here. If I can't get my ex on board with a pay agreement for the project, then I'm pretty sure the whole divorce thing will fall apart, and then I'll get in touch. And who knows? Maybe I'll do some work for Mr. Banks. Because of my background, I'm pretty good at figuring out who people are and how to get them to be on my side. I'm good at observing people. But then, I guess you are, too, right?"

Adam stood and Richard did the same. At the door, Adam forced his hand into Richard's, shook it, stared into his cold hard eyes, and did his best to put on a soft, innocent smile. "I'll be in touch."

Jade

The plan had been for Melinda to come to my apartment at six for dinner so I could update her on my conversation with Adam Kastner, and my meetings with the Walk-ins and the Irish Extra-at-birth, Erin Mason. I had concluded that we needed to go to our home in Anderson, meet with the Elders, and insist we be told whatever it was they were doing behind the scenes. This role of observer out in the world was fine but felt increasingly limited and ineffective, at least to me. However, Melinda never showed up. At seven, I called and left a message, and by eight she still hadn't called back. Since we both began working, this was a first and I found myself slipping into a classic human behavior pattern that I realized I had never before experienced so forcefully. By nine, a full-on panic set in. I drove to her apartment, knocked on her door, and when she didn't answer, used my key to let myself in.

Even before I opened the door, I knew something was wrong, and I also knew that, had I initially focused on the out-of-character pieces of the scenario and tried to see into what was happening, I would have stood where I now was, ready to enter, many hours earlier. Instead, I had jumped into an unhelpful human freak-out mode. One more lesson for the future. But what I saw next was not like anything I expected. Yes, somebody had broken into the apartment and trashed it. That much I knew. But the details. The details threw me. The living room couch lay on its back, and somebody had sliced most of its fabric into small pieces and mounded them into piles scattered across the floor. The bookcase rested on the couch at a sharp angle, and the books' covers and pages had also been cut up with the pieces heaped into more piles. The carpet: sliced. Coats and blouses from a hall closet: sliced. I looked into the kitchen, expecting piles of broken dishes and glasses, but it was as neat as Melinda predictably would have left it.

If the goal of an art installation is to immerse the viewer into a planned experience, this one was the ultimate masterpiece. My heart beat nearly out of my chest and I thought I was about to die. If Melinda had already been transformed, I knew I would follow.

I did not run away. I checked the bathroom and found nothing abnormal. The bedroom would be the ending, where my human life would finish. I stormed through the door, and again, saw nothing out of place. My eye caught the edge of a pillow with a few pieces gone, left loose on a chair. Somebody must have interrupted the demented artist, and unless they were in the last possible stronghold, they had fled their creation, leaving it unfinished. Unless…

The soft blue paint Melinda had applied to the closet door a few months earlier, the same soft color as the room's wooden trim, glared at me, red and steamy. The doorknob let me know it would burn my hands if I touched it. Still, I yanked it open and found only one collapsed human body occupying the space. At first, I didn't dare touch her, afraid I would do more damage. But she opened her eyes and smiled. I hugged her probably too hard, yet she didn't complain. She also didn't hug back. I backed away and saw her hands, fastened together with zip-ties.

"You're not cut?"

She mouthed the words. "No. no."

I helped her stand, ran into the kitchen, and found scissors—not a knife—and freed her. I shut the door to the bedroom, pulled Melinda onto the bed, and held her close while she went through the beginnings of whatever it was she needed to do. After a few minutes, she loosened her hold on me and backed away.

I said, "Let's get out of here. You can stay with me. And I'll come back and clean this up tomorrow."

"Yes. I'll pack a few things."

She went back into the closet, pulled a small suitcase off a shelf, threw a few clothes into it, and then headed to the bathroom. She was compartmentalizing like a normal human and dissociation would be next, a positive approach. Or so I thought. When she came back into the room, I had a much different impression.

"Are you okay with this?" she asked. "I mean, considering your past."

"Why are you asking me if I'm okay? It didn't happen to me."

"It kind of did. You're now in this radically altered space and your closest friend and companion was threatened in the worst imaginable way."

It was like she was way more concerned about how I felt than herself. Almost like the whole event wasn't such a big deal. "Melinda. What the hell is going on with you? You're acting like...I don't know."

"Well, I know. Are you up for another test? One that might absolutely scare the living crap out of you? I need to get an accurate read on where you're at right now."

Our brains connected. I knew a few more things. For starters, I knew the name of the demented artist. "Billy Squires did this. But why this in particular? All these sliced up things?"

"In a lit class I took at Phelps before you got there, I once complained about a part of a novel where this act is graphically described happening to people. My complaint had nothing to do with ethnicity or race or gender, although it did eventually open the door to those types of discussions. I complained because it was, for me, the most disgusting way any living creature can die. And a whole conversation went on for weeks about anything each of us found too horrible to contemplate and wished never showed up in books or movies. There was commonality but also a whole lot of individual versions of what sets a person off. Somebody passed on the info to whoever oversees Billy Squires, especially about me, for future use if necessary."

"But you're acting like you're not even all that upset about this." I waved my hand around the room.

"I'm most certainly upset. However, something has shifted, Jade, something so big."

"But why us? What's so special about us?"

Melinda grabbed my hand, pulled me into the living room, and stopped in the middle of the sliced-up piles. She put her arms around my waist and held on tight. She put her mouth next to my ear so that, when she whispered what came next—her words—went directly inside me. "When Billy Squires drugged you and locked you up all those years ago, you were a virgin, not to sex but to the true pain of the human world. And you got your dose. It trashed your life for a long time, and now the same person comes back and tries to do the same to me. First off, why didn't the people behind Billy just have him kill us? And the answer is because all of them are Extras and they can't."

She hugged me tighter and continued. "Billy Squires is just a pawn that others use to de-commission threats. Threats like us. Sad, isn't it? That he's lived such a delusional pathetic life? And I would bet whoever is behind him is afraid of us because we're not at all easy to de-commission"

Her words, her test, did not scare the crap out of me. Her voice vibrated in my held memories, dislodging useless clogged waste. She said, "I walked in and he had just started on my pillow. I told him not to bother, to instead use the knife to just kill me, and he nearly fell apart. I told him I forgave him. I told him I loved him. I whapped him on his back and watched him reassemble a little bit. I found some twist ties and told him to tie me up and put me in the closet. For his own protection from his own warped Elders, I said. He told me to never call them Elders because they weren't. Then he ran out of here."

When I'm with you, close like this, our wild thoughts calm down and mesh, and I'm infinitely more capable of staying on a steady path. That was my thought.

I'm the same. Exactly. That was her thought.

We cleaned up some of the mess, stuffing as much as we could into the kitchen garbage can, and left for my apartment. We drank tea and wine and ate food, sat on my spotless, uncut couch, and talked about what it would be like if she stayed for a week.

I remembered a part of our earlier conversation. "You said something about: first off, why didn't Billy Squires just kill us? What thought was up next? What was: second off?"

"It's a more complex question that will take our full dedication to find an answer. You asked: what's so special about us? About you and me in particular? And we can't have an answer unless we learn who is causing a Billy Squires type to act as he does. Who are they and what are they trying to accomplish? We know generally what's happening but none of the specifics."

"I might have something or many things to add here," I said. It was why I wanted to meet in the first place. I revisited my phone conversation with Adam Kastner and then my meetings with, first, the Walk-in named Jacob LeBlanc, and then, Erin Mason. I described how the first one severed his connection with the Hope people, how he had known Adam and his brother, Garrett, and how he had the sense that the whole community was at war within itself. I also shared how the young woman from Ireland knew who I was because her Elders not only knew but kept in communication with our Elders. "Including my parents and likely your mother."

"I was afraid of that," Melinda said.

I thought I knew what she was implying. "Oh no. You can't believe…"

She sounded a touch angry. "I'm not saying they're doing what they do to gain power or rule the universe or anything like that. I'm only saying that I no longer wish to play this role of observer who passes on what we see to our overlords. Like in some disturbing spy novel where the children are groomed, and if necessary, always dispensable for the greater cause. We need to know everything. We need to demand that our so-called Elders tell us everything. And we need to have a say in the path forward."

I let out an enormous sigh. "It's such a relief to hear those words. I fully agree. And if we're so special or powerful or something like that, we deserve to know exactly why."

We sat on the couch, tight together, and did our love thing. We built the energy and passed it out to the world. After what seemed like hours or days, Melinda broke the spell, made us more tea, and when she came back, said, "Adam Kastner again. Do you remember when you asked me why you kept thinking about him?"

"Yes. And you said something like, it's inevitable. The question is, what's inevitable?"

"Let's the three of us meet and see what happens."

The next morning, when Melinda got up, I was already at the kitchen table, reading emails. She said, "Morning. Hey, we finally slept. I didn't know you snore now." I didn't answer. She continued, "What's got you so wrapped up?"

"I got an email from Adam with a link to some weird stuff."

She looked over my shoulder and read—and I reread—a long and growing thread on a forum about small hidden communes around the country which practiced satanic rituals and sacrifices. It specifically identified one outside of Anderson, New York, one in Virginia, and one outside of Chicago but didn't give exact addresses.

I said, "It's a setup, isn't it?"

"There will be more on other forums. That's how it will work."

"We have to get closer to the main players in Hope. We need to meet in person with Adam, and Sara Leeds, too, if possible."

"Are you sure you trust them? Both of them?"

I shook my head. "No. The only thing I trust at this point is that you and I together have the power to send something good into the world. So maybe we need to focus part of that energy into also rooting out some of the not-so-good."

Adam

After he met with Richard White, Adam took his time returning to his parent's house. He couldn't get Jade Furlong out of his mind and wanted to call her again, to hear her voice. But he wasn't sure why. Whatever the reason, it was not like it had been so many years ago, that he liked the way she looked or acted. Something about the feeling went way beyond that. She knew about something he wanted, something he couldn't let go of. As he drove across Albany on Rt. 90, keeping his speed right around fifty-five, watching cars and trucks swerve around him, buildings and billboards pass by, he tried to visualize her face. However, instead of Jade, the other one, Melinda Breeze, showed up. He hadn't seen her in over seven years, yet there she was.

His parents were home when he arrived, and he went into the kitchen and found them preparing a fancy lunch of potato salad, fruit salad, small sandwiches, and a table set with champagne and glasses. "What's the big occasion?" he asked.

"Hey, mystery man," Clifford said. "You're going to join us, I hope. We thought it would be nice to celebrate."

"Celebrate what?"

"He's going to retire in another year," Ingrid said.

Adam looked at his father. "You can do that? You'll only be, what? Sixty."

"I won't fully retire. And I'll always do the investment thing. But not so much travel all around the world."

"You mean no more delivering baskets of cash to friends and enemies of the CIA."

Clifford laughed. "Oh, you wish, don't you? What a story that would be."

"It's what I tell my friends when I want to impress them."

They ate and chatted about unimportant things, rehashed a few pleasant memories, and when they were done, Adam offered to clean up.

Clifford helped, and when they were alone, he whispered. "Whatever you're up to now, Adam, please be careful."

"I promise you, I always am."

After lunch, Adam went for a walk down the street to a quiet empty park. His father's comment hung with him, and he couldn't lose the feeling that his father knew at least some of what he was involved with. He also desperately wanted to call Jade again but it was midday so he thought it might be a bad time. He sat on a bench and decided he couldn't wait any longer.

Jade picked up. "Adam?"

"I had this feeling you wanted to meet."

"Yes."

"And Melinda, too?"

"Yes."

"Why did I know?"

"We'll try to figure it out. It's okay, Adam. Any chance Sara Leeds would come up from the city and join us?"

"If she's not busy, she might do it. I'll ask.

"Maybe we could meet halfway?"

A few days later, on a sunny Saturday afternoon, Adam drove to Rhinecliff, a small town on the Hudson River halfway between Manhattan and Albany and met Sara Leeds at the train station. She stepped off the train onto a platform, built high above the river, greeted Adam with a warm hug, and they walked away from the tracks toward the water. "Are they here yet?" she asked.

He pointed to a lower grassy area on a small peninsula sticking out into the water. "Any minute, I think. We'll go down there, and they will find us."

A wide paved walkway led down to a manicured lawn, and stone walls protected the area from the potential of crashing waves. Sara carried a small briefcase and Adam had on a full-size backpack. "Are you planning on camping here?"

"I brought a few blankets to lay out and I bought some food at a deli. Pitas and humous and some fruit."

"Such a nice man you are. Are you nervous?"

"I'd like to say no but it wouldn't be true. How about you?"

"Oh yes. Very much."

They laid out the blankets, sat down, and stared into the water. "The river is much wider here," Adam said. "And this setup is much like when I met Garrett in Albany by the river and he took me to see the two Hope people, Max Schultz and Olivia Santini."

"It's an excellent story to share. This is all about building trust, even if we walk away after and doubt everything."

"I know it's about building trust, but at this point, it's also becoming about finding out who I am in this world. Do you feel that way?"

She pointed her finger at him and shook it, her eyes big and the hint of a smile. "Don't you go making me lose my focus. But yes."

Sara's gaze shifted past Adam and he turned his head. As the two women walked down a long ramp toward them, the same height, build, and matching gait, he thought that if their other physical characteristics weren't so different, he would have assumed they were twins. But it was more than anything physical. They exuded something, some undefined essence that wouldn't be there if they were not together.

As they came closer, Sara saw them for the first time and let out a small gasp. She stood, Adam hopped up, and they rushed over.

"Sara Leeds, it's such a pleasure to meet you. I'm Melinda." They shook hands.

"And I'm Jade." Again, handshakes.

Jade gently caught Adam's hand and pulled him close. It was different than he remembered, soft and safe. She pulled back, flashed a sweet smile and sat down. Melinda gave the same.

Melinda looked at the blankets and the food. "Is this a replay of our first meeting, Adam?"

Jade said, "But we're so much older and wiser now. And kinder, I hope."

They sat in a circle with the food in the middle and Jade added to it, pulling a few thermoses of iced tea out of a backpack. Small talk went on for a minute until Adam said, "Since this meeting is about building trust so we can possibly help each other, I had an idea that what we could do is each tell a story, a personal story, about anything related to, well, anything at all that we feel like sharing. Would it be of interest to everyone?"

They all nodded. Adam continued, "For starters, I would like to say that, although I'm still interested in doing a story of some sort on the Hope Community and still wish to learn the details of what happened to my brother I, uh, I guess I'm equally or even more interested in insights or knowledge about who or what my brother was." He lowered his voice. "And possibly learn something about myself, also."

Jade looked at Melinda and gave a nearly imperceptible nod. Or maybe there was no actual movement. Yet Adam caught something.

Sara said, "Do you want to go first, Adam?"

"Sure. I'm going to share something that happened to me, an interaction with my brother, much of which I forgot somehow but then eventually remembered. It happened the summer after high school when I was eighteen. For some reason, I now remember all the details, yet for so long I remembered nothing. And any insight from any of you about why this forgetting and remembering thing happened would be much appreciated. It's happened more than once,"

It could have been the river, the same powerful current, a bit wider there, and today with a gusty wind and rough waves slapping along the shore. "Hold on a second," he said. He stood, went to the edge, and stared into the crisp, dark flow. A quick cloud break let a smattering of light dance along the surface. Every part of his meeting with his brother, nine years before, seventy miles upstream, all the faces, the voices, the words, the subtle nuances of sensory observation, slipped back in. He could even hear Max and Olivia's strange moans and rumbles when they put him to sleep.

He sat back down, managed a weak grin, and for the next half-hour, spoke in stunning detail. He finished, slumped his head toward his chest, and let out a long sigh. "As the three of you have just witnessed, I am an observer. I watch and listen and hear and smell. And record. Yet never have I remembered or recounted an event with such clarity and precision as I just did. But previously, some kind of force clouded me so that, for years, I remembered little or nothing about it. And this has happened quite a few times. It was the same with the meeting with Old

Elwood. Something happened after it that made me forget it. Until I met you two." He looked up. "Why is…Hey, Melinda. Are you okay?"

She'd wrapped her arms around her middle, squeezing her elbows with her hands. "Uh yes. The names of the two people you met. The ones who worked on you and made you forget everything. Or, at least tried to. Max and Olivia. Olivia Santini is a patient of mine and I saw her in my office yesterday." They all leaned forward. "She said she was having migraines which is a common complaint. And the fact that a Hope-connected Extra came into my office is not surprising. But what concerns me is that, like all of us here, in my own way I am also a skilled observer and should have picked up on who she is. Yet, I had no clue, no clue at all."

A group of ten or so people, young kids and adults, came down the ramp and set up a picnic in the grass not far from the foursome. The kids behaved as if they had just ingested a bag of sugar and began running and whooping around the increasingly small space. Adam had asked a question about his memory lapses and hadn't received an answer and felt like the whole meeting was about to fall apart.

"Should we leave? Move somewhere else?"

Melinda and Jade closed their eyes and breathed quietly. Sara watched and Adam, not knowing what to do, joined in. Within a minute, the kids had calmed down and the adults moved to the edge of the water and quietly entered a discussion about parenting. The wind even softened.

"Now, that was amazing," Sara said.

Jade shook her head and smiled a little. "It's not like what you think. We may have spread a little calm energy among us and some of it might spill over onto others. But no way did we affect the weather."

"Still. Still amazing. Like we're in a little bubble."

Jade said, "I would like to address Adam's question about his memories. Because I think it can lead to a conversation about all that is happening now and maybe even shed light on aspects of who he is, and who Melinda and I are. Sara, when I was eighteen, I had an awful experience with a few young men, and because of who or what I am, I did not have the human ability to shield myself from the depths of the trauma. It stayed with me full force for years and forced me to function as a real human, with large amounts of the good, the bad, and the ugly. And, as Adam saw firsthand, I could be very ugly. It is an extreme example of how such things can work for beings like Melinda and myself. Now, Adam, I can only think that on some deep level you are connected to us and—no, I'm going out on a limb—I *know* you're connected to us. Yet your memory works unlike mine or Melinda's but also not like a normal human. Yes, you forgot so many events, likely because other Extras, such as Max and Olivia, or possibly even your brother, have messed with you a bit. However, when you do remember, your clarity, your level of observation is simply amazing."

Adam stared, wide-eyed, hanging onto every word.

Melinda asked, "Is it too much? Should she stop?"

"No, please no. I've waited years to hear this."

Melinda took over. "I can't say exactly how you're configured but I do believe, with your connection with your brother and possibly others, you've absorbed Extra qualities and it's led you to places, in your mind, and in the outer world, that must be frightening. Jade and I grew up in a commune where the whole Extra component was normal for all of us. And it was predictable because we absorbed it right after our birth. That was the whole point of our commune's existence: to create a more predictable Extra entrance into our human bodies. Which leads to what is happening now at Hope and other places. Walk-ins come en masse into humans of all types and ages and sometimes it works and sometimes it doesn't. In addition, the reasons, the intent of the Extras or the humans, are likely not always the finest."

Adam breathed out a string of words. "Are the Extras symbiotic or parasitic? That's the trillion-dollar question."

"Huh?"

"It's what the ancient Elwood Clamshaw said to me when I was seventeen. I remember that one, too."

"Oh, wow," Jade said. "Well, while we're doing this, here's one more. A student came into my office, outed himself, and said he had connections at Hope and that the whole place was at war within itself. He couldn't give more details but said a lot of Walk-ins thought of the At-Birth folks as elitist do-nothings who needed to step up and get more involved. Now, I love my group and would do anything for them and I found the comment to be most disturbing. However, I tend to agree. We need to get inside the Hope Community. We need to find out exactly who is who and what is what and Melinda and I are open to any ideas, any suggestions you may have on how to do that."

Adam turned to Sara. "Are you getting all this down?"

She closed her eyes, slowly shook her head, and sat silent for a moment. Then, with a shaky hand, she reached into her pocket and took out a voice recorder. "I didn't even turn this thing on. Nor would I want to. This has gone so far beyond anything I've ever worked on, and for the time being, I do understand that our project, our documentary, is no longer of the greatest importance. Maybe someday later. What I'm hearing is affecting me personally and I need some time to process it. Like you, Adam, I feel I am somehow connected to all this and expect I am going to be in for quite a ride. But I would like to share some information I have, stories I've been following."

They talked about the growing threads on the Bracken forum accusing a few of the small and hidden Extra groups of satanic practices and Sara added another forum to follow. She also said she had been finding in various parts of the country, candidates running for state and local government offices whose social media pages gave "likes" to the Hope Community.

"I will continue to follow all of these developments and report them to the three of you."

"Are we done then?" Adam asked. "We have a lot more food to eat here."

"I have one more question," Sara said. "How would one describe what an Extra actually is? I sort of understand it but I'm wondering if either of you women can give me a description."

Jade and Melinda looked at each other, faces tight, unsmiling, confused. Melinda said, "I guess it's a real stumper of a question. Kind of like asking what a human is. So maybe it has certain predictable characteristics but it's also individual within each person."

"How about what it is for just the two of you?" Adam asked.

Melinda and Jade had already joined, without speaking, their intent the same. They would deliver their essence to the other two. They inched forward a bit, bringing it all closer. The sun came out and heated the blankets and the grass underneath them. The river glistened and bubbled and calmed a little. Where were all the kids and the parents? Gone off somewhere, directed to a new spot. Nobody else nearby, no other witnesses. Adam and Sara also moved in, until their elbows touched and the square with four corners became a circle. They all looked at each other and watched each other shine, then closed their eyes.

Jade whispered, "Breathe in pure infinite love." They did this for some unaccountable time. They shook as one being, melting and reassembling.

Then Melinda said, "Send it back out to all of our earth's creatures."

Sometime later, they opened their eyes and saw the beginning of the parade at the top of the ramp. Thirty or so people rushed down onto the grass, then over to the water, looking for something. "I heard it," one of them said. "I felt it. Like a shock or something," said another. Some checked out the four on the blanket but most ignored them. They were just four people having a picnic.

"This I will never forget," Adam said. "Nobody will take this away from me."

Sara appeared to be choking back emotion but said nothing.

Jade

The ride home was magnificent. Melinda drove and I held the exquisite delight of the universe in each moment. "Are you able to drive?" She seemed to be fully present, but I had to check.

"Yes, yes, and more yes."

"Where are we going? What are we doing? Are we going home?"

"Home meaning what?" she asked. "Your apartment, my apartment, or Anderson?"

The mention of Anderson meant parents, her one and my two. It meant friction, confrontation, possibly even anger. My euphoria shifted into a lower gear. "I don't want to do Anderson right now and our other homes aren't calling either. What? What should we do?"

"Well, how about this? We just participated in one of the most sacred cosmic events of our lives so how about following it up with something of equal meaning? Like going to that new mall near Rensselaer and buying some clothes."

The euphoria came floating back. I said in a sing-song voice, "The mundane is sacred and sacred is always present in the mundane."

"Sure thing."

We had a minute of silence. I broke it with, "Adam is fascinating, isn't he? Unlike any of the others we've met. I wonder what his parents are all about?"

It was a rhetorical question, and she didn't answer. We knew what each other was thinking: parents, Elders, parents, Elders. Ours were full of surprises so why wouldn't Adam's parents also be walking a hidden path? The more we thought about it the more we concluded that it was not only possible but highly likely. Even so, I was glad we hadn't asked him probing questions because he needed the experience, he'd just had more than anything. Like all of us, he needed, for a change, a full immersion in something positive. Questions about his parents could wait a few more days.

We pulled into a rest area, surrendered to our quiet bliss, every detail of our surroundings still luscious and magnificent. Gas pumps danced with glow and glitter, cars unloaded magical humans and a few leashed dogs, divine even in their unaware state. Love flowed in and out of the doors of the main building and flickered in the sky overhead. We held hands, entered the building, and floated to the women's room. We took separate stalls and re-connected, sharing our bliss on our way out. And then, it all came crashing down.

I spotted him leaning against a car in the side parking lot, drinking something out of a paper cup. Richard White: many years older yet still the same. I motioned for Melinda to stop, and we backed behind a corner of the building and watched. At first, I thought he'd followed us but decided perhaps not. More likely, he'd followed Adam, possibly down to Rhinecliff, to our meeting, and now was on his way home. Better it was Richard White, who was only the lockup observer. I could handle him just fine. At least it wasn't Billy Squires, an actual lockup participant, and more recently, a couch slicer. Melinda could shower him with love energy and possibly I could, too. But, even in my pumped-up, yet quickly deflating state, I wasn't sure. Not at all.

"Shall we go have a conversation?" I asked.

"Really?"

I was emphatic. "Yes."

As we sauntered over, I realized I didn't have to, or want to, do any of my previous *on the edge of rage and fire* acts. I wasn't feeling it and it no longer served a purpose. Anybody remotely aligned with who we were—and who we are—with a little effort, could get a general idea of what Melinda and I were up to. However, it did occur to me that a good cop bad cop presentation wouldn't hurt. Guess who the bad cop was?

I stopped one car over and said, "Hey, is that you Richard? Richard White?"

He spun around and stared at me. "Huh? Do I know you?"

I was certain he was faking it. But he didn't act afraid. "Jade Furlong, remember me? And this is my lifelong friend, Melinda." The introduction was unnecessary. He knew exactly who Melinda was.

Melinda kept her energy at maximum level, and when she took his hand, I could feel it pouring off of her. He gave a jolt and seemed to relax.

"So, what's up, Richard?" I asked. "Where are you coming from?"

"I was downstate meeting with some friends."

"Rhinecliff, right? I heard something was going on down by the water."

Melinda flashed me a cut-it-out look so subtle only I would get it. Then she amped up her energy a few more notches.

Richard backed away. "Don't do that to me. I know what you're trying to do. You two think you have so much power but you really don't. And Adam Kastner. He's in way over his head."

"You followed him."

He turned and headed for the building. Melinda said as he walked away, "Nice meeting you, Richard. Say hello to Olivia Santini for me." A little snarky coming from her, so unlike her, especially then.

He flipped around and stormed back at us. "What are you people trying to do? You sit in your little Shangri-las, observing and studying for years and years, but for what purpose? And then you think you can mess with one of us, like change him up, make him like you. It's not how this world works. It's never worked that way and never will."

"Billy Squires," I said.

"Yeah, he's dead." He looked at Melinda. "You made a good mess out of that one."

This was not the Richard White I remembered. Now so forceful, angry, and scary. "It sounds like you sucked up some of Billy's more attractive attributes. Are you even the same person anymore?"

His voice hissed like a venomous snake. He held his finger an inch away from Melinda's chest, just above her heart. "This part isn't what matters." Then he tapped the top of her stomach, her center of power. "This is the only thing that's important."

Melinda froze and for a moment lost her force. She got it back and continued to spread her heart pulse to him.

He stepped away and stared at her, his head tilted, with a hint of a smile. "It is interesting, though. I'll give it that. Very seductive. But we already know all about seduction. It's our specialty."

He vanished into a crowd, and we rushed to our car. I drove now, out of the rest area, back on the interstate, and got off at the next exit. I doubted we were being followed but still drove through small towns stuffed on either side with traffic lights and modern commerce. For a long time, neither of us spoke.

We entered a larger city with nearly stopped traffic, and I said, "Are we okay here?"

"We as in we're the same person?"

"We, as in you're generally the better half. But I noticed a bit of a crossover back there. Like you absorbed some of the annoying prickly behaviors of the current driver sitting next to you. And now, let me guess, you're doing a full analysis, word for word, moment by moment, of the entire encounter."

"The guy set me off, which was what he wanted to happen, and I can't understand why he succeeded. So, I'm distracting myself with bizarro ideas about what we should do next."

"We can't just show up at the Hope Community Welcome Center, walk in, and see what they're up to."

"No, we can't. And I do have a few thoughts about other ways we might be able to gain entrance. But let's save that for a later discussion. Right now, I'm examining another aspect of Hope which is this: if they are somehow calling in large numbers of Extra overlays, and they are trying to control what the results are, they must have well-prepared Normal human recipients accepting them in."

I tried to lighten the conversation. "Which means they must have an ongoing supply of willing and ready recruits. Are you going to sign up as one of the recruiters, Ms. Gorgeous?"

She had no response to my humor, and I dropped it, aware I was only trying to diffuse my own fears. She continued. "Think of the energy you and I created between us when we tried to get sexy. If it could be flipped from negative to positive, who knows how it would affect us. I mean, even as supposedly unattached Extras, we could have become obsessed with the experience, wanting nothing else. And with just a fraction of what we created, coming from an Extra to a Normal, it could send somebody right into the arms of longing, addiction, and subservience. Richard White knows what he's talking about and I'm sure, for many, this is exactly what they are doing."

"I'm worried about Adam. He seems so vulnerable."

"Yes." She was silent for a minute, then, "You should sleep with him. Preempt so to speak."

I did not expect that one and, even less, I did not expect my response. It really upset me. "No Melinda. I can't do it. I've given him enough trouble and I don't want to add to it if it were to go wrong. I mean, what's the difference between me seducing him for my aims and some Hope person doing it for theirs? But you could. You could present it as a learning experience for both of you, you know, like an experiment."

"No, you're right. It would be the exact wrong thing to do. Also, from a human point of view, an experiment? It sounds about as exciting as watching paint dry. And besides, you're the one who's in love with him."

"If we redefine what being in love with somebody means, then we're both in love with him, aren't we?"

We rode in silence until we reached my apartment. Now that I had some space from the encounter with the newly enhanced Richard White, I reflected on how it had affected me. I had carried the trauma of my big event for so long that its sharp edges had dulled considerably. It could still poke me at inopportune times but not enough to draw much blood. And a big lesson I'd finally internalized was how much easier it is to absorb trauma when you fully grasp that the intent behind it was part of a battle to undermine a cause you would sacrifice anything to win. What about Melinda? She'd had her share of human abuse, what she described as death by a thousand cuts, yet never one gigantic pummel. Why, early on, had she not been targeted the same way I was? I had always assumed, for some reason, that I posed more of a threat to the roughest parts of the Hope people, or perhaps my abuse was meant to demoralize my parents. Now I wondered if I was merely the low-hanging fruit. Considering who we'd always been, it certainly made sense. I desperately hoped I was wrong because, what would it mean for my dearest companion?

I parked and we sat a little longer. My thoughts turned to Adam Kastner. I let out a big sigh and said, "He's going to go back to Hope. I'm sure of it."

"Sara will go with him, I think."

"Sara."

"You're having doubts."

"These days, I always have doubts."

Adam

Jade and Melinda gave their hugs, ascended the walkway and disappeared around a corner. Sara helped Adam fold the blankets and return them to his pack. They turned to the water and followed the soaring seagulls and a few distant boats negotiating the current.

Adam said. "I was raised, at least by my mother, in a sort of agnostic, non-religious household and taught to be skeptical about, well, everything. Even about your books. I read them and thought, yeah, maybe. Even if I generally decided something was for real, I still had doubts. And the whole Extra thing? It was hard to go to the next step."

"And now?"

"Now, I believe it. I believe it's as real as the water we're looking at. And I believe that, what my brother thought he was, he in fact was."

"Do you ever wonder about your parents?"

"I didn't. But now I do. Especially my father who is away so much and never talks about any of this sort of thing."

They made plans to go together for another visit to the Hope Community, but Sara needed to put it off for a few days, which was fine with Adam. He had another plan, another trip he wanted to do, and right then was the perfect time to get started. As he drove back north to his parents' house, he thought of telling them where he was going and decided against it because he didn't want to have to explain himself. Considering all the questions he had about them, it seemed like the right thing to do. He would text his mother and tell her he would be gone for a few days. It would have to be good enough. He pulled into a gas station, filled his car, and entered into his phone the tiny, nearly hidden town of Marion on the southern coast of Maine, where he had stayed with his brother and parents ten years earlier and hadn't been back since. It would take five hours, the early autumn sun would still hover overhead, and he would be able to walk the path that swept by Old Elwood's house before the night terrors set in.

Over the years, he had thought about going back many times, but never allowed himself to put a plan in motion. He had never wanted to confront the reality that what had happened in the funny little town might have been real. Now he'd crossed over, he was a believer, and if the two women, Jade and Melinda, were who and what they said they were, which he no longer doubted, who was he to question any of it?

Before he got back on the road, he searched his phone for a motel in Marion, found one on the town's main street, and booked a room for the night. He had everything covered and was able to relax into the trip. He found an NPR station and settled into an interview with a writer he was familiar with. Good stuff. When it was done, he turned off the radio and began composing his own story about Old Elwood. Maybe it would be something that would happen on this trip. The motel could even be called Old Elwood's Motel and he would check people in and put them in specific rooms where they would embark on a mythic quest specifically geared to their own way forward.

An hour from his destination, his mood switched, and, as usual, doubts came crashing in. Doubts about everything: his new-found beliefs, this hastily planned trip, what he thought he was going to find there, people telling him who he was and trying to control him. What was it that Melinda had said about his Extra connection? Or maybe it was Jade—it didn't matter because they were scarily so much the same. He'd gotten pieces of it from Garrett? Or others around him? Meaning who? His mother and father? Dreams? Fantasies? This time, somehow, he sat with his confusion, and after a while, let it go.

He arrived at the Ocean View Inn around seven, checked in, and went off on foot in search of a good place to eat. The street had already adopted its post Labor Day off-season personality and was nearly deserted. The streetlights had come on but the storefronts were all dark. A few cars passed and a couple walked by, lost in conversation. Further down the street, a small group stood on the sidewalk outside one of the few places still open, and he remembered it was a bar he had been too young to go into. It could be his first stop. Before he reached the bar, he passed a restaurant, called Crabby's, which he'd eaten at a few times, hesitated a moment, and then went in. He entered and a host, standing behind a kiosk with a pile of menus, greeted him.

"If you're here for dinner, you're just in time," he said, handing Adam a menu. "Sit wherever you like and a server will come by shortly to take your order."

The restaurant appeared exactly as he remembered, a somewhat corny tourist destination with nets, buoys, and nautical rope affixed to the walls and ceilings, and a long menu of endless varieties of seafood. As the restaurant's name implied, dishes involving crab were many and diverse. Except for two other couples, still eating at a far table, the room was empty. A door from the kitchen opened and a server came right over.

"Hello, how are you doing tonight? Can I get you something to drink?"

She wore designer jeans and a white blouse, had short brown curly hair, blue-gray eyes, and a thin-lipped smile. She looked familiar.

"Water will be fine and I think I'm ready to order."

At first, she didn't answer. "Have you been here before?"

"Oh, yeah, a long time ago. I came here a few times in the summer. I…wait, are you Christina Luft?"

"I am. And you're Adam Kastner. And your brother is Garrett."

"Uh, yeah. Can I get a few crabmeat rolls and some coleslaw?"

She hesitated, looking at him. "Sure. I'll be right back."

A few minutes later, Christina returned with the food and carefully placed it in front of Adam. She included two pieces of apple pie, one for him and, she said, one for her. "Do you mind if I sit with you? My shift is done. And the pie is on me."

"Thank you. Yes, please sit. It's such a surprise to see you. So, how are you doing? Were you here just for the summer?"

"No, I live here full-time now. My parents split up and couldn't decide who would get the house so I took it over. What brings you to town? Are you renting the little cottage again?"

"No, I'm only here for a night. I'm staying at the motel down the street."

They made small talk for a few minutes and Adam settled in, enjoying a simple conversation. His biggest concern became not wanting to drip the insides of the crab roll all over himself.

Eventually, she changed the conversation. "I have a question for you. That night, when you and your brother came over and Carrie was there. Why did you leave? I knew you weren't going fishing."

"That night? It was more than ten years ago."

She put on the cutest smile. "Seems like yesterday, doesn't it?"

He couldn't help it, he returned her look and relaxed into the story. "Okay, here's the reason why I left. You and Carrie were both drooling all over my beautiful brother, right? Like hanging on to every word he said, and you couldn't take your eyes off of him. I mean, it happened all the time with him so I figured…you know."

She laughed and shook her head, drawing him in a little more. "Really, Adam? Really? Oh, you read that so wrong. You see, we both knew Garrett had no real interest in either of us but we'd planned on going all stupid gaga over him because we thought it might make you jealous and you'd try harder for one of us." She reached across the table and touched his arm. "I guess it was the wrong strategy."

"Oh well. I was just a kid. What did I know about such things?" And with every word she spoke, the hand on his arm, the looks she gave, he rapidly became the same seventeen kid who didn't know about such things. Except, now he did know. Yet, still like his younger self, he did not know how to stop what he was feeling.

He ate slowly, not wanting to be sloppy and have food fall out of his mouth, or in any other way turn her off to him. "Hey, Christina. Are you hungry at all? No way can I eat two of these crab rolls."

"Oh sure. Pass one over."

She had no problem with the mess. The crab mix fell on her plate and the table and got all over her hands, and she repeatedly wiped her mouth with a napkin. "You just have to go for it with this meal," she said.

He tried not to watch her eat but was fascinated that there was actually something alluring about her messy abandon. The apple pie came next, sweet and tart, crunchy and spicy. He couldn't take his eyes off her. Especially her eyes. Every time they met his, she made them grow a touch bigger and hinted at a grin.

"Did you know I was coming here?" he asked as if he was joking.

"Now how could I have known that?"

"Because this is the best apple pie I've ever had."

She invited him to her house for a drink and maybe to play cards or listen to the sounds of the ocean, and he eagerly agreed. And although he still remembered his way around the area, he followed her in his car. He passed a long dark driveway to the cottage where he'd stayed as a kid, then the one to Old Elwood's rotting home, and after passing two more houses, he followed Christina's turn down a neat, straight, well-maintained drive to the Luft family property. He got out of his car and walked with her to the house. She led him inside, showed him around most of the elegant and well-maintained rooms, poured glasses of wine, and they went out to the deck overlooking the water.

The same deck he had sat on ten years earlier. He had forgotten how the far end nearly reached the water's edge, how the waves slapped at the shore almost underneath them, how the distant foghorn made its quiet moans. A glorious multi-colored sunset bled through and around patterns created by a blanket of wispy clouds. He looked for boats out in the expanse but saw only the slowly disappearing horizon. A chill wind blew off the water and she pulled a thick wool blanket out of an outdoor closet, directed him to a cushioned outdoor couch, moved tight against him, and covered them both up. The glasses of wine sat on a small table in front of them. She leaned forward, picked up a glass, and handed the other to him. They drank silently. He liked the taste and quickly emptied his. Her shoulder pressed into his, their knees touched, and she placed her hand on his forearm. She smelled like woods and flowers. Delightful. Magical.

"Which one of us were you most interested in that night?" she asked.

"I remember telling Garrett it was Carrie but it was definitely you."

She pushed a little closer, took his hand, and rested her head on his shoulder. "We were in some stupid teen competition to see which one of us could snag you."

He returned the pressure on her hand. "And I was too young and dense to pick up on it. Do you still know Carrie?"

"We keep in touch." She stayed silent, then, "When you left here that night, what happened?"

Her words ripped a chunk out of the magic. He hung onto his observer mode enough to notice she had changed the tone of her question. So subtle but still apparent. She knew. She knew what had happened that night, knew where he'd gone.

"I waited for Garrett outside the cottage. I waited until he came back. He was angry because I left. He's dead, you know."

This time her response was genuine. "Oh my God. What happened?"

"Supposedly he committed suicide," he whispered. He sat up, pulled his hand away from her, stared at her, and with a touch of anger said, "But I imagine you know that wouldn't have been possible."

She threw off the blanket and backed away. "And why would I know that?"

"Because you're an Extra."

"And you are, too. So, what?"

"Actually, I'm not."

"Okay, Adam. I don't know what's going on here. I'm really sorry about your brother. My impression even then was that his Extra part didn't line up correctly and he was having a hard time." Her words speeded up. "I don't know. I don't know. I try not to think about any of it anymore." Adam didn't respond. She slowed down and lowered her voice. "You know all about it yet you're not one. It's so unusual."

Adam took both her hands. "I've been told that a few times. I'm sorry Christina. I didn't mean to imply anything. The thing is, and I do think you might know it, after I left that night, I took the path, and three houses down, the light was on. I met him and then forgot and then remembered. Over and over. And I always wondered what this strange little town was all about and why my parents came here."

"This strange little town. It about sums it up. This strange little town is an outlier and people come here to escape, to forget, to remain neutral, to live a simple Normal life even though it's not what we are. That's why I'm here. Why anybody is here." She waved at the ocean. "We don't want to be part of the chaos out there." She giggled. "But we do need some entertainment and Old Elwood sure could tell the stories."

Adam frowned and raised his voice. "Do you know about the Hope Community?"

"I've heard of it. Everybody's heard of it. But I don't follow any of it. Why are you asking me that?"

"Why were you being so seductive just now? What did you want?"

She jumped up and raised her hand like she was going to slap him. He backed further away "What do you think I am? One of those programmed catcher types who spots their marks and then does the magic so they have to have more? What the hell is wrong with you, anyway?"

"I, I'm sorry. Maybe I should leave."

She lowered her voice. "Well, you can leave if you want but not before I tell you a few things, explain a few things, and, and maybe even humiliate myself." She took a deep breath. "Okay, so you asked me what I want. From you. You see, you suddenly show up off-season, one of a handful of customers, and you're a good-looking, nice kind of guy—or I thought you were nice—and I'm living in this beautiful oceanside house all by myself, looking ahead to a nasty cold winter and…what am I supposed to do? Once, a long time ago, you had a thing for me and I did for you so should I have just said hi and walked away? I am lonely, Adam, really, really lonely. Do you know what that's like?"

He knew exactly what it was like.

"Is it so terrible that I wanted some company? And the other thing, too, which I wasn't even going to mention is, I've read a lot of your articles over the years and I figured it was you. So now, you're not only good-looking, occasionally nice, intelligent, and once a long time ago very funny, but also some kind of creative master." She stopped, moved a little closer. "Should I keep going?" He nodded. "All right, here is the biggest draw of all. You know all about Extras, you know what and who I am, but you aren't even one yourself. You're a Normal with a capital N which makes you normal with a small n. Not too many of those around here off-season."

He got his humor back. "Are you saying I could be some kind of hot catch for lonely Extras?"

She smiled but her eyes were sad. "Please don't leave. Not yet."

The wind picked up and the chill sent them into the house. Christina poured two more glasses of wine and they sat on a spacious couch. "If you want to stay here tonight, you can. But you'll be sleeping on the couch because," and she gave him a big sweet smile and a gentle poke on his shoulder, "I'm sure as hell not going to try any more of my so-called seduction tricks."

That was it. Those were the words. He understood exactly how she was feeling, and he had felt the same way for so long. Always alone, always distrustful, always wishing something was slightly or a lot different than what it was. Until today, until his gathering that morning on the grassy lawn next to the Hudson River with Jade, Melinda, and Sara. It was the first time he'd ever felt so connected, so loved, so *in* love.

Jade and Melinda, the strangest yet most wonderful creatures he had ever met, had created it and passed it along to him, and at that moment, he began to believe it had changed him, given him a new meaning and a real purpose. He watched Christina's mouth move, her subtle breath pass in and out. Jade and Melinda had given him something so vast and magnificent and maybe the point was that he should now pass some of it on, pay it forward. It would be in a different form but still with the same intent.

"I would love to stay here and the couch will be fine. But I left on a whim and never packed a thing."

"Not a problem. Not in a house like this. I can likely even find you clean clothes that will fit."

She told him again how much she enjoyed his writing and asked him to tell her stories, anything that came to mind. He knew, though, what she wanted—to know what had happened to Garrett. He started with the night he left there, ten years earlier, and described in detail his experience with Old Elwood.

He asked her, "Did you ever have a private session with him?"

She rolled her eyes. "Everybody here has had many, usually more than they ever wanted."

"He's still alive?"

"Well, his house is still standing but most of us here long-ago, came to the conclusion that he was never alive. Unless you go in the house at just the correct time, you won't even find him there. A few of the more philosophical locals will tell you, 'Don't worry, he's only an extension of your mind.'"

"He had a few choice words for me," he said. "About Extras."

"Like what?"

"Something about whether you're symbiotic or parasitic."

She shook her head. "Yeah, well there's not a single one of us who doesn't have that thought rolling around in the extensions of our own minds. Pretty damn insulting for him to say it."

"But if my mind created him then I'm the one who said it. If so, I'm sorry."

She laughed. "Keep on with the story of Garrett. He was a sweet guy and I'd like to know. That is, if you want to."

He wanted to. He talked for another half-hour without distractions or interruptions. He recounted in detail every meeting he'd had with Garrett during those next four years and Christina's attention never wavered. When he described his meeting the first time in Albany along the Hudson River and his strange session with Max Schultz and Olivia Santini, he glanced at her a few times, looking for hints of recognition or surprise. She had no response. He ended with the news that Garrett was dead but omitted the fact that he was in Anderson, home of Jade and Melinda, when the call from his mother came. He wasn't sure why but Jade and Melinda were off-limits for this discussion.

"What a story," she said. She took his hand and squeezed it. "I truly am sorry. For most of us it's not easy and for some of us it can be downright awful."

"It's a strange thing, this far along in your life, to continually have it turned on its head. I mean, this is a town filled with Extras. Which means, why did my parents always come here? My father, okay. He's mysterious and weird and always away somewhere so I can believe it. But my mother?"

"Maybe, like you, she's not one. She's heard the words but doesn't believe any of it is real. Even here, we've got a few of them."

"I mentioned the people I met who had influenced Garrett—Max Shultz, and Olivia Santini. Did they ever pass through?"

"Max and Olivia. Yes, a few times. But more recently, like the last five years or so. Kind of pushy as I remember. Some of the folks here thought they were a big deal for some reason. I served them once in Crabby's and they were very chatty and left a good tip. Who knows? They're Extras and these days defining an Extra is as confusing as anything the Normals cook up. It's hard to know what anybody is all about anymore."

"Hey, look," Adam said, pointing to the glass doors leading to the deck. The moon is up."

They walked over and pressed their faces on the door, and the moon angled above them, shining onto their faces. She leaned into him and he put his arm around her, they hugged, kissed, hugged some more, and flopped onto the couch. They stayed pressed together, their clothes on, content to feel each other's warmth and energy. She wanted them to keep eye contact, and in a growing state of ecstasy, he followed her lead.

As they progressed, he tried to find the energy source from earlier and when they locked together, naked, she said, "We'll try it this way."

A soft and gentle pulse, now familiar from his earlier encounter, same day, different group, lifetimes ago, crept through his entire body. She tapped his chest with her finger, maintained eye contact, and he traveled dreamily to some new space, fully present yet removed from all the rough edges of his life. He thought of Jade and Melinda and then all thoughts vanished. How many hours? Time stopped. No performance, only transfer and connection.

Sometime later, he woke with the moon, now much lower in the sky, reflecting the light from an unseen day directly in his face. His first thought was of a conversation he'd had once on one of his journalist travels with a heroin addict. The man had described his first time with the drug as a thousand blessings and a direct meeting with God, and every time he shot up after, he desperately wanted to recapture that first experience, but it would never happen. Adam carefully turned to the naked Goddess, now sleeping next to him, parts of their bodies still in contact, still breathing her air, her taste still in his mouth, and he desperately wanted to wake her for more. He wondered if he was now the same addict, that same man.

He slid off the couch, found his clothes, and slipped still naked through the front door, into a darkness the moonlight couldn't find. He pulled on his clothes and dug in his pockets for his wallet and keys, both thankfully there. He started his car, knowing the noise would wake her, turned on the lights, and slowly drove out of the driveway, apologizing to her in his thoughts which she might be able to hear. His heart pounded and he could barely hold the steering wheel. Because he knew what his next stop was going to be. How could it be otherwise?

He passed two driveways, pulled into the third one—dark, rutted, wet, and overgrown— and barely made it to the end. He stood at the back of Old Elwood's house, the moonlight shining around the edges, the back pitch black. As he ran around a side, he saw the glow from a window bouncing off the thick scramble of weeds and brush. He ran to the front and onto the porch, still rotted yet still standing. He opened the door but stayed away from the doorway.

An ancient voice said, "Hey out there. No need to worry. No shotgun this time. Come on in."

Adam passed through the door and into the living room, again empty except for the old couch and two folding metal chairs placed front to front, in one of which sat Old Elwood. Elwood pointed to the other chair. "Have a seat. Long time no see, as the saying goes."

Adam sat. "You look exactly like the last time I saw you. Haven't aged a bit."

Elwood waved his hands around. "If I aged any more, I'd disappear. Well, then, what can I help you with today? You who just left a fine young woman stranded after you seduced her and got what you wanted. Have you no shame, m'boy? No sense of kindness? Or is your fragile little mind flying all over the place making up stories about who this fine young woman really is and what she wants?"

"I know I'm just conversing with myself. I get it now. This house is real but you're just something I'm creating."

Elwood let out a throaty, raspy chuckle and again waved his hands in circles in the air. "Oh, oh, oh. What a crock of shit it all is. I am an extension of your mind. This house is not, yet I am? A crock of shit. Where does it all end, Mr. Kastner? What's real and what's not? You know that bar you almost made it to last night? I think you should stay another day in our fine town and make a trip there tonight. Have a few pints with the crowd. Hear what all the Extra rednecks, just like in an Irish pub or a western tavern, dance to, sing about, and talk about after they've had a few too many. Just like this."

He forced out an ancient croak that somehow followed the tune of Twinkle, twinkle little star: *Dreamy, dreamy what is real, dreamy, dreamy how I feel. I made you up inside my head and now I'm going to make you dead.* He moved his face inches from Adam. "Philosophy. Spirituality. Artistry. Take it from an old man, all bullshit. Don't get sucked in. Run away from it like you always do."

Adam didn't back away. "That's right. I'm going to make you dead right now."

"Please do. I'm so ready to go. And I will cooperate, but only if you agree to a test. I want you to try to make this entire old rotten crumbly house also go. See if you can do it. With your mind. Try hard. No, no, no, wait a minute, that's asking too much. I'll make it easier. When I go, another object will appear in my place, and I want you to try your hardest to then make that object disappear."

"Huh?"

"Get rid of me now! Close your eyes and do it, right now! Before I go all nutty on you!"

Adam closed his eyes for a few seconds, and when he opened them, Old Elwood was gone. But his seat was not empty. In his place sat a large, thin book, like a children's book. He jumped up, looked closely at it, but didn't touch it. On the cover was an illustration of a glorious sunset merging with distant hills and the book's title superimposed, *The Story of Old Elwood*. No author was listed. He leaped to the door, stopped, turn around, carefully picked up the book, real in his hands, ran to his car, and threw it in the trunk. As he drove away, the morning sun was just coming up.

He stopped only once on his drive back to Oakwood, pulling into a rest area to fire off an apology text to Christina Luft for leaving so quickly. He got a quick response assuring him she understood and to please come back when his life settled down. He promised he would and then obsessed for the rest of the trip about what *life settling down* meant for him. When he arrived at his parents' house, he left the *Old Elwood* book in his car, not wanting any questions from them about it, and hurried inside. His father was out and his mother was perched at her usual seat in the kitchen, looking at something on her laptop.

She looked up and said, "Adam, you're home. Still on secret missions?"

He sat next to her and said, "I'm done with the secrets, Mom. What I need now are some answers."

"Oh, are you okay?"

"I'm going to tell you where I was last night and then I want you to tell me why we used to go there when I was younger."

"Adam. What are you talking about?"

"I went to the funny little town on the ocean and ate a crab roll at Crabby's. And guess who my server was? Christina Luft. And guess what she refers to herself as? Are you one, too?"

She tensed and scowled. "Oh God, Adam. Stop it. I've had to hear about this Extra stuff since before you were born and I had really hoped I'd never hear the term again. We went there because your father insisted and, no, I am certainly not one of them and nobody else is, either. Because it's all just some crap somebody made up and people latched onto. You know, like some of the idiotic conspiracy garbage that's so popular now." She put her face close to his. "You don't believe in any of it, do you? I don't think I could stand it again."

"No Mom, no need to worry. And Christina says hi. She lives there full-time in that house."

He went to the sink, poured a glass of water, and sat back down. "Hey. On this other thing I'm working on, and I will tell you about it soon, I came across some names. I was wondering if you've ever heard of any of them."

"Okay, sure."

He almost said Max Schultz and Olivia Santini but caught himself because it was likely that Garrett had mentioned them at some point. And it would have given his mother a huge lead into what Adam was up to. Instead, he substituted, Damien and Therese Furlong, and Josephine Breeze.

"The first two don't ring any bells but the other one, what was her name? Josephine Breeze?"

"Uh huh."

"You don't forget a last name like Breeze. It must have been about twenty years ago and I went with your Dad to some dinner with a bunch of investors in something. It was boring, I think, and I met a man there whose last name was Breeze. Maybe Josephine was his wife or sister or cousin or something but I don't remember meeting her."

"Do you remember what he looked like?"

"I do. He was quite striking. Tall and thin and all that. And he had an accent like he was Indian. Or from Pakistan, maybe? Yes. Now that I think about it, I remember something else. He had quite a handshake. It made my hand tingle."

Jade

Melinda and I went into the apartment, found a bag of peanuts, and sat without speaking, the only noise coming from the cracking of the shells and the munching of the goods inside.

"What a day," Melinda finally said, "What a day."

"And it's not over yet because we have some more planning to do. Like how are we going to get inside the Hope Community and see for ourselves what's going on?"

"Do you have any ideas?" Melinda asked.

"No. But you said you do."

"Yes. Let me review this a moment." She shut her eyes and stayed silent. Then, "All right, here goes. I have one idea to try first and it's a wild one. You know how Adam talked about forgotten incidents, how they came and went, over and over? Well, our parents, in their infinite wisdom—and yes, please excuse the sarcasm, they were only looking out for our well-being—did it to us once. Or actually, many times. But this one instance is what I'm referring to. The first time you and I built an animal fort and we slept in it, can you recall what we tried to do? And what we were able to do briefly?"

I had delightful memories of those early days with Melinda, many of them happening in the forest and our forts, but I didn't know what she was referring to. It was my turn to stay silent. I examined the full scenario of her recollection and what she was now searching for until the connection came into focus: Melinda was searching for powers, in particular, ones we might have discovered on our own and which our parents would have discouraged us to use. As kids, we always explored the boundaries of what was allowed, and when we crossed those boundaries, we would confess, our parents would give us a lecture and sometimes erase the memories.

I remembered this one. "We became deer. Or not actually became them but entered into two different ones we spotted running by. We left our bodies in the fort and went for a romp in the woods."

"But we quickly knew it was a bad idea so we zipped right back."

I knew where she was going and it seemed, at first, so outrageous. Such an action would be a strong slap at the moral structure of our upbringings, and how we strived to act toward ourselves and the rest of our planetary species. We did not have the right to invade others in such a way. Also, it could be terribly dangerous.

"And now it's a good idea?"

The insistence of her reply shocked me. "We don't have much choice. We have to get in the front door and at least part way into the inner workings. But first, we must practice how to do it and hopefully make it less treacherous."

"The question is, who will the hosts be?" I knew the answer to that one, also. "We wouldn't be able to tell them so it would be kind of...no, it would be *seriously* invasive."

She looked down at the floor and whispered, "The ends justify the means?"

I sighed. "I don't know. Even a year ago, I wouldn't have cared much. But now? I guess the cosmic morality police have finally had some success with me."

"Yeah, I know, but…"

"Oh, to hell with it," I said. "I'm going to try it with you."

We sat together, quietly, our eyes shut, and I brought a part of myself into Melinda's pathways. She stood and walked around the room, looked out the window, then went into the kitchen, and picked up a round container of oatmeal.

I kept my eyes closed. "Directions on the oatmeal container." And I read them aloud as she did the same, except she didn't speak.

Next was a cookbook. She thumbed through until she came to a recipe for a pesto pasta dish.

"Haven't had that for a while" I said. "Let's do it tonight. But we might not have the ingredients to make the pesto from scratch."

She went into the bathroom, closed the door, and brushed her teeth. This small act upped the experience to a whole new level. I heard the sound of the water and the toothbrush pushing back and forth on her teeth. I could also vaguely smell and taste the toothpaste and even feel a tingle from the action like it was on my own gums.

Melinda came back and sat. "It's so very strange. I think if I hadn't known you were doing it, I wouldn't have known you were there."

We needed to practice on others. We left the apartment and headed down the street toward a grocery store. We knew what was coming next. If we hadn't discussed and then determined that this power we were playing with was *not* within the framework of the abilities of other Extras we knew, I believe we couldn't have continued. We likely would have experienced a large portion of human guilt for even being Extras. It was easier to justify when we convinced ourselves we were unusual in our abilities to so easily do such an activity. And, of course, what we were doing was for the good of everyone's future.

We kept it simple and basic. We chose individual shoppers, turned toward the shelves, closed our eyes, read their lists, and watched their hands pull items off the shelves. We tried younger, older, someone with minimal English skills, and all were easy. We moved far away from them and still could hear the voices of the other shoppers next to them. Our only failure happened when both of us attempted to enter the same person, an elderly woman carrying a small basket. She twitched and scowled, and we backed away, feeling a touch of headache and nausea ourselves.

"Good to know," Melinda whispered.

That night, Melinda called Adam, and I called Sara. We split it up that way because, even now, after our exquisite experience in Rhinecliff, I didn't trust the chemistry between Adam and me. We shared a specific type of edginess that I wished to imagine I had finally learned to control but was honest enough with myself to not take chances. And besides, he was not the one I was preparing to invade, the unknowing recipient of my potentially disastrous act. Common sense had designated Adam as the mark for calm and reasonable Melinda.

I talked with Sara for less than five minutes and told the biggest lie of omission in my life. We knew they were planning an entrance into the Hope compound, we knew Adam could get them a few levels deeper into the bowels of the institution, and I expressed fear and concern about their trip, which thankfully was not a lie. I asked Sara to call us when they planned the trip, to text us when they entered the building, and again when they came out. For our peace of mind. So, we wouldn't worry. Again, it was not a lie, but it was also a long way from the truth.

Two days later, on a Saturday, our day off from our jobs, I received a text from Sara indicating an approximate arrival time at the Hope compound. As the time approached, Melinda and I arranged mats, cushions and blankets on the living room floor so that we could improvise ideal positions for our tasks, switching from lying down to sitting if needed. We would need to keep our eyes closed, noise to a minimum, and most importantly, maintain a masterful amount of presence. Our levels of observation would be more focused than ever, and chatter interfering with our thoughts had to be kept under perfect control.

Sara texted when they reached the Hope building, and for the next minute, Melinda and I kept our laptops open, hers to a photograph of Adam and mine to one of Sara. We absorbed the visual presentations of our hosts and entered into the essence of who they were. Then we climbed in as gently as possible and began the journey.

I saw Sara's hand on a large wooden door. I saw her push the door inward. I saw the inside of the room as her eyes moved around, stopping at each detail. Adam stood next to her and then in front of her.

"Quite a space, isn't it?" he asked.

His face moved up and down as she nodded. He showed her a card, some sort of business card with the name, Nicolle, and a phone number. His phone appeared and he called the number.

"Hi, Nicolle. This is Jaime. I was here about ten days ago."

Adam grinned. Gave a thumbs up with his free hand. "Okay, thanks."

Jaime? It seemed kind of dumb.

Adam shook Nicolle's hand, introduced Sara using her real first and last name, and they also shook hands.

Nicolle said, "So nice to meet you, Sara. I've read a few of your books. You're a wonderful writer."

"Thank you. And this is so interesting to be here."

Nicolle turned to Adam and said, "Jaime, the last time you were here you indicated what your interests center around and I have somebody who wishes to meet with you. However, he is busy for another half-hour, so perhaps you could show Sara around. And I'll find you when he is ready."

"Oh yeah, sure."

"Jaime?" Sara whispered.

"I know. I did it on a whim. Seriously stupid. I'll confess. I wonder who we're going to meet?"

For the next half-hour, Adam took Sara through the line of introductory displays in the first room, and they quietly discussed each one. When they finished, they moved into the next room and sat at the farthest table. Adam got the video going, and within a minute said, "This is not what played for me the last time."

In the video, a man introduced himself as Russell and delved right into the basics of what it means to be an Extra. He covered the differences between Extras-at-birth, later-in-life Walk-ins, the many ways in which humans with the Extra layer can be different from ones without it, how Walk-ins can sometimes—oftentimes—need assistance as their lives go on to keep a correct balance, and how the Hope Community offered such assistance. The term he used for the process was Reconfiguration.

To me, the name was as blasé as the name, Hope Community. Reconfiguration? It didn't say much. But then, what did the name, Land Trust, have going for it?" The Hope people had carefully picked their titles for specific reasons just like we did.

When the video ended, Nicolle appeared next to them. "He's ready now. Follow me."

Nicolle opened another door and led them down a short hall into a quiet carpeted room, about the size of an average living room, with-floor to-ceiling windows on one wall. A feast of goldenrod, sunflowers, and evergreen bushes decorated the outside, dabs of sunlight illuminating the colors, and caught Sara's—and my—attention so much that we didn't at first notice the man sitting on the couch. He looked about fifty and had graying hair, a comforting roundish face, and a funny gray and white beard. He stood and walked over, and from a description Adam had given or possibly some other reason, I knew who he was.

He took Adam's hand. "Hi Adam, remember me? Max Schultz."

If Adam was surprised, he hid it well. Sara stepped forward and introduced herself, and Max motioned them to sit on the couch. He picked up a small dining room style chair, set it across from them and sat facing them. I heard the door gently close and figured Nicolle had left.

"What a beautiful room," Sara said. The other three walls had large semi-abstract floral and forest type paintings, and a few live plants in simple but large ceramic pots sat in the corners. I had to agree with Sara, it was a beautiful room.

Max spoke first. "Yes, this is my sanctuary. I love it in here and spend as much time cloistered as I can get away with. Now, before we get going here, I want to ask you both a question. I know you both just watched the video about Extras. It's kind of like Extras 101 and is designed to give anybody requesting knowledge on the subject a place to start. My question is to both of you. Do you, at this point, believe that what is discussed in the video is possibly real, or are either of you still skeptical? Please try to give an honest answer and know there is no judgment about what you say. It will only affect the way I word answers to some of your questions."

Sara said, "I can say I'm eighty to ninety percent there."

Adam glanced at Sara with a hint of a grin. "I'm the same. I'm wildly skeptical of everything so it's saying a lot."

It was a slick opening on Max's part and excellent answers.

"Adam, I know some of the reasons you are here, and Sara, you also, and I would like to suggest that we stop trying to hide from each other. If you both wish to do a story of some type about Hope Community, it likely can happen at some point. And Adam, I need to apologize for not coming to you a long time ago and trying to shed light on what happened to your brother. To be honest, I did not know myself and still don't for certain. But now I believe I have a much clearer picture of how it might have happened." He stood and said, "Would you like some water?"

They both said yes and he went to a side-table with a large plant resting on it. He leaned behind the plant, and I could hear the drizzle of liquid into cups which he brought over and handed to them.

He sat and continued, "There are so many stories circulating in the outside about Hope and Extras in general and the one thing I am positive of is that, just like the Normal human race, those with the Extra overlay, no matter how they got it—at Birth, early Walk-in, later Walk-in, a Normal asking for an Extra to enter, a Normal not even knowing an Extra has entered them—we are not a uniform group of beings. We come in all different flavors, so to speak, most wishing to add positivity into the world and a few, not so much. We've had to deal with some of the negative ones trying to latch onto our organization. Now, one of the major stories circulating is that late Walk-ins are coming in with exponentially increasing numbers. I will tell you that the numbers are increasing but nothing like the rumors say they are. And many of these folks need help, and that help cannot be a public matter because the public would not understand. Which explains the secrecy. And the hesitancy for a story from either or both of you."

Adam asked, "Is it true that Extras cannot consciously kill themselves or anyone else for that matter?"

"Well, like so many seemingly simple statements, it's not simple at all. It might be true for most of us, but again, just like Normals, there are always a few who likely can. However, I do believe your brother committed suicide and I believe the reason he did was because his Extra layer departed, and he just couldn't go on without it. This does happen sometimes."

Adam had no response.

Sara said, "One of the stories out there is that Hope grooms Normals with the intent of having them receive the Extra layer. Is that true?"

"Again, another misleading story. If we know Extras are waiting to enter somebody, anybody, we believe we are doing them a service by finding them a good host. The ideal situation would be for people like yourselves, who know all about what we do here, and who understand the Extra concept, to offer. And we have ways now to make the match work amazingly well for both beings."

"Interesting," Sara said. "I would love to learn more about how it could work."

Sara looked at Adam and I saw him nod.

"First, I would like to bring up another subject," Max said, "that may be even more sensitive than what we've already talked about. I'm aware that you know about the more hidden groups of Extras, what I've called Extras-at-Birth, generally from communes, and how some of them have certain abilities to transform a situation into something akin to a blissful state. It can be almost like a drug, maybe like Ecstasy at a rave. Now this, in my opinion, is similar to techniques the Moonies used years ago which they called love-bombing, meaning they showered potential recruits with bombs of love to suck them into their group. In modern times, the term has been coopted and applied to any situation where one seduces another with good feelings with the long-term intent of establishing control. But certain Extras with special abilities can literally create what they call Love energy and pass it on to others. It's a powerful form of energy and it all feels so wonderful. But you have to ask, what is the point? And even more important, what is the purpose?"

My full attention focused on every word Max Schultz said. Even though he was blatantly referring to me—to Melinda and me—it was almost like I became Sara Leeds, seduced, revisiting opinions I had only minutes earlier, ready to reexamine an experience I'd had only a few days earlier. So, so powerful. This person was actually seducing me into believing something about myself that I knew was so far off. Or was it?

"Even more interesting," Sara said.

When she spoke, I heard a different tone, felt a different energy, and another aspect came into focus. Adam Kastner was searching for who he was. That was why he was there. Sara Leeds knew exactly who she was and had known for a long time, maybe forever.

Max broke into a grin. "You don't have your recorders on, do you?"

His grin turned to a scowl. Or, at least I thought it did.

I saw Adam, frowning, a slight twitch in one eye. "We wouldn't dare," he mumbled.

Max continued to look into Sara's face, those all-knowing eyes inspecting. I opened my own eyes and jumped out. Melinda heard me move and waved her hands for me to keep quiet. She kept her eyes closed. She wasn't ready to leave.

I rolled onto my back and breathed quietly. Melinda was about two feet from me and I could have touched her if I dared. The idea that she was still attached to Adam Kastner, inside the wiring of his being, connected to all his senses, fifty or more physical miles away, made me so uncomfortable that I thought I was going to throw up.

Finally, I felt Melinda's touch on my arm and I sat up. "I'm never doing that again. Not ever," I said.

"What happened?"

I tried to control my breath, racing in and out like a panting dog. "He knew I was there. At least, I think so. What he was saying…I can't believe it. What happened after I left?"

"Not much. Max said he had an appointment, and they agreed to meet again."

"He didn't go into more detail about them receiving Extras?" I asked.

"No, he cut it short."

I forced myself to calm down. "We should be able to tell who is bullshitting and who is not. We should have the ability to determine exactly where somebody is at."

"Yes, we should. But it's impossible if they don't know themselves."

"I think Sara Leeds knows exactly where she's at."

Adam

Adam left the Hope building through a nearly invisible door, silent, expressionless, Sara at his side, and followed a rich garden path around the building to the front parking lot. They climbed into Adam's car and drove a few minutes, and he said, "Why do I feel like somebody has been inside my head?"

"Because they have been."

"And you knew all along?"

"Only near the end."

He waited for her to say more but she kept quiet and stared out the window. He pulled into a gas station, stopped at a pump, and filled the tank. Sara got out and said, "I'm going inside. Do you want money?"

He grumbled, "No."

When she came back, he'd turned the radio on with the volume up and they didn't speak until they had reached the Albany bus station. He parked and she tried to get out but the door was locked.

"Can you unlock this please?"

"Not until you tell me something and I tell you something."

"All right," she said. "You tell me who you think was messing around with us and also tell me how it made you feel."

He raised his voice. "How it made me feel? Are you kidding me? Max Schultz is the most manipulative fuck I've ever met in my life. He's talking about Moonies? Sun Meung Moon has nothing on him. And the other two? Jade and Melinda? They're obviously every bit as bad, and no way in hell am I going to get in the middle of whatever war they have going on between them. So, I'm what? Their human video connection? No fucking way! And then there's you, Sara. You're the biggest mystery of all. The only thing I can figure is you're after the biggest story of your lifetime and—and you know way more about this whole shit show than you're letting on. I mean, who the hell are you?"

"Adam..."

"No, no, don't answer because, guess what, I'm done with all of it. So, goodbye, Sara, and don't ever contact me again."

He unlocked the door, she got out, and he drove away.

I'm done with it, I'm done with it. The problem was, he could never be done with it and he knew it. He wound through the streets of Albany with no real destination, killing time, trying to settle himself. He parked and walked quickly through different neighborhoods, looking for something, or nothing. Slowly, the force of what was behind his confusion revealed itself: disappointment. Not with Max Schultz or even Sara Leeds. The biggest crushing letdown was with Jade and Melinda. He had wanted so much to believe in them and they had used him in such an invasive way. His other revelation was that, if his father was somehow connected to Melinda's father and probably also her mother, then what did it say about who he was? Another conman always on the lookout for new followers? He would confront his father right away, and if he wasn't home, was off on one of his unexplainable absences, he would track him down and get some answers.

As he neared his parent's driveway, his phone rang. He pulled over and checked and it was Melinda. He couldn't bring himself to answer it and let it go to voice mail. He wanted to delete it but couldn't bring himself to do that, either.

He listened: "Hi Adam. I'm calling to apologize for something you likely know I did, and if not, I'm going to confess to doing. I used you without your permission, without your knowledge, to monitor your meeting with Max Schultz. It was invasive, unkind, and against everything I have previously believed about such actions. The ends do not justify the means, and I can't in any way excuse what I did. Again, I am so sorry. Please be safe. You are truly a kind and special being."

If it had been Jade who had left the message, he might have had an easier time categorizing it as more manipulative bullshit. But coming from Melinda, it was harder to dismiss. He flashed back to seven years before when he had hacked into the Creative Writing class student folder, read Jade's story submission, and would have also read Melinda's had it been available. Wasn't it a similar action? Also, wrong? It was similar perhaps, but this was a thousand times worse. He listened to the message two more times, tuning into the exact words and the vocal tones. She did not try to explain why she had done what she did, she did not ask for forgiveness, she didn't even try to defend herself against Max Schultz's love-bomb spiel. She only owned that what she had done was wrong and she asked him to stay safe.

He didn't know what to think. As he re-started his car, another vehicle drove past, in a hurry, a little bit over the speed limit. He recognized the vehicle, and its driver: his father, Clifford Kastner. He watched Clifford pull into the driveway, go into the house, and a few minutes later, come back out and drive off in the other direction. Adam followed.

The sky darkened and a thick rain began to pour, hard enough to nearly obliterate the visibility. Adam lost track of his father's car but he sped up, knowing that the torrent would disguise his own car. He spotted the blurry taillights and hoped he wouldn't lose them when they turned corners. Within a few minutes, Clifford entered an on-ramp to the interstate highway, heading west. Adam wondered if he could be going to the Hope Community, but he got off after two exits and drove into a neighborhood with newer townhouses and condominiums. When he pulled into the driveway of a duplex, Adam stopped on the street about a hundred yards back.

He watched his father walk onto the porch of one of the units, knock on the door, and enter. A few minutes later, another car passed him and parked on the street. Two women got out and Adam quickly left his car and walked toward them. The rain had slowed enough that he could see how they were dressed: both wore casual jeans and short raincoats, and one wore a baseball cap. If they would just turn toward him so he could see their faces. He walked by them, and they turned and he said "Hello."

They both returned the greeting, and at first, he thought it couldn't be possible, could only be a coincidence. One was a Black woman, likely in her late fifties or early sixties, and he would not have associated her with Melinda, as the woman was much shorter and did not share the same facial features, except that the other woman, a white woman, probably the same age, looked exactly like Jade Furlong. He kept walking, then stopped and turned around. They also knocked on the door and this time he could see a man's outline letting them in.

The rain stopped and the clouds parted in preparation for another sunset. If the group in the house came out now, he would surely be seen by his father, and since now anything was possible, he might even be recognized by somebody else who he had known from somewhere at some other point in his life. He wasn't ready for any of it. Not now. He needed to go back to his parent's house and hide out in his room.

As he drove, the sun set behind him, and the glow lit up store windows, car windows, and his rear-view mirrors. The light seemed to push him forward, like an invisible giant hand and he wondered if any moment it might grab him and make him stop. Colors began to dance and flicker and he saw masses of huddled shadows lining the sidewalks. Another hallucination. But why now? After what he'd been through in the last few days, driving through a suburb of Albany, New York shouldn't be weird enough to trigger one of these moments. He remembered he wasn't the only passenger in the car, he had another companion still stowed away in the trunk. Maybe it was only a book or maybe it was Old Elwood himself, ready to give a commentary on his current actions. Whatever or whoever it was, it wanted to come out.

His mother's car was gone and he thought cynically that she could be the one out having an affair of some sort. He grabbed the book from the trunk, rushed into his bedroom, closed the door, and tossed the book on his bed. He rarely turned on the overhead light, usually content with just his bedside lamp, but he switched both on now. He also opened his closet door and pulled the chain on the overhead light inside. For his final preparation, he closed the curtain on the one window, blocking out any possible interference.

He sat on the edge of the bed and pulled the book into his lap, relieved that the cover was exactly as he remembered it. *The Story of Old Elwood*. He opened it, skipped past the title page, and leafed through illustrations with backgrounds portraying Scottish hillsides or English country lanes and Old Elwood looking like a character from a Dickens novel. At first, the story itself held little interest: a young man, Jonathon Deerfield, wandered into an old house—in this situation, a rundown stone farmhouse surrounded by empty fields—and met the cantankerous Old Elwood who gave him advice about his life. However, as the story continued, the language gradually shifted to Elwood using phrases like "outside spirits finding a home in the unsuspecting human," or "they tell you they're helping you out, but in truth, m'boy, they only want a free ride." The final statement let Adam know he was going to lie awake for the night, with no chance of sleep anytime soon: "Dear Reader, we hope you enjoyed Jonathon Deerfield's experience with Old Elwood Clamshaw. Now, we would love to hear about your experience. After all, no matter how similar the external events, the human interpretations are never the same, are they?"

Jade

After our experience with Adam, Sara, and Max Schultz, Melinda and I munched on a few things, drank endless cups of a sedative herbal tea, and tried to sit quietly. But Melinda, usually calm and centered, was wound up like an old clock about to spring apart.

I tried to fill her role. "It wasn't our most noble act, but I believe they will understand," I said. "Or, at least Adam will."

"No, he won't. And why should he? It was my idea, and I need to take responsibility for it."

"Okay, maybe it was your idea. But I certainly went along with it."

She stood and pulled on her coat. I said, "Let me come with you. You never even cleaned up the mess from Billy Squires."

"I can handle it."

She gave me a quick hug and was out the door. I later learned that she left a voice mail on Adam's phone, owning her actions, taking responsibility, and deeply apologizing. Knowing her as well as I did, I was sure it was sincere, and if anybody could claw us out of the hole we'd dug, it would be her. I sprawled out on the couch, in an unusual haze, drained of energy. I wanted to sleep, but when I closed my eyes, my amped-up wiring made it clear that a night snooze was not on the agenda.

I focused on Sara Leeds and came to the conclusion that she was not who she said she was, or more accurately, she had much more going on, much more knowledge than she was letting on, about who we were and what the Hope Community was all about. However, this in no way meant I had conclusive evidence that she was aligned with the Hope people. My only more definite conclusion centered on the possibility that she still had a continued interest in a powerful and revealing story, and perhaps had always planned, for the fame and glory, a slick end run around Adam. I let all thoughts of Sara slide away and put my attention on our greatest obstacle: Melinda and I still had no way to easily and safely get inside the Hope Community compound.

Safety and ease. Neither was going to be a part of the plan I was creating and I abandoned them as descriptors. I had other ways to get inside, or one in particular, and I intended to pursue it. My plan would again involve the use of a power I believed I had. But, unlike the last one, when I climbed inside somebody else's brain circuits, and had at least once done similar acts with wild animals, I had never attempted to use this ability. And, without Melinda's accompaniment, I would only have half the strength to pull it off.

As children, the Elders often reminded us to never indulge in practices that could be interpreted by outsiders as special powers, ones that might draw unnecessary attention to ourselves. Many of these powers were shunned primarily because they were invasive and rude— and, yes, the Elders would have been critical of what we did to Adam and Sara with our ultimate invasion. But there was one power that the Elders vehemently discouraged because it could potentially disrupt or even destroy our Extra and human configurations. I'm referring to the practice of one's soul/spirit leaving one's body, which was exactly what

I planned to do. The Elders considered children especially at risk because their Extra layer would not have fused sufficiently with their human body and mind. But I was now well on my way to twenty-eight years in this human container, so how much more fused did I need to be? After all, it wasn't like my entire Extra component would just fly away. If I did the process correctly, enough of it would remain housed in the Jade body, and a key part of me would set off on a wild adventure. At least I hoped so.

I had never before tried it—had hardly ever thought about trying it—and had no idea if it was possible, but the act didn't seem much different than taking a piece of myself and inserting it into another live being, whether it be Sara Leeds or a deer in the woods. Except, when I traveled into Sara, it was a much smaller and more secure piece of me and I still had a human host. Now I would be flying free, much like dying—although, at actual death, much more of the Extra component untangles from the human—with the hope that I would be able to return, still alive. I told myself it was a necessary risk for a greater cause. I laid on my back, tuned into my Extra self, easily rose far enough out of my Jade body that I could see it about five feet below, and became so excited that I snapped back in. Altruism for a greater cause is all well and good but I was rapidly becoming the less rational, more impulsive Jade Furlong of many years before. It didn't help that there was no Melinda Breeze around to calm me down.

I forced myself to focus and tried to dampen the rush of euphoria. First, I needed to establish my destination and what I intended to accomplish there. I opened my laptop, went to Google Earth, and honed in on the Hope Community. When I reached the maximum enlargement, I could identify the community outlines and how the various buildings were placed. The main building housing the Welcome Center, where Adam and Sara took Melinda and me, was easy to identify, as were the open areas I assumed were different types of gardens. Toward the back of the property, much smaller structures formed what appeared to be a living area of sorts, likely with a layout much like the one I grew up in. Three larger buildings in the center grabbed my interest. These were the ones I would go for. I randomly picked one of them as a starting point.

Now, what did I expect to accomplish? I wanted to gain access to each of the buildings, one by one, and examine their contents and the activities of anybody inside. A memory, something Adam had shared, paid a visit. He had once sat behind the property, far up on a ridge, and seen large excavation equipment digging deep into the earth as prep for some sort of gigantic foundations. Would it be possible that what the satellite shots showed me was only a small part of the whole operation? Could there be more underground? Oh yes!

To pacify my human aspects, I mapped out a route with distances and directions. However, ultimately, I am an interdimensional being and in the actual mode of transportation I was about to climb into, concepts of time and space had no relevance. I closed the laptop, lay again on my back, visualized the space above the Hope Community, and off I went.

In a second, I blew through solid physical plane material—the ceilings of my apartment and the one above, then through an empty attic and out the roof—and in another second, I hovered above the three buildings in the center of the Hope Community, as if I was one of Google's satellites taking the photos. I put the thought forward in my mind, *go inside the first building*, and there I was.

The space was cold, dark, and empty, a gigantic warehouse containing nothing. I hovered around, looked in the corners, and along the ceiling, and became aware of a dim light coming from an undefined source. The light revealed nothing. The longer I was inside, the more this descriptor, *nothing*, morphed into an overwhelming feeling of profound emptiness. I began to simultaneously experience intense claustrophobia and a spatial vastness stretching to infinity. The feeling increased until the force was both crushing me and blowing me apart. I needed to escape, but if I did, I would have failed and I couldn't bear the thought. I put my attention on the vast concrete floor, slid my being part-way into it, and sensed an entire world below.

The floor gave way and I flowed into a room below, this one filled with a mass of something I couldn't at first identify. It was more of a feeling, a sensory experience closing in around me, that exuded familiarity, connection, and peace. I drifted aimlessly and fell into a bottomless stupor, not caring if the mass absorbed me into itself. My visual sense began to awaken, bringing with it an odd form of survival instinct, likely connected to the bits of humanness still swirling around inside me. When my vision perceived the color or multicolor array of the mass, I understood what I was stuffed in the middle of—a tight but enormous number of Extra beings, unconnected to humans, somehow dialed down like bees when the weather turns cold, and likely waiting for their human host assignments. How did they get there? Why were they there?

I scrambled, I struggled, I fought hard to get out. I learned that even a disembodied soul/spirit can access some form of cosmic adrenaline when confronting its demise. The floor/ceiling, combined with a type of energetic suction from the captive mass of Extras, presented the biggest challenge. But once free, I slammed back into my body, still lying on the couch in my apartment, with a near atomic force. I lay on the couch, shaking, crying, in full despair, and I desperately wondered what I could do next.

The next day, I didn't leave my apartment. I read, slept, watched a movie, and ate very little. Melinda didn't call and I couldn't find the motivation to call her. The day after that was a Monday and I pulled myself together for work. The first two classes dragged by in a blur, and at the beginning of my in-office free period, I heard a quiet knock, saw the door open, and Jacob LeBlanc walked in. I hadn't spoken privately with him since our first meeting weeks earlier when we discussed the goings on at the Hope Community.

"Have a seat, Jacob. How are you doing?"

"The real question, Ms. Furlong, is how are *you* doing?"

"Spoken like a true observer. Things have been a little rough. And you can call me Jade."

"Let me guess. You've had dealings of some sort with the Hope scene and it's shaken you up."

"Very impressive." My entire focus, my sour defeated mood, shifted in an instant. I put aside my self-obsession and tuned into this person sitting in front of me. "You observed me in front of the class and got a perfect read. Now I'm doing the same to you and I see you are also quite upset. Please tell me why."

"Wait, first I have to say, I made that comment about the at-Birth communes being elitist and all that stuff. But I know you're not like that at all. You're…I don't know what you are but it's something special."

I didn't expect that. "Oh c'mon. Not really."

"Something about you is different."

"I don't know, Jacob. But maybe that's why the Hope people dislike me so much."

"Two of my friends disappeared and I think they took 'em. They love a certain type— around my age, nobody younger than eighteen so they don't get in trouble that way. They want them old enough to handle what they put them through but still young and stupid enough to go along with the brainwashing."

"When did they disappear?"

"About a week ago. Nobody knows what happened."

"Has anybody gone to the police?"

"We don't dare."

"Are your friends all Extras?"

"No, only one other. And we never talk about it. I overshared once, even did some ridiculous magic trick, and now all the Normals think it's the thing to do. Like it's cool or something."

His hands shook and I took them and squeezed and they settled down. I went into teacher mode. "Here's what you can do right now. Team up with your other Extra friend and you each take half of your vulnerable Normal friends and go into super-observer mode. Try to be subtle but always there."

"I know a few other Extras but I'm not sure where they're at so I don't want to include them. Do you have any plans yourself?" His level of concern, his fear, verged on panic.

My words rambled out. Anything to help him feel safer. "We're in it now. Past the point of turning back. Yes, I'm a bit shaken up but a small group of us has assembled who believe we can stop this thing."

My God. A group of us? What a lie. But I was glad I had put it out there because the creation of a group was essential, and it was up to me to make it happen. Jacob left, and a few minutes later, another hand tapped on the door.

Adam

A delicious moon shone through Adam's bedroom window and cast a powerful light on his face and into his dreams. It transported him back to the seacoast, sitting on the deck with Christina Luft, absorbing a mix of her essence and the mighty ocean waves. Except, it wasn't Christina huddled next to him, it was Melinda Breeze, fumbling around in his brain, trying to chase him out of his own body so she could become him. And Old Elwood sat across from them, alternating between maniacal laughing, and snorting out his warped suggestions and observations. Adam twisted awake, hopped out of bed, and pulled the curtains tight to shut out the light.

What to do? What to do next? He lay awake in the blackness for the rest of the night, got up at dawn, went out for a long walk, and came back to a quiet breakfast with his mother, neither of them speaking much, both lost in their upset worlds. His father had never come home, and he knew that sharing details of where he was would only create a further disturbance for his mother.

He spent the rest of the day glued to his laptop, reviewing everything he had read about all the different characters, organizations, and locations he had brushed up against in the last few weeks. He also tried to hunt up new material and had his first hit with another forum called Clurid, similar to Bracken, with more hate threads related to small hidden communes throughout the country engaging in satanic practices. He scoured the internet for local news related to violence or protests against any communes or communal members and only found a short video clip of a gathering of about ten protesters outside a building in San Francisco. The signs the protesters held, and their speech mimicked what he'd read on the forums but no more information was available.

He did a more thorough search of Sara Leeds and Carter Freedman and learned on an old blog post of Sara's that they had collaborated on two other projects, neither of which were ever completed. He could find little information of substance about either project and was about to give up when he did a YouTube search including both their names. He found an obscure video of a ten-speaker lecture, which Sara and Carter were both a part of, titled *Beings Among Us*, and began watching. He realized he had viewed part of the video years earlier, wanting to learn more about Sara, but at the time, he had never heard of Carter Freedman. He remembered watching for about five minutes and abandoning it because it was boring. This time he would carefully view specific sections.

He fast-forwarded through the clip until he came to Sara, and she predictably re-hashed concepts and information that could be found in her books. He found it interesting, but he heard nothing new or unexpected. Carter Freedman followed Sara with philosophical ideas about the relationship between spatial infinity and the concept of multidimensional reality. He then asked Sara specifically what she thought about it. Her answer was again educated but somewhat predictable. Carter then spoke for a few minutes about "something he'd been hearing about." He mentioned hidden communities of people who believed that their body/mind/soul/spirits were the products of a human bodies and highly evolved sentient energy beings who had merged with them. They referred to these beings as Extras and called themselves Extra-normal. He asked Sara if she had ever heard of this.

Sara's hesitation was brief, and Adam caught it and froze the video. He blew up the image and studied her facial expression. She hadn't expected the question, and it disturbed her, but she responded quickly and moved on.

"I have heard something about what you're referring to," she said, "but I didn't take it seriously. You know how people are these days with the fantasies they like to create."

At the end of the discussions, the videographer continued to film, asking some of the speakers further questions but attempting to surreptitiously collect "hot mic" footage from a few of the others. He stood a distance from Carter and Sara, locked in a close discussion, and zoomed in. Sara's facial expression and body language suggested to Adam, *disturbance* and *unease*. Carter said, "I'm sorry, Sara. We'll talk more in private. We have a lot more in common…" The final words were inaudible, but the overall footage clinched it for Adam. Sara Leeds maybe wasn't lying about who she was. But she sure as hell wasn't telling the whole story.

The next morning, as Adam laid in bed not ready to get up, his father came in, rustled around in the kitchen, began what sounded like a heated conversation with his mother, and after about a half-hour, left again. Adam wanted to confront his father but chose to wait for a time when his mother was not around. He based part of his choice on his desire to first meet with either Jade or Melinda so he could verify that the women he'd seen entering the townhouse where he saw his father, were, in fact, their mothers. By the time he went downstairs, his mother had also left for some unknown destination, and he ate a bowl of cereal, drank a glass of juice, and headed out on his next journey. He would have preferred to meet with Melinda, not because she was easier to get along with, but because she was the one who had crawled inside his brain. He had lost most of his anger and now only wanted to hear her talk about it. But she would be busy at her work so he drove to Clark College, hoping to find Jade.

He parked on a side street, took a reusable grocery bag out of the back seat, and walked across the campus. When he reached the door to the building Jade's office was in, he spotted what looked like a familiar face walking toward him. He couldn't put a name with the face and was about to walk past when the person said, "Are you Adam?"

They both stopped and examined each other. "Yes, I am. And I'm sure I know you. But from where?"

"You knew me when I was much younger. Like twelve or so. And Garrett was trying to help me out."

"Oh yes. You're Jacob. Jacob LeBlanc." Adam grabbed his hands, pulled him close, and hugged him. "So how are you doing?"

Jacob backed up a foot. "I don't know, man. Everything is kind of crazy."

"You know about Garrett?"

"Yes, and I'm so sorry. That guy helped me out so much when things were bad. I mean, we lived a whole summer underneath a bridge, homeless, trying to get away from those whack-jobs in the cult. And he got me back with my Mom."

"But now you're going here to college, right? Are you more uh…settled?"

"You meant to say Reconfigured, right? And I guess in a lot of ways I am. But no thanks to the cult freaks. I did it mostly on my own."

Adam looked at the door to the building, then back at Jacob. "You just came out of there, didn't you?" He nodded at the door. "Can I ask you who you were seeing?"

Jacob gave a little laugh. "I bet the same one you're on your way to see."

"What do you think of her? With all you've been through, you know as much as anybody about the whole Extra thing. I mean, is she for real? To you?"

Jacob frowned and shook his head. "Oh man. I hope you don't mean what it sounds like you're saying. The first time I met her, I was snarky and doubtful, but I always watch her with eagle eyes every class and she is something amazing. She's like the nicest person I know."

Adam fought back a laugh. If this kid only knew the whole of it. But he was an interesting one, a street-smart Extra who likely didn't miss much.

Adam softened as much as he could. "You know what. I totally agree with you. She's for real and she's an absolute gem of a being. I just wanted to get some outside input."

He knocked on her office door, heard Jade's voice, and entered.

She nearly jumped out of her chair and moved toward him, her face revealing a flood of emotions—sadness, fear, and a lot of concern. Before he could speak, she said, "I'm sorry, Adam. I am so sorry. We never should have done it."

He laid the bag on the floor and said, "Yeah, well now, my biggest question is, why did you pick Sara and not me? I'm kind of insulted, but I guess we would be too much alike for you to handle."

"Huh, what do you mean?"

"Jade, I'm joking. I'm not angry, I don't blame you, I even think I understand. I was off-the-wall pissed at first, but mostly at Max Schultz who is a, you know, horrible person. Then Melinda left me a genuinely contrite voice-mail, Jacob just assured me you're the nicest person he knows, and now I'm dying to know how you did what you did."

"You met Jacob?"

"Yeah. He seems like a good one."

"Yes, but once again, a huge mis-truth came out of my mouth. He's way tuned in to all this Hope and Extra stuff, really disturbed, and I told him I was working with a group who was figuring it all out. Like I had some big Elder connection who could make miracles. Adam…"

She grabbed onto him and pulled him close. They went silent, held onto each other, breathed together.

Then Jade said "I have something big I need to tell you. Something…" She couldn't get it out.

"I do, too. A few things."

"Maybe you could go first."

They sat back down, still close to each other. He described his developing concern about his father, questioning who he really was and why he was gone so much of the time, and then how he followed him through a raging rainstorm to a nameless townhouse in a development somewhere outside of Albany.

"I watched him knock on a door and go in. Then a car passed me and parked ahead of me. And Jade, two women got out, so I casually walked by them. They were probably my father's age, and one was short, thin, and Black. and the other one was taller and white and had on a baseball cap, and she looked a whole lot like you."

She shook her head and looked down at the floor. "It figures, doesn't it? I mean, why would we have ever thought any different, right?"

"I wanted to run after them and make a big scene."

"Yeah, well, I wouldn't have blamed you for that. It's good you didn't, though. But keep going if you have more to tell."

"After the meeting with Max Schultz, I kind of took out my annoyance with the whole meeting on Sara. The thing is, I'm not sure if you could pick up on it, but I felt like she knew what was going on right from the beginning and she was playing along with it because…I don't know. She just seemed like she wasn't completely upfront about who she is. What do you think?"

"Exactly what you just said. I saw a look on your face when she said something that made me think the same thing."

"So weird that you were inside her, looking at me."

"Never again, I promise you."

Next, he described the video he had seen with Sara and Carter Freedman. It emphasized what they both were feeling about Sara.

He finished and Jade asked, "What's in that bag?"

He slowly pulled out *The Story of Old Elwood* and laid it on Jade's lap. "A present for you."

"Oh, holy shit. Where did you ever get this?"

"I went back to Marion, you know, the little town on the Maine coast." Adam described his trip, going into every detail about Old Elwood, but omitting the part about spending the night with Christina Luft. "Do you want to hang onto the book? It might be safer with you."

She laid the book on her desk and stared at him. "Okay, sure, but it's my turn now. I only have one thing and it's awful, awful, awful."

She slowly, quietly shared her last adventure, the specifics of each piece enhanced by her accompanying feelings: the ecstasy of leaving her body; the profound discomfort within the walls of the warehouse; and the horror she found below.

"How many do you think were in there?" he asked.

"Hundreds, thousands. I don't know."

"How did you know how to leave your body like that?"

"Again, I don't know. I just thought it and it happened."

He sat up, eager. "I want you to help me do it."

She grabbed his hands, tried to be commanding, but could only express more fear. "Oh Adam, please. No."

He gently squeezed back. "Jade, listen. If Extras are in one part of the complex, humans will be in another part. I know you know that. And I know you will go back, as will Melinda. I'm not an Extra, at least not in the way you are, but I believe I have enough of whatever is needed to accompany you. And here's a good reason why I should. I'm a journalist and this is a big story. I would know how to write it in a way that suggests that strange cult practices, such as housing people against their will, are happening there, and need to be investigated."

Jade

My office time ran out and I told Adam he could wait there if he wanted, read my strange books, or stare at the small watercolor of the Extras floating around, the one that freaked him out the first time he saw it. Nothing seemed to bother him anymore. Not even leaving his body to break into a cult compound. And do what? That was the question, the one we needed to have a solid answer to before we broke through the wall again.

One idea we were in solid agreement about was the need to round up our parents and have a serious conversation, one which would likely change the trajectory of our lives. If we could get Melinda on board, we planned to meet late afternoon the next day, and unannounced, go to our home in the woods, and have a sit-down. We knew Adam's father wouldn't be present, but my parents and Josephine most likely would. We would start there and haul Clifford Kastner into the mix at a later date.

The next day, Adam came to my office at the arranged time, and we put our plan in motion. The first stop would be to pick up Melinda. I agreed to drive and had just started the car when I received a text from her saying she had already left in her car because she planned to stay overnight, and this would give us more flexibility. I still hadn't seen her since we burrowed inside Sara and Adam three days earlier and had only talked to her for a minute on the phone. She seemed a little off but I didn't think much about it.

The ride was almost fun. Light and playful with Adam Kastner—who would have thought? I desperately needed it to be that way, anything to escape the knowledge of who the monsters at Hope had trapped in their underworld. For most of the trip, we avoided all the heavy stuff, and even when we talked about aspects of the Extra world, we managed to do it from the part of humanness that can be joyful and fun.

I think I started it. As soon as we left Clark College, heading southwest toward Anderson, the onset of fall showing in the clouds, the changing trees, and the delicious hint of a wispy breeze, I said what I suspected, "So you spent the night in Marion. I don't imagine you stayed in the cottage or at Old Elwood's house. Where did you end up?"

"Is it all right for us to talk about this sort of thing? What do you think?"

I suppressed a grin which, since he was looking at me, I'm sure he noticed. "It's fine with me."

"Her name is Christina Luft. I had a schoolboy crush on her when we used to stay there and it was her house that I left when I met up with Old Elwood. The first time and again this last time. She's an Extra, but like many of the townspeople apparently do, she strives to be as human as possible. She's a kind being, and like you, Jade, she's gorgeous."

It got a full laugh out of me. "What was the sex like? Was it human? Or something else."

"Wow. You're going for it."

"I know." I put on a serious tone. "But I am genuinely interested, not just for prurient reasons. I'm trying to figure out a few things in my own life."

"Well, then, here it is. It was so intense, nearly overwhelming, not like anything I'd ever experienced, and, uh, you know what I mean. It got me wondering about you and Melinda. With you two, it must be earth-shattering. I can't think of a better word. Oh, wait. I'm just assuming you're that kind of couple. Sorry."

"It's okay. You can assume it. We're about as in love as any two beings could possibly be. But sexual contact has been problematic. You know what it's like when you're trying to jump a car battery, and you mix up the positive and negative?"

"Really?"

"Imagine that times a thousand. And we haven't been able to figure out why. One major plus came out of it, though. With our experiments, we did create the so-called love bomb."

"Let's not defile it with the name. I think it changed me, Jade. It woke me up to something."

A few minutes later, Adam said, "Maybe you and Melinda can't match up sexually because she's just too pure of a being. She goes inside my brain and does something she never should have done, yet I feel honored, like I had some sacred visit or something. It's almost like she's not real."

"Oh, she's real all right. You can say I'm gorgeous all you want but she's the real deal."

We stopped for gas and Adam drove. I drifted around, half asleep, and then something jabbed me, a message of some sort from Melinda, most likely, which wouldn't have been surprising. I sent her a text, saying we'd be there shortly, and didn't receive an answer. The closer we got to the gate to my home, the more the scary vibe closed in around me.

Adam felt it, too. "Is something going on?"

I couldn't answer. "We're almost there."

We passed through Anderson and the main street was deserted. We heard sirens behind us, Adam pulled over, and two state trooper cars rushed by. A minute later, it happened again, and a fire engine whizzed past.

"Keep driving," I whispered. We had another minute.

The imagery screen lit up and my mind saw some but not nearly all of it. First the bunkhouse and the library, both burning. Then a few of the cabins. Something prevented me from seeing more. Flaming trees and grass but no bodies anywhere. I willed myself to see my cabin. And Melinda's cabin. I only caught a glimpse of hers—nearly gone, the flames already dying down.

Up ahead a fire truck, an ambulance, and three state trooper vehicles were packed into the parking lot, surrounded by troopers keeping order among the crowd of onlookers. The smell of smoke made its way through the closed car windows, and I could see a bit of white and gray haze lifting out of the woods. A trooper stood in the road directing traffic wishing to drive by. As we got closer, I recognized a few of the dear ones from my commune and I slunk down in my seat.

"Just drive slowly by," I said. "You can look but I don't want anybody to see me."

"Where are we going?"

"A backway in."

After we passed, I asked, "Did you see Melinda?"

"No. And I tried to figure out if either of your mothers were there. But I couldn't tell."

Another half mile ahead, I sat up, looked behind me to make sure nobody saw, and said, "Turn left here."

We pulled onto a ragged dirt road, made it a few hundred yards in, and had to stop. We got out and ran along the road as it quickly turned into a winding forest path. I knew these woods as well as anybody and left the path to make a straight hike to where I desperately hoped I would find my people. I had to go slower at a few steep rocky parts and direct Adam to the safest way down. As we got closer, I could smell the blaze and smoke, like the entire forest was on fire. I thought of the animals who I shared my life with but knew they had instincts beyond ours and would have escaped. However, the people, my people…

We crashed into the opening, the magnificent stone plaza where we came for our baptisms and any other celebrations, and found it empty. I grabbed Adam's hand and we ran across the flat stones, our footsteps making hollow thumps, and came to the small lake with the walkway and the temple perched on the little island in the middle. Adam let go of my hand, stopped, and gasped.

"This is it," he said. "My God, it's real. Just like the picture."

I gave him a moment, then took his hand again. "We have to go inside."

When we entered the temple, a group of about twenty people, all of whom I knew intimately, greeted us. They thronged around me with hugs, tears, and pained greetings. Adam moved back, staring at the walls, looking into the other room at the enormous window overlooking the lake.

I turned to him and introduced him. "This is Adam Kastner." I gave them his last name and because of who his father was, watched for reactions. Even in the midst of what I knew was going to be a trauma to surpass all, I was already looking for suspects. If anybody there knew Adam's father, they hid it well.

I followed with, "Where are my parents?"

A woman I'd known forever named Cynthia Louder rushed over to me. Her eyes were red and swollen and her face wet. "They went somewhere early this morning. We've tried contacting them. By phone and even other ways. In this situation, we had to."

"Whatever it takes, do it. Did Melinda get here?"

"Melinda. No. I haven't seen her," Cynthia said. She turned to the group, asked if anybody else saw her, and a chorus of voices said, "No."

"She drove separately," I said. "She was ahead of me."

The room went quiet and I knew what had happened, not everything, not the details, but most certainly the general idea. Melinda had finally had her truly awful experience. The big trauma had finally arrived, no longer a slow death by a thousand cuts, but one hard stab into her heart. I turned to Cynthia for more information and our thoughts merged. She held me and we shook and sobbed.

Adam touched my arm. "What?"

"Melinda's mother. Josephine."

"Oh no."

I disconnected from Cynthia and headed to the door. "We have to find Melinda."

As I opened the door, I saw that Adam was not directly behind me. Cynthia was saying something to him. At first, I wondered what she said but forgot when somebody else said, "You can't go into the housing area. The police have it all blocked off." Everybody was reading each other's thoughts, or at least mine. We were so far beyond manners and protocol, and they all knew what I wanted to know. "They came through the woods, about twenty of them, masked, with guns. They lit the fires. Only the outer edge of the woods burned but they got the houses they wanted. Almost all of us got away, coming here or back through the front gate."

Somehow, I controlled an emotional blowout and slid into an unfamiliar role—serious, controlled feelings, like a cop on a TV show. "And how many didn't make it?"

"Only one that we know of. Josephine."

"Where is she now? Her body?"

"An ambulance took her."

"We're going to go back the way we came through the woods and leave going the other direction. We're going to find my parents. And Melinda. We're going to find her. She must have followed the ambulance."

But I already knew she didn't follow anybody. I could feel her presence like it was right next to me, almost inside of me. Was she also gone? The thought made me crumble around the edges, but the cop persona held on a little longer.

We went back outside, down the short peninsula path, across the stone plaza, and back into the woods. "She's here, Adam, I know she is."

"I agree. In these woods somewhere."

"Do you feel it, too?"

"Yes, like she's right next to me."

I didn't know what to make of that. If I hadn't been so scared, I might have had a twinge of jealousy.

It didn't take long to find one of the animal forts, our childhood favorite. I stopped, bent down, and then backed away. I couldn't do it. Adam gently moved me aside and crawled in. I heard cries and moans and soft words. I wormed my way in, and at first, didn't know where to sit. Adam had his back against the tree that the fort was built around and Melinda lay with her head in his lap. Light came from his phone, face-up on the ground, casting an eerie glow through the darkened space and onto Melinda's face. I saw way more of her than I should have, her features distorted in my awareness by her trashed being. I wormed my way behind her so I was pressed against Adam and she was mostly in my lap.

"Can we be in the dark?" I whispered.

Adam turned off the light, but I could still see everything about Melinda. Or maybe only feel her. We stayed silent for a long time, holding onto each other. I was so close to falling apart, to joining her in a pile of mush. But I held it together. I noticed a pulse flowing between us and figured Melinda and I still had something to offer. After a minute, I realized it was coming from Adam, and I wanted to pull away from him. How could anything like that come from him? He had no awareness that he was doing it and my curiosity took over and I tuned into it as much as I possibly could.

Melinda sat up and said, "Stop it. It's annoying."

I'm not doing it. I didn't say it out loud and doubted she had picked up on my thought.

She pushed toward the opening. "I'm getting out of here." The tone of her voice was unlike anything I'd ever heard from her.

I tried to grab onto her hand as she hurried off but she shook it away. In the gloom, Adam didn't notice, and when he did the same, she let him hold on. The woods were now nearly black and she must have been accessing some kind of night vision, her inner owl or bobcat or something, because she hopped and trotted through the brush and scramble, making a direct line to the war zone.

"We can't go in there. The police will stop us."

She didn't answer. The smoke smell grew stronger, and we saw the glow through the forest, but now the dancing orange from the fires had been replaced by white stadium spotlights. The closer we got, the closer I came to having the imagery from my earlier visions switch to the hellishness of this new reality. We heard the voices of the fire squad and whatever police were still there and stopped. We fell to the ground, and like snakes, slithered face-down through the dirt and moss and puffy wood scraps from transitioning trees. Melinda led because she moved the quickest, obviously now the most eager to plow ahead. Her feet were sometimes near my face and sometimes far away and the flits and glimpses I caught of her movements triggered memories of my past progressions. After my sordid event eight years earlier, it had taken me a few weeks to fully embrace rage as a way forward. For Melinda, only a few hours had passed, and she was already deep inside it.

We stopped our forward motion at the edge of the glow and tried to overhear any conversations between the few remaining authorities. We caught part of one that a trooper was having with a fireman, something about the troopers needing to leave, but they first wanted to make sure the fires were fully extinguished. Another trooper said they had arranged for a few vans to take about eighteen residents to Ithaca to stay in a hotel for the night.

A firefighter asked the trooper, "Any word on the one who was taken out of here?"

"I haven't heard anything."

In the final conversation, the agreement became to leave a trooper and firefighter in the parking lot overnight and to check back on the crime scene—they used that description—every hour or so. They dimmed down one of the spotlights, turned off the rest, and left.

We waited another ten minutes, circled to a side of the area, and crept in. I questioned why we would want to go further into the mess, and it didn't take long for me to receive an answer. I only had to step back and watch the movements of the two of them. Melinda had crossed over to a whole new way of being and Adam easily glommed on, his movements and language every bit as aggressive as hers. He stayed at her side, absorbing her—and my—sadness. But being in the center of the action seemed to excite him, letting him slip back into who he was—before the love-bomb, before the trip to Marion—only a few weeks before. His ancient rage came back in full and the two of them in the dull light were like a pair of pumped-up police dogs. I imagined somehow tossing a love-bomb at them right then and what the furious responses would be.

Melinda went directly to the remains of her cabin. She circled the wet, black clumps of former logs and beams, not getting too close, with enough awareness to preserve any of the evidence. A nearby structure still standing displayed red, spray-painted letters reading, "Satan's spawn must die." We went next to my family's cabin and found the same smoking stink of a mess. I circled it one time and turned away, trying to stay calm. Altogether, only two other cabins were destroyed to the same degree as ours and they may have only caught fire because they were too close to the bunkhouse and library infernos. It was blatantly obvious who the primary targets were. It was intentional. One more message from the Hope Community designed to destroy some myth about the greatness of Melinda Breeze and Jade Furlong.

She turned to me, wet, dirty, a face filled with war-anger, and said, "Never, never will they take me down."

Adam didn't answer. I didn't answer. Adam had already entered her arena, and within another minute, so did I. We rushed back through the woods, using our phones as lights when needed, and debated whether we should go back into the temple, to let everybody know Melinda was with us. Melinda said no, I said we should, and Adam offered no opinion. I thought I would go along with Melinda's wishes and text Cynthia once we were on the road. We were almost past when Melinda stopped.

"I changed my mind," she said. No explanation. She turned toward the plaza, nearly jumped down the steep section, and raced across the flat stone to the path to the temple. She opened the door, hurried through, and I followed. Adam waited outside.

The group inside let out a range of sounds, all expressing relief and sadness. She put aside her current vibe and allowed herself to absorb the hugs and condolences, and after a few minutes, said she was going to leave with me and stay with me. Cynthia stood at the door and was the last to comfort us.

We went out and spotted the outline of Adam, in the center of the plaza, looking up at the sky. Melinda said, "He better not call anyone in. Any Extra. This is not the time."

"Oh." I thought she was joking but why would her humor surface now? "What do you mean? Why?"

She hissed out a whisper. "Cynthia in there is Garrett Kastner's mother."

"How do you know that?"

"I can smell it all over her. But don't tell Adam. Not now."

It wasn't possible, she had to be wrong. But I remembered seeing Cynthia whisper something to Adam. What did that mean? I shoved the whole idea out of my brain and concentrated on getting us back to my car. Adam offered to drive and asked us if we wanted to both sit in the back seat so we could be close, Melinda didn't answer and I said, *yes*, opened the door and directed her in, then followed and pushed close next to her. She didn't move away and instead, slowly slipped down in the seat until her head rested on my shoulder. I smelled the dirt and forest, her sweat and salty breath, and a hint of some new shampoo she had tried. I took her hands and gently squeezed them.

Adam slowly backed the car down the rutted dirt path until he found a space large enough to turn around. He faced forward, sped up a little, and a bump pushed Melinda and me together. I got her and held on tight. She did the same.

"Our mother is gone," she said. She didn't say *my*, she said *our*. Adam stayed respectfully silent but heard every detail of our collapse. The rage thankfully left but the space behind it was filled with all the other stuff, all the fixings for a long rough ride.

Adam

Adam drove through the dark, composing and saying silent prayers. At first, he wanted more than anything to stop and hold them, comfort them, and try to take their pain away. But when he looked in the rear-view mirror and saw them bundled together as one, he saw them as something so exquisite that he knew it was best to just stay silent and try to put out positive thoughts. Mourning was such an elusive practice. Yet so important. Had he ever actually mourned his brother? Or did he just stay wildly angry for years and years? Even in all the emotion and chaos, he had watched Melinda carefully as she moved through the different ways of being in her initial meeting with grief. *She moves through it quickly because that is who she is*, And Jade took over as the more grounded, rational half, even though she also grieved. *They're both so interesting. Unlike anybody I've ever known.*

Yet he doubted the stubborn in-your-face anger had made a final exit. He had seen it and knew so well that, once it makes an appearance, it never leaves. He'd even observed himself latching right on when Melinda let it out for all to see—although, only two humans and a crowd of forest creatures were there as witnesses.

261

He recalled a phrase he'd heard somewhere that he used to dislike but he had now begun to understand its worth and beauty—*Do what you must do with others but never throw them out of your heart*. He imagined the two women in the seat behind him applying the phrase's philosophy to whatever was coming next for them. We'll tear your fucking walls down, destroy your entire operation…and then rain love-bombs all over you. He wasn't even close to being there yet, but he wanted to believe they were. The more he thought about it, he had to believe they were because who else had enough insight into what was happening in the Hope insanity and had an actual ability to get inside and document it further? A most disturbing thought came next. You collect all the information, organize it, make it into something, and then what? Who, in the outside world of Normals, who might have the power to shut Hope down, was ever going to believe it was real?

They arrived at Jade's apartment and decided they would all stay there. They scrounged a few things to eat but nobody was hungry, and they went to bed early. Jade and Melinda slept in the bedroom, Adam set up on the couch, and nobody slept more than an hour at a stretch. Around three in the morning, Adam woke out of a dream in which he'd been back standing in the middle of the stone plaza, looking up, this time into a bright night sky. He was conscious now, but the vision continued. The multicolored bands of light shimmered overhead, hovering, surrounding, preparing. Was one of them ready for him? Wanting him? It was still too soon but he was getting close.

He fell back asleep, woke with the sunrise, and sat up, trying to prepare for his day. He carefully folded the blanket he had slept under and the sheet he'd laid on, filthy from his clothes which were still crusty and dirty from crawling through the woods the day before. Jade came out shortly after and sat next to him. He told her about his dream or vision or whatever it was.

"I'm almost ready," he said, "and if we can make it through these next few weeks without crashing and burning, I'd like you and Melinda to call it in, however it is you do it."

"The problem is, I don't even know how it works anymore. Do we have a choice of who comes in? Did we ever have a choice?"

"As Old Elwood might have said to me, that's the trillion-dollar question. But I trust the two of you, I guess, more than I've ever trusted anybody."

"Do you, Adam? That's saying an awful lot because right now I do not have a whole lot of trust in myself. And Melinda, my life-long hero. She's a mess, a real mess. She moaned some things in her sleep that were so out of character, like scary, angry things."

"Yeah, but I observed you both through the whole insanity yesterday. Like really watched. "You're both...."

She shook her head and changed the subject. "What are you doing today?"

"Not much. What are you doing today?"

She begged. "Adam, please. Please don't try to get into Hope with us. They will do something so awful to you if they catch you."

"Okay. But this is what's going to happen. If you get in trouble in any way, you will contact me. It doesn't matter how. You will just do it."

"And then what? What would you do?"

"If I did nothing, I couldn't live with myself anyway so something, anything, is better than nothing."

Jade drove Adam to his car, still on a street near the Clark campus, they said their goodbyes, and he headed toward Oakwood, toward the sanctuary of his bedroom. He parked on the street in front of his house because his father's car was blocking the driveway as if he'd come home for a minute to pick something up and was about to leave again. His mother's car was gone. His father's car. It triggered something that had happened, a small ten second interaction he had forgotten about amidst the chaos of the day before. When Cynthia Louder touched his shoulder, leaned into his ear and said just loud enough for only him to hear, "Take care of those two girls. I know how much you love them." Cynthia Louder, not Cynthia Kaster. But still Cynthia. And she had Garrett Kastner written all over her face.

He heard his father in the kitchen, went in, and found him shuffling through a pile of mail. "Morning Clifford, where's Ingrid?"

His father looked up. "It's one of those days? First names and all? What have you been up to?"

The last sentence, coming out of his father's mouth, flipped a switch, activated all Adam's anger circuits, and made him finally ready for the confrontation he'd imagined for weeks. "Helping to put out fires."

Clifford stopped and looked hard at Adam. "What do you mean?"

"I also got to stand in the big stone plaza and look up at the sky and imagine what could be on its way down to wrap itself inside my entire being and help me be something special. Right? And then, I got to help Melinda Breeze deal with the death of her mother, who I know you were tight with because I followed you the other night. Who else do you know down there in Anderson? Jade's parents? The Furlongs" He called up the other name, the one that matched somebody he'd known about for years but never met. He took a shot at it and spit out, "Maybe you know Cynthia. I met her in the temple. Is she your ex? Garrett's mother?"

"Stop, Adam. Stop. Just sit down. Please. Just sit."

"I can't sit down. I don't even know who you are. What father would not tell his own kid what's been wrong with him his whole life?

And even worse, what was wrong with his brother? Because, if I give it any more thought, I will begin to understand what Garrett meant when he told me a body like mine would have been more suitable for him. He wasn't talking about just the physical body, was he? He meant the entire Adam Kastner package, didn't he?"

Clifford stood and tried to put his hands on Adam's shoulders, but Adam backed away. "We tried, we tried so hard. But it all went backward. Nothing worked as it was supposed to."

"Wait. Are you telling me that my mother, Ingrid, who thinks this whole Extra thing is not even real was there right after my birth participating in a baptism? Or—or—how would you have ever taken a baby, less than a week old away from his mother? Is that what you did? She wasn't even there?"

Clifford sat back down, slumped into his chair, and closed his eyes. He whispered, "You were already ten months old. And your mother didn't know. The Light that was meant to go to you was a very special one, but it flowed into Garrett instead of you. We tried so hard to have it work for him but he could never contain it."

"We? Who's we? The Reconfiguration people?"

Clifford jumped up and raised his voice. "I am not talking about those people at all. And you need to back away from this. You and those girls. You think they're something so different from all the rest of us and you're right. They are that. But you saw what just happened in Anderson. They are no match for the people who did it."

"What about Sara Leeds?"

"Is that who you've been working with?"

"Yes."

"She is the worst of all of them."

Adam went to his room, laid on his bed, and eventually fell asleep. An hour later he heard his father's car leave and he got up, took a long shower, and made an eggs-and-toast breakfast. When he finished, he looked through the refrigerator and the cabinets and decided to go grocery shopping. He worked up a list, collected some reusable bags, and left. He turned a few corners and noticed a new-looking white sedan following him. When he pulled into the parking lot, the sedan stayed close behind him. They weren't even trying to be subtle. They wanted a confrontation so they could deliver some nasty threats. *Bring it on, creeps.*

The white car parked next to him and he got out and walked toward the driver's side. Before he got there, the door opened, and Sara Leeds stepped out. She was dressed much differently than he had seen her before: a knit ski hat pulled down to her eyebrows, a winter coat, and baggy pants, likely pulled over long underwear.

He scanned her in a way she would relate to, observing every detail. "It's not that cold up here. And your car. Is it yours or a rental?"

She forced a smile. "Have you seen enough? I can spin around if you like. Or raise my arms and you can search for weapons. I dressed like this because I generally don't leave my apartment when it gets cold and, yes, the car is a rental. I don't need to own one in the city."

"Should I be flattered that you came all the way up here and tracked me down so you can see me in person?"

"I don't know about flattered but it should establish my level of concern."

"Sara, let me just say that it is becoming increasingly clear who and what you are and exactly why you're here right now. My biggest question now is about Carter Freedman. Was he in on it from the beginning, this plan to ultimately either suck me into the Hope cult or divert me far away from it? I get it that my whole idea of a story never had a chance in hell of happening."

"Whatever I answer, you're not going to believe me. But I'll still give it a shot. Carter Freedman is way too busy with other projects to get so involved in this one. Although, after yesterday's event in Anderson, he might change his mind. And then there is this. You said you think you know who and what I am. The only response I can give to that is, you do not know."

"I asked my father just twenty minutes ago what he knew about Sara Leeds and his response was, " 'She's the worst of all of them.' "

"This from the man who never told his own kids exactly who *they* were."

He wondered if the dreamy feeling was about to start, the travels away from himself, the sleepiness, the forgetting. No. He was past that response. He stayed present, tamped down his anger, and fear and asked in the calmest voice, "Why are you here, Sara?"

"To tell you that the best and safest course of action right now is to step away from Hope, from Jade and Melinda and anybody else involved with Anderson, and even from your father. Go hide out somewhere for a few weeks. And when all of this craziness settles, I know what you want and I can facilitate it. I know there are Extras of the best sort out there who would be honored to have you as a host."

"Except that, the idea of you or my father or somebody from Hope or even an Elder from Anderson fucking around with me in that way is absolutely repulsive. No, no way. You just keep away from me. The time will come, and either the only two people I would trust to help will be there, or if you wipe them out somehow, I'll do it myself."

"Well okay, Adam. All I can say then is good luck with that."

He couldn't tell if she was fighting back a smirk. Whatever she was doing, the look on her face was unpleasant.

Jade

When Adam left, I wondered if I would ever see him again. So much about our relationship made sense now, yet so many questions remained unanswered. I was beginning to enter a deeply connected relationship with him and one of the results was that the thought of real harm coming his way was unbearable. I closed my eyes and reflected on the concept of harm. It had visited us in a horrific way and likely was not finished. It hung now around the edges, eagerly awaiting its next chilling move. I begged for a space where I could go and gather up the threads of acceptance for whatever came next. I would weave a blanket, not to shield me, but to keep me a little bit warmer if and when the next frigid blast roared through.

I texted my parents and they both responded. I told them Melinda was with me at my apartment, and we were taking care of each other. I knew what to do to process what had happened and we would stay together, there, for as long as it took. I didn't ask where they were or for any other details. I didn't want to know.

I opened my eyes and Melinda stood in front of me, trying to smile but looking like absolute hell. I suppose I didn't look any better.

"What do we do now?" I asked.

"We change the sheets and take a shower. Dirt and leaves are everywhere."

We took a shower together, something we hadn't done since we were little kids. We gently washed each other's skin, scrubbing off the muck and slime, and then shampooed each other's hair. At another time, the whole process could have been something romantic, and I suppose that even then it was still a version of it, but as I washed her, my overriding desire was to soap away some of the pain.

After we dressed, I made pancakes for breakfast and insisted we both eat. Then I insisted on something else.

"Melinda, listen. We're not going in there today. Not, not, not. We can practice if you feel up for it because we do have to figure out a few things. But nothing dangerous today."

"Jade."

"No!"

"Hey, chill out. I agree with you. I'm exactly where you are. Except, I didn't get to say goodbye to Adam."

"Are you in love with him?" I asked. "I mean big picture love kind of thing."

"I am most certainly that." Her eyes teared up. "It would have been much worse yesterday if he hadn't been there."

"He asked me if some time in the future we would help him find an Extra. He says he's ready and doesn't want anybody else to do it but us."

"Oh. What does that even mean anymore?"

The grief came in waves. I sat next to her, distracted, and then we would hold onto each other, mostly crying, and sometimes remembering and laughing. When one of the rounds had run its course, she said she was ready and wanted to practice. We again laid out mats and pillows and stretched and meditated. Ultimately, we wanted to leave our bodies at the same time and somehow stay connected to each other. But we didn't know how it would work or even if it was possible. I suggested we first try to only go as far as the apartment ceiling because I knew it would be easy individually since I had done it only a few days before. After that, we could experiment with establishing our connection.

We lifted out and rolled over to see our bodies below, quiet, unmoving, seemingly asleep. I looked at whatever it was next to me, this essence of Melinda, and examined it—her—this aspect of her being. She was mostly transparent but if I looked at her a certain way, I could see outlines of her body parts, especially her hands and face. Oddly, it was the same when I looked at myself, something I had paid no attention to—or maybe it wasn't there for me to see— the last time I had done this. Melinda swished her hand over mine and I felt a familiar tingle which caused some concern about the process being too strong in certain situations.

The thought entered my mind that I wanted to return, and Melinda voiced her agreement directly into my thoughts. Oh, what a charge that was. Our minds had connected. One of my biggest fears going forward, that we wouldn't be able to communicate through speech or actions, gently slipped away. With this new awareness, I allowed myself to acknowledge how great my fear was of what we were planning. The idea of entering any of the Hope warehouse buildings again, by myself, was just too dreadful to contemplate. But, teamed up with Melinda? A whole different adventure.

We sat—back in our bodies—went over the details of what we had just done, and decided on the plan for round two. This time we would pass through the sidewall of my apartment and hover over the streets. We wanted to see if we could move from one point to another and coordinate our movements with each other. We left our bodies and stayed so close together that our essences touched. I felt an energy surge, hot, zingy, and unpleasant, and moved away. *"Oh well*, she said. *We'll still be okay."*

We slid through the apartment wall to the bright outside and marveled that, like nosy crows from high above, nobody could see us as we observed them. We rose about a hundred feet and followed the sidewalk to the first corner, then turned, and kept turning until we'd gone around the entire block. We re-entered the building and our bodies, and compared notes, even though we both knew what each other had thought about everything. We just wanted to be sure.

"Sunlight," she said.

"Yes. Beautiful colors coming through us but it's hard to negotiate."

"Shadows."

"We will visually disappear in the dark."

"Yet still see other objects."

"Any other sensory input?"

"I could hear quite well but feel nothing."

We both began to receive numerous texts and phone calls from our group's members and did our best to respond immediately. We emphasized that we were together and were spending the day in a healing process. At this stage in our lives, nobody would question us about it, not even my parents. I imagined at some point we would be contacted by police investigators, but right then, I couldn't focus enough to put together a plan. I believed that, since I had not been spotted by the police in Anderson and Melinda possibly hadn't either, we might have a few more days to come up with the best response.

I brought it up and Melinda said, "This is a unique position for us. For once, the best response is to tell the simple truth. Not about who we are and all that and certainly not about what we're about to do. But we have to remember, all we did was drive to our home to see our parents. There's nothing wrong with that."

"You just said, *what we're about to do*."

"I did, didn't I."

We nodded, sighed, and shook a little. I hugged her so tight I thought we would both break and she returned it. We stayed together for a long time. The word, forever, flitted by and I didn't dare think what it might mean.

I opened Google Earth again on my laptop, the same as before, and again zoomed into the three Hope warehouses. In case we could only make it through one of them, we picked the center one. We laid down again on our mats, made ourselves as comfortable as possible, Melinda kissed me on the cheek, I squeezed her hand, and off we went.

We entered through the roof of the middle warehouse and into a new sensory experience, the overwhelming power of smell. We were in what looked like a produce preparation room, with large cubicle areas for the different types of produce. Some had industrial sinks, some packaging apparatus, and almost all had crates, large bags, and shiny metal tables. We saw beets, carrots, potatoes, squash, pumpkins, and so much more. It would be a perfect room to bring newcomers, tourists, beginners—or whatever the innocent types might be called—because it looked and smelled wholesome and harmless. Three workers, obviously well-versed in their jobs, rushed around below. We hugged the high ceiling in case one of them looked up and had some special ability. Just in case.

We burst through an inside wall to a larger area containing a row of small offices and various types of agricultural machinery such as tractors, harvesters, and hay balers. To the side sat a large backhoe. About ten or so people milled around doing different tasks. We considered going through the floor but had a powerful sense that whatever was below was not of much interest. We floated around, again clinging to the ceiling as much as possible, and exited at the far wall to the outside.

We entered the final building which was devoted to experimental ways to grow produce indoors including water, air, or soil for the plant roots to anchor in, many lighting configurations, and complex structures to support the different plants. A few of the water-based structures contained fish that would supply plant nutrients with their waste. Again, the room's entire operation was a perfect cover for what we knew was still happening elsewhere on the property. And again, what lay beneath the vast room did not call out to us.

I transferred to Melinda that I wanted to leave for a bit, go back to our physical bodies to regroup. She agreed and a moment later we re-entered ourselves, shook and twitched, and sat up. We looked at each other with squinted dazed eyes, mouths hanging open.

"I can't believe we just did what we did," she said. A glimmer of happiness swirled around her.

"We need to think carefully about our next step. We know where we have to go and it will be much more intense. And then what? What do we do with the info we gather? Information is useless if it can't be used to end the whole operation. It's not like we can go in there and unlock doors and let the humans out."

She let out a long sigh. "Adam is the only possibility. He'll have to put something together and get it out to the media or the police or something. I imagine the mess in Anderson is all over the news, so if he connects it with Hope, at least it might drum up an interest for the authorities to investigate."

"But the mess at our home means whatever craziness Hope wants to do is just about to happen."

"I'm going to try to contact Adam."

I felt like my body had a layer of mud clinging to it. "I'm going to take another shower."

I stood under the water and visualized a police raid on Hope liberating maybe ten or twenty humans and then we would sneak back in and set free all the Extras. How could it possibly work? It couldn't. It was all too late. Adam Kastner meant well but this was so much more complex than something he could pull off in the next day or so. I finished the shower and Melinda said she'd had a good conversation with him, that he would come by later after we returned from our next travel round, and we would work on the next step. They had also discussed a few other items, but I didn't learn exactly what until much later.

We waited until the sun slid away, took up our positions, and prepared to go. While still in our bodies, we didn't hug or say much of anything. We now had experience and believed we were ready. We didn't use Google Earth to pacify our human doubts because we knew exactly where we were going.

The empty warehouse greeted me with the same sensation of nothingness I had experienced before, this time with an even more potent feeling of existential horror. We didn't need or wish to re-enter the section containing the drugged-out Extras and planned our entrance to be directly above the concrete floor at the other end of the building. I transferred to Melinda that we should go right through. I received no response. I tried again and still no response. I moved upward toward the ceiling and tried to scan the entire blank area, but like the last time, only encountered nothing. My essence felt as if it was about to come apart and I dipped to the concrete floor. I didn't want to go through and realized I couldn't anyway. Real-world time lost its meaning. The space had me trapped, waiting, waiting for something. I only wanted to leave but didn't dare try. Not without Melinda. Never without her.

Adam

After Adam's meeting with Sara Leeds, he couldn't bear the thought of returning to his parents' house and instead drove to a motel north of Albany with an early check-in. He psyched himself up to spend the rest of the day writing but wasn't sure what he would write about. He sat for a while and then started a timeline of what had happened every day for the last three weeks. First, he created headlines for the major events, such as his meeting in Rhinecliff by the Hudson River with Jade and Melinda and then went back and wrote a detailed paragraph or two about each event. Considering what had happened the day before, the process filled him with anxiety, and a few times, he had to stop and distract himself with daytime TV shows.

In the early evening, when his phone screen lit up with Melinda's number, the knot of tension drained out of him. She assured him they were okay and promised they would get together within the next day. All good. She gave a one-minute synopsis of their out-of-body travels. A little tension seeped back in but, what did he expect? Now that they knew where to look, they were going back to observe the entire Hope underground operation and they hoped Adam could put something together that would be suitable to present to Normals in positions of authority. He said he could do it and would do anything she wanted. She asked if he would consider hosting her Extra layer should something happen to her. He choked out an affirmative. She told him she loved him and Jade loved him and he said the same.

What if something happened to Jade? If her Extra came his way, of course he would welcome it in. But what if something happened to both of them? Maybe then, his entire world would just have to fall apart.

A few hours later, his phone rang again, this time with a call from Sara Leeds. He knew he shouldn't answer but he couldn't resist. "Are you back in the city?"

She sounded desperate. "Adam, I need to see you again. I have something I want to give you."

"You're still here, aren't you?"

"Yes. Please. I beg you. If everything goes to hell, which it likely will, I want you to have a backup."

"A backup. Like a backup plan or an actual thumb drive or something?"

"Both."

"You gotta be kidding. This is like something out of a really bad movie. Like, when we meet, two huge creepy dudes are going to grab me and stuff me into the back of a black limo."

"We can meet in a safe place. Anywhere you want."

"Sara, if I'm going to do this you have to tell me why."

"I don't have time. Please come get this."

Ten minutes later, he walked into a coffee shop connected to a department store in a crowded mall. Sara sat at a small two-seat table against the far wall, sipping a latte, a half-eaten scone on a plate in front of her, and he rushed over and sat across from her. She stayed silent, handed him a thumb drive, and started to get up. "No way, Sara," he said. "You can give me three minutes to explain what you're up to. And before you start, are our phones tapped?"

"Our phones are not tapped, we're not being watched, and we weren't followed. Extras don't need to do any of that, do they?"

"Tell me what's on the drive."

"Everything. Voice recordings, event outlines, even photos."

"And what are you going to do with it?"

She took a gulp from her cup, looked around the room and back at him. "I don't have to do anything. They already have it."

"They meaning…"

She didn't answer the question. Instead, "Within the next day, I believe a massive influx of Extra layers are going to transfer into at least fifty, possibly as many as a hundred people. People who are currently being held in parts of Hope and other locations. People who suddenly disappear for a few days and then come back all ready to go. All programmed to follow the leader. This is the start and it can't happen, do you understand? It will spread everywhere like a nasty virus."

It couldn't be possible. No way. She had been undercover the whole time? If it was true, then he now understood who she was, or who he hoped she was. He had come on the scene, her scene, thinking he was going to do some great story and had been, at the very least an annoyance, and possibly an outright danger.

"How did you do it, Sara? I know you're an Extra, but didn't Max Schultz and Olivia Santini and many others know what you were doing?"

She whispered, "We all have our special powers, I guess."

"And the people who have your info. Don't tell me who they are. I only want to know: they're not Extras, are they?"

"I sure hope not."

"But why are the Hope monsters so fixated on Melinda and Jade?"

"The same reason they were after your brother. When you have as part of you an Extra layer that big and powerful, they want it for themselves. And they know it's a long slow process to get it undamaged."

Adam rushed out of the mall and drove as fast as he dared back to Jade's apartment. He had to warn them to not go into the Hope property. There was no need and there was nothing they could do, anyway. He parked and hurried to the door, knocked a few times, then tried to open it. It wasn't locked and he pushed his way in and ran through the rooms. All empty. Where were they? He stepped back and scanned, first the kitchen, where nothing seemed out of place, and then the living room, with the mats laid out on the floor and the cushions strewn all over. Jade and Melinda were both fanatically neat and it seemed unlikely that they would not have straightened up before they left. And they certainly would have locked the front door. He picked up a few of the cushions and under one found an object that erased any doubts about what had transpired: a large hypodermic needle with a small bit of liquid still in its tube.

Jade

My own life force desperately wanted me to stay whole, to stop this foolish disconnection I had believed was so necessary, and it sucked me through the floor with unimaginable force. As I came through the floor/ceiling, I caught a micro-second flash of my new environment, my new home: a sterile white windowless hospital room with machines, tubes, monitors, and two white-sheeted beds. In one bed was the Jade Furlong body, my body, appearing whole and undamaged as if she was enjoying a pleasant sleep. In the bed next to her was Melinda Breeze, and her body had a different presentation. As I reentered Jade, I brought with me the knowledge that my life companion, lying so close next to me, was seriously broken in many ways.

Our captors could easily kill us if they wanted to. This myth about Extras not being able to kill humans is not entirely true. Oh sure, somebody like Max Schultz or Olivia Santini can't give a direct order, but they can give a hint to a Billy Squires type who then passes it on to an even more deranged Extra, or possibly a Normal, and they will do the job. As I lay there, back in my body, about to set sail on the stormiest ocean imaginable, what these people wanted from Melinda and me presented itself with perfect clarity: they wanted our Extras and they wanted them to leave our bodies of their own free will. If they killed us, the Extras would leave so quickly, they would be hard to contain and likely get away. If they somehow forced the Extras out of us, they likely would become seriously damaged and of no use. So, in the warped minds of these Hope people, the most workable solution would be to slowly and carefully destroy our minds and bodies so the Extras would slip out quietly and gently, with just the right amount of abuse to keep them submissive and agreeable to enter a new host.

I finally admitted to myself that my Extra configuration with my human body, this Jade Furlong being, was indeed something special, something unique, as was the one lying next to me. At first, the awareness caused me to cling to a belief, a wish, that ours were so integrated and loyal to their complete beings that nothing could sever us. I wanted a predictable controlled outcome and the thought brought me comfort. I quickly learned that this infinite ocean I was about to enter would have none of it. No life raft would be bouncing around in the waves to grab on to, no helicopters circling overhead to pull me out, no distant shore I could possibly swim to. Well, actually, there was some of that, but I knew if I clung to any of it, the whole game was over.

A man I had never seen before came in the room, turned on a few machines, and attached electrodes to parts of my head and some kind of heart monitor to my chest. Then he fussed around with my arm like he was about to shoot me up with something. Whatever somebody had given me earlier still put a freeze on my body so I couldn't pull away. But I spoke, although I'm not sure if it was out loud.

"What are you giving me?"

He eagerly responded. It was part of the fear plan— scare me to near death, literally. "An interesting mixture of a high dose of

Ayahuasca, LSD, and a rough and unpleasant psychedelic we created here. We call the mixture, Disintegration. Have Fun."

As he put the needle in my arm, I said, "I love you."

"Not a chance."

He left. He hadn't bothered with Melinda which was both a relief and a concern. Was she that far gone?

My first musing was about the relationship many humans have with some of the more sentient and physically powerful members of non-human species. When I was around ten, I had a brief obsession with elephants who are sometimes in tight relationships with humans, usually in a subservient role. Circus elephants and those helping forest loggers do exactly what their human overseers command them to, even though, with one sweep of their mighty feet or trunks, they could knock these puny humans aside and refuse their orders. When Extras enter, are they subservient to their human hosts in the same way elephants sometimes are? Even when their hosts are awful? Why do they bother with us? I never thought of my Extra layer as subservient, only that it was an integrated part of myself. Which made me what? Special? Was I special when I was twenty years old and yelled and screamed and hated? How could it have stood me?

The next paragraph of my musing switched to something wonderful, beautiful, sacred even. My Extra layer didn't ever have to nervously and awkwardly put up with me, because it *wanted* to be with me, tight within me, acting on its primary purpose which was to teach me, and likely also itself, how to love. Unconditionally.

Next up. Nothing like a fearful string of dark thoughts to flip the script in your mind. Cosmic bliss to cosmic dread, in one millisecond. *They will never get this out of me. Never! Or will they? What about Garrett Kastner? They removed his layer and then he ended his life. Because he could when he went back to being a Normal. Where did his Extra end up? Why is this thought pestering me right now, moments before my final destruction? Oh yes, Adam Kastner, the Extra being without the layer. My new best friend who is just another Normal human yet so much more, waiting, waiting for what is…what? What is rightfully his? Oh, no! Now I get it. He will ride in on his great white stallion, coming to our rescue, and the lovely evil Max and Olivia will usher him into his new golden palace and bribe him with a prize he can't resist, the Extra his brother briefly wore, the one his brother couldn't handle, the one the evil ones tore out of him and have been saving for just the right moment. For Adam, the only Normal being who could possibly be the perfect match for an Extra layer so unique and powerful.*

I tried to invade Adam Kastner's mind and warn him to keep away. *Do not come here! It is far better that we die. For us and everyone else on the planet.* It was a pathetic attempt. I surely understood the purpose of the warehouse's space of empty hell above me, designed to skillfully block such small efforts. Who was I to think I could change the outcome of one more classic battle between so-called good and evil? This is how humanity began and this is how humanity will end, and what was happening now would only be a small chapter, a few pages, in the trillion-page journal.

In another shift, I lost full control of what poured through my thought paths. Next came a 3D video with no end, with clips of the worst nightmares, and for added effect, the greatest joys a human can imagine. The first one was a dramatic replay of my own deep trauma, and after so many years of processing it, examining it from every angle, extracting every nugget of knowledge possible from it, I answered with a snotty response: *big fucking deal, Hope Devils. Is that all you got?* I must have said this out loud—or perhaps it was just me speaking back to myself— because I heard: *A snotty response to your own worst experience? Not very respectful, Jade.* However, the interaction served to open up something inside me which I'm sure ran contrary to the intentions of those behind the controls. At that key moment, I was able to grab onto the truth—just like life in our vast universe, I couldn't control what was coming my way, but I could still control my reaction to it. It must have been me talking to myself because the voice, now without a trace of snottiness, continued: *Your survival depends on your presence and acceptance. Focus, Jade, focus.*

A high-pitched noise, an amped-up tinnitus, rattled my hearing. A smell that passed through my nose and into my lungs made breathing unbearable. All designed to enhance the disturbance of the following clips which would certainly be much worse than the last one. I got it now. My only defense would be no defense at all, and I would mix it up with a brew of love and kindness toward all the horrible and sometimes wonderful things we humans are capable of. I asked myself where this simple and powerful potion, this way of being that might be salvation, had come from, and the answer stood right in front of me. The part of me I still can't fully understand and never will, my blessed Extra being, delivered it as its most honored gift. It allowed me to enter a space where one cares so deeply for all things yet still views them as only passing clouds in the sky, sometimes stormy and sometimes bright. But even with all the help from my Extra layer, this space was slippery and illusive, and when I got off track, the added pulse of another Extra, housed in the bed next to me, snuck in a few choice morsels to get me righted again. The movie, and our entire existence, would go on and on with nothing to stop it, and right then, I finally comprehended, even embodied, that the best I could do, as I was about to die in so many ways, was to always strive, with love, to lessen the suffering of all things.

Something began to crash above me, rough, metallic, and consistent, like a hammer beating on a metal garage door. That was it. Somebody above was beating in the doors to the Room of Nothingness, the Existential Hell Hall, trying to let in the life of real, outside, planetary atmosphere. When the noise stopped, I imagined people rushing in, but I couldn't hear footsteps or voices because the floor/ceiling had purposely been built to isolate the above from the below. I tried to sit up but my body could not respond. A minute later, the man who had shot me up earlier came back with two others, each pushing an empty gurney. The man gave me a shot and that is the last thing I remember until I woke later in entirely new surroundings.

Adam

Adam called his father and it went to voicemail. He begged him to call back, that it was urgent. He had another idea, went into the bedroom, and found phones on nightstands on either side of the bed. Either one would have numbers for Jade's parents. He tried one but he needed a thumbprint to unlock it. The other one required a few numbers, easier but still likely to take hours to hit the correct sequence. He tried one, two, three, four and it opened. He had a flash of amusement that it belonged to Jade, whose concern with such minor details was not always there. He leafed through her Contacts and found only two Furlongs with male names, and since he didn't want to call Sam, her younger brother who was thankfully out of the country, he tried Damien. This again went to a voice mail, and he again asked for a return call as soon as possible.

He got through to Therese Furlong. "Oh, hi Jade. Is everything all right?"

"Mrs. Furlong, this is Adam Kastner, Jade's friend. I think we have a problem."

Her voice tensed. "Is Jade with you?"

"I'm sorry. I just got here and they're both gone and I think the Hope people took them."

"Oh no, oh no." Silence. Then, "Do you know how long ago it happened?"

"I talked to Melinda, let me think, about three hours ago. And they were together. Do you know where my father is?"

"He's here meeting with some people. Maybe you should come here."

"Where are you?"

She gave him the address. It was the same townhouse he'd followed his father to a few days earlier. He wound through the dark streets, becoming increasingly upset, confused, and desperate. Anger took over. These Hope characters, the same ones who had taken his brother from him, had now taken the only people he had ever imagined could replace him. He had let Jade and Melinda into his heart and now they were about to be savagely ripped out of it. He considered driving directly to Hope and forcing his way in but how stupid would that be? Another possibility emerged. He pulled off the road and called Sara Leeds.

"Adam, are you all right?"

"No, not at all. They broke into Jade's apartment and took them both. I even found the hypodermic needle they used to knock them out. Sara, if it will do any good, I'll go to the police right now. Or anything you say."

"No, no. Oh my God, Adam. This is so horrible. I can do something. Possibly, I don't know. I'll try to get in touch with my main connection. I usually can. I'll tell him two women who grew up in the Anderson Land Trust were just kidnapped and likely being held at Hope."

"Will he believe it's true?"

"Not unless there's some verification. But he'll believe I think it's true. Which might be enough to get the whole thing rolling."

"He can call me if it helps."

"I'll tell him that. And I'll call you if I get any further information. Adam, please don't go there."

He drove the rest of the way, parked under a tree across the street from the townhouse, and sat for a minute, watching to see if anyone came or went. He grabbed his backpack from the back seat, crossed the street, knocked on the door, and went in. Four people, two men and two women, surrounded him. One of the men was his father and one of the women was Jade's mother. And the other woman, Cynthia Louder.

Clifford, his father, introduced everybody: Therese and Damien, Jade's parents; and Cynthia, who he now was positive was Garrett's birth mother.

Therese said, "Just use first names, Adam. It's easier that way."

They led him into the living room, a sterile middle-class American space looking like it was straight out of a home goods magazine. The artwork on the walls broke the stereotype. On each wall was a large painting, possibly all by the same artist, depicting a different story behind the merge of a human with their Extra layer. The one facing him showed a young man on his knees, his eyes closed and hands folded in prayer, with the glowing band of light turning the part of his body translucent where it had already entered. All around him were darkened skeletons of buildings like in a nighttime war zone.

They had him sit in a wooden chair, somewhat in the middle of the room. He counted four open laptops on various tables, and by instinct, reached into his pack and pulled his out. They all sat and looked at him expectantly.

"I don't think I have any information. I'm sorry."

"Just recount anything you experienced," Damien said.

He didn't want to reveal what Jade and Melinda had been doing, sneaking into Hope, but what other option did he have? They had a right to know and any far-fetched possibility of getting them back needed to be discussed. He told them everything. Except for anything to do with Sara Leeds.

"In my last conversation with Melinda, she said something about going back to the empty warehouse, the one Jade first entered. They planned on exploring the entire space underneath. Where all the secrets are, she said."

Damien broke in, "We have to go to Hope right now. We don't have a choice."

They all agreed, and Adam realized he also didn't have a choice.

He pulled the thumb drive out of his pocket and said in the calmest voice he could muster, "I have something here we might want to look at first." He turned to Clifford. "Dad, when I asked you about Sara Leeds, you didn't have a positive response. And maybe you're right and she's only been playing me. But she gave me this thumb drive, and said she's been undercover for a long time—not as an Extra and I do believe you know she is one—but working with legal authorities who she wouldn't name, as a concerned citizen. These authorities supposedly have all this information already and are about to make a raid on Hope."

He looked at each one of them for a response. They all showed various degrees of surprise. He put the drive into the port on his laptop and looked through the files. Everybody else gathered around. He didn't get far before everyone agreed it was real and potent.

"Why does Sara think they're about to do a raid."

"She said they've been planning it for a while. I told her about the kidnapping, and she said it just might be the final bit of information they need."

Clifford said, "We need to get updated information."

"I have an idea," Adam said. He did searches on Facebook until he found two neighborhood groups in the area of the Hope Community, joined them, and looked for recent posts. He found one describing a police roadblock on a road leading to Hope and another saying police cars, ambulances, and a Swat vehicle were spotted in the area.

"Now we do have to go," Damien said.

They all agreed. Clifford left his car and drove with Adam, and the three others drove together. The sun had set and full darkness was quickly moving in. Clifford searched his phone for shortcuts and faster routes and Adam focused on his driving. They didn't speak much but Adam found, as the trip progressed, that he appreciated the company. About five miles from the compound, on a deserted back road, an ambulance, with no flashing lights or sirens blaring, stormed around a curve from the other direction, slid out of its lane, and swerved, just missing Adam's car. An inside light dimly illuminated the cab, and he caught a glimpse of the driver. He slammed on his brakes and twisted into a u-turn before he was completely stopped, shaking Clifford into the passenger door.

"What the hell are you doing?"

"I saw it. I know I did. You're not going to believe me, but I did."

He sped up until he tailgated the ambulance. He put on his flashers and smacked his horn a few times. The ambulance tried to speed up, to get away, but he stayed right with it. They came to a long straight stretch, and he went into the other lane and pulled alongside the ambulance.

"Dad, roll your window down. Make sure I'm right."

"Oh my God. How can this be? She's pulling over."

Adam slowed way down and slid to a stop behind the ambulance. They both jumped out and ran to it just as the driver's door opened. A small woman with dark curly hair, dark skin, and an attempt at a smile, climbed out and ran to them, hugging them and crying.

"They're in the back," Josephine said. "Both of them. And they're not good."

Adam flung open the rear doors and climbed in. Two gurneys, one with Melinda and one with Jade, both strapped in and unconscious, occupied the entire space. The gurneys were also strapped and locked into place.

"Can we move them?" Adam asked. "Is it safe?"

"Jade will do better," Josephine said. "Melinda had a broken foot or something, I think. And something else is way off with her. But we have no choice."

They unlocked Jade's gurney, unstrapped her, and tilted the gurney platform so that she slid into the waiting arms of Clifford and Adam. They carefully positioned her in the backseat of Adam's car and then repeated the operation with Melinda. Josephine climbed in and sat between them. A few miles later, a state trooper's vehicle zipped by in the other direction. Clifford opened his phone and began looking for a way off the road in case the trooper came back, looking for answers about the ambulance he would surely notice.

"You have a signal?"

"Not much. One bar."

Adam spotted a seasonal dirt road and swerved onto it. "I have no idea where we're going."

He drove for about a mile and stopped. Clifford fussed with his phone trying to find their location. Josephine sat still with her eyes closed.

Adam had to know. He leaned over the seat and whispered, "How did you get the ambulance? What happened to you? We all thought you were gone."

She moved forward, her mouth inches from his ear. "I know. I'm so sorry. For all of you. When they came to our home, they got me first. I was a prize they wanted, I believe, to mess with Melinda and Jade. They were hoping to take Damien and Therese, also. They came in first, dressed like EMTs in this same ambulance. They didn't hurt me, only sedated me, and spread the rumor that I was dead. They had me in a private cell below that warehouse. I heard all this banging up above, I tried the metal door, and it just opened. I made it outside and ran like hell. I made it to the road and the same damn ambulance went by. It pulled over and I thought they were going to get me again. But when these two characters jumped out, they tore off on foot through the woods. They didn't even turn off the engine. So, I got in and floored it, and when I looked in the mirror that showed what was behind me, you know, in the back, I almost went off the road. My babies. Such a mess but at least they're still alive."

"I can see where we are now," Clifford said. "It's okay."

"But where are we going to end up? Any ideas? What do you think?"

"I wanted to go to Anderson, Josephine said. "We could do more there to help Melinda." She sighed. "No, it's way too far."

"We'll just go back to the townhouse. I'll direct you."

He sent a group text to the others and quickly received responses with words of joy for Josephine and concern and prayers for Melinda and Jade. Every few minutes for the rest of the trip, Josephine undid her seat belt, scrunched her legs onto the seat so she squatted toward Melinda, and whispered a different sound into her ear. She touched her head, heart, and shoulders a few times, and then their two foreheads together. Adam wanted to ask how Melinda was doing, but didn't dare interrupt, and was also uncertain he really wanted an answer. The longer they drove the more worried he became and he continually played back his last conversation with her. She'd asked if he would host her Extra if something happened to her. How did she know to ask that?

They arrived at the townhouse and Adam parked behind the building in a spot close to the rear entrance. They carried Jade and Melinda inside and put them next to each other on a bed in one of the rooms. Within the next half-hour, the rest of the group returned and, after an emotional reunion with Josephine, began their vigil and healing processes for the other two.

Melinda

When the Hope people came into Jade's apartment and took us away, somebody dropped me hard on the stairs, and bones in my foot and maybe other places shattered. They had already injected my body with a strong sedative so I felt nothing. I didn't even know my body had been moved until my essence was sucked back in at a much later time. I attribute this lack of awareness to the horrific space in the warehouse where I lost Jade and lost all sensation of time and space. I came through the floor first, and back into my body just as the Hope people injected me again, this time with something much too harsh for my body. As I watched myself begin to transition, and all the way to those final moments, my educational experience of what it means to be in a human body continued. On the one hand, I had made my decision and joyously embraced it. Yet, I also observed vestiges of fear, longing, regret, and sadness and concluded that those parts are always companions on the final human journey. They will always be there in some form for all beings. I blessed the feelings, let them be, and got on with the tasks at hand. The Extra aspect of my being took over and the process of dying became an active event.

The full and final awareness of who and what I was in this lifetime came to me before it arrived at Jade's door. But I knew Jade's full being, when she finally regained consciousness, would rapidly assimilate the same knowledge about herself. What wonder, what joy, what love. In the body of a Normal human, so much love for oneself would be labeled narcissistic, yet for us, for our combined self, it is the opposite because it fully transcends our sense of self. It is so much bigger than this Extra and Normal combo of Jade and Melinda, Melinda and Jade.

As I drifted, I explored the connection between love and acceptance, how the two are ultimately conjoined in such a way that they create a conundrum similar to many other conundrums humans contemplate. We play with the unfathomable beginnings of time and the non-existent point where the universe ends. We theorize about the seeming nothingness that is the building block of sub-atomic particles and therefore all matter. We endlessly study the relationship between an unobserved and observed object. And now I find that, to create and become pure love, one must first fully accept and forgive its opposite. Yet one cannot fully accept and forgive its opposite unless one first creates and becomes pure love. I'm close. I'm so close.

This human body named Melinda Breeze was too broken to continue to contain her half of our unique Extra component. The Elders had come to the same conclusion, and I overheard their plan. They wished to reconnect the two halves within the Jade body. Oh, if only. Three of them are our birth parents so their wishes perhaps should have been respected. Yet I knew it was still not possible. For I could at that moment remember the details of my baptism, in our commune outside of Chicago, twenty-eight human years earlier. I remembered how one Extra component, more magnificent, more joyous, more powerful than most, was scheduled to enter my tiny human body, recently named Melinda Breeze. The Elders believed I could receive and contain such a special gift within my body/mind/soul/spirit, and Jade's parents traveled from Anderson, New York to witness the event. Jade's human body also attended, still snuggled inside her mother's sacred womb, not ready to enter the world for a few more weeks. Her father stood next to them and held her mother's hand.

The multi-colored band of light hovered over my human body, began its descent, and before it wrapped around me, split lengthwise neatly into two parts. One half quickly surrounded me and merged into me, and the other danced around Jade's mother for a moment and then faded away. The Elders gasped and sighed and cried but the Extra band knew where it needed to go, where it could thrive, where it could best deliver its cache of wisdom. It knew that its power could never be contained in one human body and was content to divvy up the goods. The remaining half waited a few more weeks, waited for the birth it was best suited for, and claimed its host in the human world.

Yet, even as Extra-normals, our human minds never knew. We might have suspected, we might even have wished, but nobody ever laid it out for us. My body was dying and, as happens with humans, I could finally remember every detail, and vowed to pass the information directly into Jade's consciousness. *My dear Jade, we've been nearly the same being and our parents never told us. Our world cannot continue this way. All this will change. There is no other way. Honesty is honesty and stories need to be told.*

No way was I going to let my Extra half attempt to join hers. I knew her better than anyone of any type anywhere because I nearly was her, and I had no doubt that the act of fully re-joining the Extra in her body would seriously harm and likely kill her, too. Adam sat quietly, so still, so present, knowing and ready. What a lovely being he is. For so long he didn't know this about himself, he had struggled hard in his human-ness, and I was honored to have him accept this part of me, interconnected with the similar part of Jade, into who he was. I only wished I could explain to her what was about to happen, but I feared my body would have stopped functioning long before hers woke up. Yet, a potent essence of Melinda Breeze would still be with her, inside of her, inside of Adam because that is how Extra-normal works. I know this now. The Extra layer influences the human, and the human influences the Extra. We need each other to move forward. We need each other to grow. We need each other to survive.

Jade

I could hear chatter around me but didn't understand its meaning. I switched to a different sensory mode, one based on touch, and had better reception. The Elders: my parents, Josephine—Josephine? My other mother? How did she get there? — possibly Adam's father, and somebody else. They danced around, their hands playing with the currents, doing something, trying to create something. I couldn't sufficiently re-enter to grasp the full scenario and only knew it all had to do with me.

I directed a fragment of awareness, all I could muster, to Melinda and her message came roaring in. "They're trying to re-unite our Extra selves back to one. It will be much too much. It will overwhelm your Jade being. Trust me, please."

"Of course, I trust because, because…oh, that's it." Like it was no big deal. Like I always knew. "We're the same being, aren't we? We have the same Extra component. But why are they trying to unite…Oh, what? What's happening? Are you hurt?"

"This is a big one, my dear Jade. You will let your attachment to this Melinda Breeze being loosen and then slide away. Her essence is already in you and will be forever. And her Extra component, seasoned with Melinda's human self, will always be close by."

I wondered if my instant hysteria only smashed around inside me or if those who stood outside of me were picking up on it, maybe backing away because my screams were too loud. I needed to wake up. Wild, dark currents held me at the bottom of an ocean trench, and I needed to fight my way through them. I struggled through moss and coral and angry white sharks until the surface above me lightened, and then my breath came back to the outer world. At first, I didn't recognize where I was but figured out it was a room in the townhouse Adam had told me about. I was laid out on a bed, and I sat up, bumping into Melinda sprawled out next to me. Her eyes were closed, and she exhibited no movement. Lifeless? Across the room in a fluffy lounge chair, sat Adam. Why was he there? His eyes were also closed, and he lay with his head back, breathing heavily. His face began to twitch and then his whole body began to shake. Now the same thing happened to Melinda and the magnificent colors of her Extra slid out of her and danced around each one of us. When my turn came, I felt the pull of my own Extra, so strong I thought it also might leave. But it was only acknowledging its other half. It left me, floated directly to Adam, and disappeared inside him.

Everyone crowded around Adam, laughing, crying, in different states of shock. I agreed, it was a most wonderful, blessed experience. And now, Melinda Breeze moved on. I turned over and lay nearly on top of her. I put my face to her nose and still felt the tiniest trickle of air going in and out of her lungs. I lay the side of my head onto her chest and listened to the fading thump of her heart. I pushed next to her and held her. I wanted to be angry at the others for letting her go so easily but anger had fled and the bitter note of acceptance took its place. An image flashed by of my past experiences with healing energy. She had sent it to me many times and a few times I had done the same to her. Successfully. I thought I could at least try, even though it probably wouldn't work and might muck up her peaceful exit.

Yet, I heard it as if it was my own thought because in many ways it was. "You can try if you want to. Who knows?" I thought I saw the hint of a smile form on her lifeless mouth, and I knew what I had to do. I stood up, wobbly, dizzy, and latched on to my three parents. They all teetered on the edge of a breakdown, a collapse into an emotional mush, and who could blame them? They had been and still were in the middle of war trauma. Homes and land destroyed, friends and family missing and then dying. Awful, awful. I expected to join them but first I had to try this one thing a final time.

I told them to hold me tight and give me all their best energy. Everything they had. They backed away, confused. I latched on to their gaze, one at a time, and caught an inability to refuse my command. Our power structure had flipped. Nobody cared but it was still nice. They squeezed and loaded me up. Next, I went to Adam and put my face inches from his. He wandered in some kind of trance but I knew the Extra would hear me. I whispered, "Adam, give me love." The Extra, so familiar, part of me still, forever part of me, knew exactly what to do, even if the human Adam didn't. He put his hand on my heart, thumped my back, and touched my forehead with his and the force jolted me backward.

Again, I lay next to Melinda, squeezed her hands, worked up some heat, and sent everything inside me directly into her. I put my hand on her heart, tapped her back, put my forehead against hers, and then snuggled up close to her. It took a minute or so and I heard a few breaths. Josephine sat next to her, took a hand, and did some more magic. One more minute and Melinda was back. But so different. Like me, like most of us in the room, she had never existed without her Extra.

She sat up and tried to stand and Josephine gently pushed her back. "Your foot is broken. We need to wrap it up and get you some crutches."

Melinda grabbed her hand and pulled her nearly on top of her. "My precious mother. Still alive. And you rescued me." She looked across the room. "Adam, can you come here?"

He opened his eyes and came out of his trance state. "Melinda?" He leaped up. "Melinda!"

Josephine moved aside and let Adam get closer. He gently hugged her. "How did this happen?"

She latched on tight, putting her arms around him, not letting go. It took me a few moments to understand. She was overjoyed to see Adam but she also wanted to stay close to this new part of him that had left her.

Then he also got it. "If you're still here, why did I get this? It shouldn't have come to me. We have to reverse it."

He turned to his father. Clifford shook his head and said softly, "It doesn't work that way, Adam."

"But Melinda, please." He was frantic.

She wasn't much different now. She came back as herself more than ever. She looked at each one of us, slowly, carefully, with so much love I thought I would melt. Her smile turned into a laugh and her entire being lit up. She forgot about her foot, began to stand, then remembered and laughed again.

"Look at me, everybody. I'm still alive. I am so happy. Still in this wonderful Melinda Breeze body with all you people. You blessed gorgeous beings. And my Extras are here and here," she pointed to me and Adam, "and all the rest of you." She swept her wild arms around toward the older ones.

She was full of it now. On a free roll. Melinda amped way up. We all watched, amazed, as her persona gradually morphed into one none of us had ever seen before. An element of almost childish hyperactivity found its way into the grown-up Melinda we were familiar with.

She turned to me, put her hands on my shoulders, and pulled me closer. She kissed me full on for about ten seconds, stopping only because of a joyous giggle.

"And I can do this now. We can do this now."

It was outrageously exciting, even in front of my stunned parents, but I began to experience some concern. I caught a look from Adam, wide-eyed, a hint of panic, surely thinking, "am I next?"

My parents stood to leave and Josephine followed. "Wait," I said. "Where are you going?"

Josephine answered, "It's after three in the morning. There are two other bedrooms and a living room couch. We're all staying here. Melinda, I have to wrap up your foot and we'll take care of it tomorrow."

They all gave their hugs and kind words and left. Adam stayed in his chair with his eyes closed. Josephine came back with bandages and Melinda directed her on how to get her foot set for the night. At the doorway, Josephine said, "Jade," and she nodded at Melinda who said, "Yes, mother, she will take care of me."

Melinda laid back, finally exhausted, and seemed to drift off. I scooted over to Adam, took his hands and said, "Hey. Are you all right?" His hands buzzed like Melinda's used to.

"Jade, I am so confused right now. Please tell me this is okay."

"It will settle in and I'll help you. It will integrate and it will calm you down and give you amazing gifts."

"I feel so guilty. But she did ask me if something happened to her if I would take it on."

It crushed me. She'd asked him without me knowing. Now I was confused. However, I was going to rise to meet whatever this was about.

My hurt and confusion could be acknowledged but my real concern needed to be this lovely man sitting in front of me and the precious one over on the bed.

Adam

The sun came up and shone through the townhouse windows. Adam opened his eyes and began to plan how he could quietly sneak out of the room. He thought he hadn't slept at all, but couldn't be sure. He tried to scan his entire being, to carefully observe every detail, physically and mentally, believing it was his only chance to make it through the day and still keep his sanity. He didn't feel all that different, he was still the same Adam Kastner as the day before, and what he needed the most was to get somewhere by himself and chill out. Jade and Melinda lay side by side on the bed, still fully dressed, both on their backs, their legs overlapping and heads touching. They were so beautiful together and needed to remain joined. If he could, he would help them stay that way. He reflected on past ideas he'd had about a romantic—physical—relationship with Jade. The desire for such an arrangement had left them both, yet occasionally he still felt the twinge and was sure she did also. Now it would be impossible and he liked the relief that accompanied the thought.

He left the room, happy with the potential for these two beings who were now so intricately connected to him. However, when he entered the living room and saw his father sitting on the couch, drinking a cup of coffee, a lifetime of questions came roaring in. They quietly left in Adam's car, Clifford driving, and headed toward their home. They didn't speak and Adam, this time, did fall asleep. About half-way home, he woke, said he was ravenous, and asked if they could stop somewhere to eat. They found a breakfast café, perfect for quiet conversation, and settled in at a table with more coffee and a good meal.

They ate for a few minutes, silent, until Adam said, "Dad, I'm losing my appetite because what I really want right now is to hear you talk. Tell me things."

"Oh Adam. I don't know."

"Please. Right here, right now. Just tell me something. I'm ready."

Clifford took a deep breath and began. "All right. But if it gets too much, you tell me to stop. I'll start with this because it's about Garett. Cynthia and I were never married, we were only a couple for a short time. We were both part of a sort of secret group, all Extras, all Walkins, and when she got pregnant, I had this idea that she and I would move to one of the communes we kept hearing about. We even went to Anderson but they were so wary back then that they didn't let us stay more than a few days. Then, after Garrett was born, Cynthia got really depressed and confused and took off. With Garrett. I finally tracked her down, got her stabilized, and although I didn't live with her, I helped her raise Garrett. Then I met your Mom, we got married, and you came along. But Cynthia began to disassemble again. Fortunately, by then I had established a good relationship with the Land Trust and she moved in, we took Garrett, and you now had a big brother."

Adam looked down at the table and brushed at his eyes. Clifford said, "Adam?"

He looked up, pushed back a sob. "Keep going, Dad, I need to hear it. I can imagine what's coming next, somewhat, anyway, but I still need to hear it."

"The whole time, I had been meeting with my other Walk-in friends at least once a month and we planned on forming a group to help the ones who were having difficulties. We experimented, developed a whole protocol, and believed we were doing something amazing. And when a few of us had kids, we discussed doing our own baptism ceremonies. We called ourselves the Hope Community."

"What? Are you kidding me?

"Adam, don't judge yet, please. It wasn't the same then. Damien Furlong was even involved for a while."

Adam closed his eyes, opened them, looked around the room, sipped his coffee. "This is so strange. I'm not judging. And for some reason it all makes sense." He closed his eyes again. "Wait, wait. Why do I know this? Garrett's Extra really *was* meant for me, wasn't it?"

"You were nearly a year old and I took you and Garrett to the ceremony. Your mother said she didn't care if it was so important to me. She didn't believe any of it was real and stayed home. The group I was with thought we had it all figured out but the Extra was confused or, well, we couldn't understand what happened."

Adam began to shake. He hugged himself and squeezed and felt chills all over his body. "I remember it. I remember the whole thing. It came to me, curled up inside me, stayed a minute, and then slipped out and into Garrett." He started to laugh but stopped himself because he was still sitting in a restaurant. Then he remembered what came next and his mood went the other direction. "He couldn't handle it. He never could. It must have been so awful for you."

Clifford stared at him, his eyes wide and mouth open, stunned. "You're not angry right now. Why?"

"Why would I be? Oh. Oh my God. You're right. I'm not. This is amazing."

They had a few minutes of silence as they picked at their food. Then Clifford said, "Max and Olivia were at the baptism. They were new in our group, and at first, came across as so helpful to everybody. They worked with Garrett a few times, but I began to have a bad feeling about them and wouldn't let them do any more. Within a year, I and a few others could tell that, more than anything else, they were hungry for power. They had their own ideas and were so charismatic that a lot of our group wanted to follow them. Damian left and eventually I did, too. After a while we formed a new group which sought to keep the peace between the Hope people and any other groups of Extras. We bought the townhouse so we could have a neutral meeting spot."

"It's also why you brought us to the ocean, to Marion each summer, isn't it?"

"Yes."

"And what about Sara Leeds?"

Clifford slowly shook his head. "I guess you could say she's brilliant. All of us so-called observers? She fooled every one of us."

"And we're lucky she did."

Jade

I slept well into the morning and woke entangled in Melinda's arms and legs, both of us still wearing the same clothes we'd put on the day before. No brushed teeth or washed faces, not even a before-bed trip to the bathroom, and I thought I would burst. I unhooked from Melinda and saw the empty chair. The other half of my Extra layer had gone off somewhere unknown to me. I wondered why I cared so much, considering I'd only learned a few hours before about this new configuration. Oh well, I would just have to get used to it.

I visited the bathroom, cleaned up as best I could, went into the living room, and entered a discussion about how to handle the inevitable media fascination with the police raid of Hope and the fire at the Land Trust. Somebody, other than the police, would make the connection and would track us down for interviews and many other annoyances. I figured the most likely candidate would be Sara Leeds, and when I mentioned it, the response of my parents shocked me. Also surprising was that, with all the chaos the day and night before, I had no idea why or how the Hope Community compound had been raided. Sara Leeds had worked undercover for many years and none of us knew. I wondered if Adam had more information, and I wished he was here to ask. One aspect I was now positive of was that she had her own strange Extra story she'd managed to keep well hidden. Someday she would share it.

My parents, all three of them, and Cynthia created an enormous healthy breakfast, and we were just ready to eat when Melinda came out. She and I ate an absurd amount of everything and watched our parents giving subtle expressions of approval to each other. When we finished, we sat in the living room and discussed approaches to dealing with reporters. We all agreed that no purpose would be served to let any media person know about our kidnapping. Most likely, the police would do an interview in the next few days. Or, depending on the level of confusion leading up to the raid, maybe not. Josephine's experience was another matter, as the authorities had been told by the ambulance driver and EMTs when they left the Land Trust with her, that she was dead.

Damien's phone beeped and he scrolled through something, reading a news update. "We need to turn on the TV."

He flipped to an area station and an announcer began with, *News from the latest breaking story about the police raid on the Hope Community compound.* Clips flashed of police vehicles packed into the Hope parking area, police escorting dazed and drugged young men and women into ambulances, terrified people being shoved into police vans, and a helicopter circling overhead. Another clip of Max Schultz followed, his hands in cuffs and his arms behind his back, being helped out of a police car and led into the county jail. At one point, he faced the camera, and what he might have hoped was an innocent smile I interpreted as the evilest grin. Then I did something which stretched the limits of my entire configuration. I actually wished his heart to open and experience love. It was a small attempt and I didn't do it very well. The report also showed a quick snap of Olivia Santini's face inside another police car and I repeated my wish for her.

Other than a walk around the neighborhood, I stayed half the day in the townhouse, reading books I found scattered around, or finding updated news stories about the Hope raid. Melinda contacted the office manager at her work, said she needed to take a few days off, and then went with Josephine to an out-patient facility to have her foot x-rayed. She returned a few hours later with crutches and a boot and happily reported only a cracked heel.

"I'll be back at work maybe by Wednesday," she said.

I wondered how she could be so upbeat. But I also wanted to get back to work. I wanted to be in my office the next day when an inevitable throng of a certain type of student would come knocking on my door. I stayed another night, and early the next morning my mother drove me to my apartment. I poked around for some clean clothes, tried not to focus on the horror of the last time I was there, and headed back to school.

I had done no prep for any of the classes and the first one was a bit rough. Yet I concluded from the information my observing eyes took in that nobody cared. However, four of the students showed a high level of concern for my well-being and this touched me in an unexpected way. I wanted to stop the class, pull them aside, and assure them I was okay, even if I wasn't. As expected, a line of four students stood waiting at my door when I came back to the office. One of them was Jacob LeBlanc, which I thought was a good thing. I took a big chance and invited them to all come in at once.

"Is this all right for all of you to be in here?"

Jacob answered, "The Hope thing, holding all those people against their will. It's so fucked up."

Another young woman responded angrily, "I don't think you know what you're talking about. It was fucked up, all right. But not in the way you think it was. Whoever fucked over Max and Olivia is going to pay a price."

The students broke into an argument.

"Are we all Extras here?" I asked.

They quieted down and a student said, "We all are and we shouldn't be arguing about this."

The door opened and Erin Mason walked in.

I went way out on a limb. "This is what I believe about myself and everyone here. I believe our Extra components themselves have a specific orientation and it's the human impulses that cause us to argue. And, right now with all that's happening, we must use the most positive aspects of our Extra layer to find ways to get along with each other. Hi Erin, what do you think about what I just said?"

She teared up and said, "God bless you, Professor. God bless you."

Jacob said, "I heard something about another little community getting attacked and burned or something, down south of Ithaca. Do you know anything about that?"

Erin stared at me, tears now flowing down her face. She gave a nod and left the office.

I knew I had to hold it together. "I don't know enough to feel comfortable talking about it. Actually, if admin even knew we were having any of this conversation, I would likely get fired."

I made it through the day, and after going back and forth in my head about what I needed to do next, began to plan a new mission. First, I went back to my apartment and vacuumed, dusted, or wet-wiped every surface. I opened all the windows, not caring that the approaching night air would surely drop the temperature to a deep chill. I cooked up a vegetable soup, going heavy on the garlic and onions because I wanted the smell to overpower any lingering odor I imagined from my kidnappers.

Then I did my preparations. I ate two large bowls of the soup, endless pieces of bread and butter, and even slugged down a glass of wine. I found a tiny powerful flashlight, punched directions into my phone for Siri to give back to me, dressed warmly in a fleece coat, knit hat, and gloves, and set out on my next adventure. I got in my car and drove through the dark roads, reflecting on the fact that a day earlier, other beings, who were also Extras, had subjected me to the worst sort of trauma. And now, I was calmly driving back to the scene of the crime. I remembered my first trauma and how angry I had become when the concept of, *whatever doesn't kill you makes you stronger*, made its appearance. I tried to observe possibilities for what was moving me forward this time. The first one I hit on was an attitude of, *Ahhh, who cares anymore? I'm, still here. What difference does it make?* It might have sounded hip and hard-ass years earlier but now did not feel good at all. It was way too defeatist, too empty, almost like being in that cosmically vacant Hope warehouse before somebody smashed open the door.

As I passed by the Hope Community parking lot—dark, empty except for one sheriff's vehicle, the entrance to the building cordoned off with yellow tape— I found my true reason for this visit back to this horrid place. Most likely, in the underground of the same building where I had been held hostage, a large number of non-human beings were still hovering, waiting, confused, not knowing what to do next. And I loved those beings so much, so much. I would do anything and risk everything to help them along.

I drove another couple hundred yards, found a small dirt patch to turn onto, got out of my vehicle, and slid into the woods. The sky was clear and stars were out but a moon hadn't yet made an appearance. The woods were so thick here that, even after my eyes adjusted to the darkness, I could see little. I didn't bother trying to come up with some magical power to guide me and instead used the compass app on my phone. I probably should have spent more time figuring that one out because using a compass, especially in the dark, was more complex than I thought, and I got way off track. But I did make it. I broke out of the woods and into the village, now also dark and empty. I rushed through the streets until I saw the scary outline of the first warehouse, and I overpowered any hesitation by running fast toward the smashed-in door.

The upper section was still empty, but the awful energy had left. I had no idea how to get through the floor to the lower area and did not want to leave my body again and enter in that fashion. I ran back outside, around the perimeter of the building, and found a stone-step stairway, hidden by well-crafted hedges, leading into the earth. I ran down, opened an unlocked door, ran through a few more rooms, including the one where Melinda and I had passed the time the day before, and finally came to the last wall. I opened another door and stepped in.

The space was absent of artificial light, yet I could see everything imaginable. No words were spoken, yet I received a glorious welcome and understood everything this mass of beings wished me to understand. If I thought of words in English, my Extra layer translated them and placed them within the entire group. The same system seemed to be in play coming from them. Although I had knowledge of such experiences, primarily from my group's Elders, I had never witnessed it on such a vast scale and I doubted my Elders had, either. The beings swirled and danced and flickered their phenomenal colors all around and even through me. They caressed me with the gentlest, kindest bliss imaginable. I was not there to help them. I had come so they could help me.

I asked them how they had all come there and they said they were young and foolish and the humans tricked them. I asked them why they were still staying in that dreadful space, and they said they wished to purify it. I asked how many of them there were, and they said it didn't matter, numbers didn't matter. I asked why they didn't intervene in all the awfulness that had gone on and they said it was up to us humans to figure it out. I asked them what happened to Garrett Kastner's Extra and there was no answer. A shape slid through the mass, circled me, and hung around my neck like a gigantic scarf. I asked it where it had been and it said the humans had kept it locked up but now it was free to help these young ones and also me. I asked it why it never merged with another human and it said it acted up so its human captors were afraid of it, and now it was waiting for just the right one. It began to make clicks and sounds and rhythmic light pulses and softly stroked my face. Its power was enormous and gentle, and its love poured out, seemingly unlimited.

That was when I crumbled, when I fell apart, when even in this building that was the chamber of horrors, I finally felt free enough, safe enough, to let it all go.

As always, though, there was a catch. It said it wanted to see Adam and my instant response was, "Why?" It said it wanted to see Melinda. Again, I asked, "Why?"

Of course, I knew why, or thought I did. It wanted to switch things up again with Adam and Melinda. More confusion but I didn't dare to object.

"Okay. Should I bring them here?"

"No, I would like it if you could help me to prepare Melinda Breeze. You know her better than anybody. Your companion, best friend."

I didn't understand. The conversation had become overly human, and I sensed a touch of humor.

It said, "Do you think it's a good idea?"

Then I got it. It slid away from me and danced and twisted, and in human terms, grew so big that I stepped away from it. But its colors twinkled in a funny way and its rhythmic sounds reminded me of a children's nursery rhyme. It was acting playful, funny. It was teasing me.

"Yes," I said with a touch of Elder authority. "I will help her prepare. But the final choice is hers. Do you agree?"

"Always," it said and then disappeared.

Adam

He had to somehow reach Sara Leeds, to check up on her. He texted, called, and sent an email, all with no response. He had spent enough time around Jade and Melinda that he understood the protocol for some of the more exotic forms of communication they had access to and he was a long way off from daring to experiment with any of it. He paced his room, tried calling a few times, even left a message with Carter Freedman's secretary, and then succumbed to his concern.

He lay on his bed, closed his eyes, and imagined Sara's face. He imagined the sound of her voice, watching her mouth move and words come out. He heard her say, *I'm going to call you. A number you won't recognize will come up. Answer it.*

His phone rang. "Hello? Sara?"

"My God, Adam. When did you learn to do that?"

"I can't believe it worked. But it sucked the energy right out of me."

"Yeah, well it's no fun for me, either. So, use this number. And, yes, it is secure."

"I assume you've been following the news."

"I hope you kept out of it."

He told her about the last twenty-four hours, and she listened with no response. "Hey, are you still there?"

"That is the most bizarre thing I've ever heard of. Every bit of it. Welcome to the club, my dear brother and friend. All I can say is it's a strange, strange world. And what you now have within you? Coming from Melinda Breeze? Oh, what a gift."

"I know. It's hard to process. Hey, you're not safe, are you? Like out in public."

"Not at all. And I want to share a few things I've come across. The guy Richard White works for who was running for State Senator dropped out. Turns out a whole lot of other Hope connected characters all over the country, running for similar state-level jobs, also dropped out. And apparently, quite a few folks, mostly college kids from around New York and other nearby states, who were reported missing, were found, all drugged up, in the lower level of that one empty warehouse."

"Should I destroy the thumb drive? It's still in my pocket."

"Hang on to it for now."

Every day for the next four days Adam stayed in or near the house, sometimes writing for a few hours, or listening to music, and occasionally going for walks around Oakwood. He liked to go into stores or walk through a park where he could observe others and observe his reactions to others. He often felt as if he were adopting aspects of Melinda's generally sunny personality, and as his tolerance for minor annoyances increased dramatically, he decided it was a blessing.

At least once each day he called first Melinda and then Jade to update them on his progress and find out how they were. Jade had reclaimed her apartment and her parents were still staying in the townhouse. Melinda had also moved back to her apartment and Josephine was staying with her.

On the fourth day, Melinda called him and told him she had been interviewed by a reporter from a local news station and that the clip would be aired on the evening news. He politely said he was eager to watch it and would call her later when it was over. When he hung up, he ran downstairs in a panic, found his father in the basement getting food out of a freezer, and tried to tell him.

Clifford cut him off, "I know, Adam. Josephine just called me."

"Does she think this is all right?"

"No. She's quite upset about it."

Adam's phone rang and Jade's name and number appeared. "Have you heard about Melinda?"

"I just found out."

"Could you come over and watch it with me?"

"How about you come here and have dinner with us after?"

Adam helped his father cook a lasagna and a little later welcomed Jade at the door. His mother, Ingrid, still oblivious to all that had transpired, naturally assumed Jade was a new girlfriend and treated her as if she was a queen, showing her around the house, telling stories about Adam when he was younger, and asking Jade if she'd read any of his writing. She played along and, when they came back into the kitchen, Adam said, "What awful stories are you telling her about me?"

"Oh Adam. You know I wouldn't do that."

When the time was right, Clifford, Jade, and Adam went into the living room and Clifford flipped on the TV. Ingrid came in and asked what they were watching.

"A woman Adam and Jade know is doing an interview. She's from the Land Trust group in Anderson that got attacked."

Ingrid answered, "Oh?"

"Jade also grew up there. The woman, Melinda, is her closest friend."

"I'm so sorry. It sounded horrible. And then this whole business with that Hope group. I don't understand the connection."

"I'm not sure I do, either," Jade said.

The news began with a newscaster reporting on a few unrelated stories and followed with an update on the raid on the Hope Community and a possible connection between the attack on the Land Trust in Anderson.

"And one of our own, Todd Miller, had an exclusive interview in our studio earlier today with a woman who grew up in the Anderson Land Trust, Melinda Breeze."

The interview began in a room that looked like it might be a quiet area off of the lobby of an upscale hotel: comfortable chairs and a couch, a low table for drinks, and a window view of trees and a touch of blue sky. Melinda sat in one of the chairs across from Todd Miller. She had her hair tied back, unusual for her, and wore a simple yet dark red dress and a cardigan sweater. She also wore a subtle gold necklace and matching earrings, and her makeup looked professionally done.

Todd began, "I have with me today, Melinda Breeze, who grew up in the Anderson Land Trust which was subjected to an attack last week by arsonists. Thank you for coming, Melinda."

Her eyes brightened and she put on a hint of a smile. "Hello, Todd. Thank you for having me."

"Wow," Jade said. "I've never seen her quite like that."

"She's kind of perfect," Adam said.

Todd first expressed his sympathies for the damage to her childhood home and then began with a few general questions concerning who she believed was responsible for the attack.

"Unfortunately, Todd, what you're asking is part of a police investigation and it's best if I do not try to answer anything specific. Although I have not yet been contacted by the authorities for my input, I imagine at some point I could be. Is that okay?"

"It's fine. Perhaps I could ask more general questions about what it was like to grow up at the Land Trust. I know a lot of people are trying to figure out the connection to the Hope Community so maybe you could speak to that."

"That was pre-planned," Adam whispered.

"Yes, it was," Jade agreed.

Melinda said, "I know over the years a dialogue went on between my home and the people at the Hope Community, but I was never aware of any deep connection. Would it be all right if I only speak about what it was like to grow up in the Land Trust?"

"Absolutely."

She picked up a glass of water on the table, took a quick sip, and began. "As children, one of our most important lessons centered around learning to observe the world around us, and our most important observations were always about ourselves, how we felt or acted at any given time, or how we treated those around us. This allowed us to more easily take a step backward when something happened or was happening that we didn't like, and if it wasn't something possible to change, then we learned to accept it and move on. We were taught that trying to always micro-manage outcomes in any situation was generally a losing battle, and a much healthier approach to life was to learn to control our responses to outcomes. And our ability to act as observers of ourselves made it much easier for us to integrate this idea of not controlling everything. For example, if a tornado is going to come, headed our way, bearing down on us, then there is nothing we can do about it other than prepare as best we can and afterward accept the outcome. In the bigger picture, I think if we're honest with ourselves, we can surely see that the underlying nature of the world is that it is continually in flux, and nothing is ever entirely predictable or permanent. And there's a big payoff to accessing this acceptance because it opens the door to the one constant I was taught to believe in, which is love."

"That's quite an answer. How would that approach to life be different than what was taught at the Hope Community?"

"I can't speak specifically to what was taught at Hope. But I can say this. The more a person or group attempts to control all outcomes, the more they cling to the acquisition of power, which is so often power over others. And the more they cling to this power, the easier it becomes for them to lose their ability to access love, which then leads to it being replaced with the opposite. My closest friend from the Land Trust has spent her entire life studying every aspect of human history and she would be the first to tell you that power is never permanent in any culture, government, or individual. In fact, few other aspects of humanity are less permanent than power over others. It has, and always will, come and go. Yet so many of us so desperately cling to the idea that it's eternal. Again, the only force I believe has permanence is love. True love can always find its way through the mess of humanity if we just give it a chance. It heals us, it brings us together, and it makes us whole. It's the only constant in our world and ultimately the only safe space to hang out in. It also teaches us about empathy, kindness, and compassion. What could be better than that?"

"Do you believe this extra being inside you helps you with your understanding of all of what you're talking about?"

She tilted her head, scrunched her eyes a touch, and gave the hint of a questioning smile. "Actually, Todd, I don't have an extra being inside of me. For me, right now, it's only a wonderful guiding idea, a metaphor if you will. Now, about what others believe? The specifics, the fine points don't matter so much, do they? It's quite easy to love and accept somebody, anybody, no matter what they believe, when you have this one piece in common, when you are both guided by the power of this universal love."

"Melinda, you and your group just had a horrific experience perpetrated, it seems, by people who have extreme hatred toward you. Did this put your beliefs to the test? How are you personally dealing with it?"

She paused, took a deep breath, looked down at the floor, and then back up at Todd. Although tears were visible on her cheeks, her face stayed relaxed, calm, and, I thought, nearly angelic.

"You're correct, Todd. It was an extreme act and I know how I'd like to respond but I'm not quite there yet. It was a fierce reminder to me and most of us that we are still works in progress and we need to accept that fact because perhaps it's what we always will be. We can think we are permanently free of any of the vestiges of the opposite of love, but it's not how our world works, is it? However, we can never give up trying to achieve such a goal. At least, that's what I believe."

She finished, she left, and we shut the TV off. We sat in an awed silence for a minute and then Ingrid said, "That young lady is truly something special, isn't she?"

Jade

Melinda was the hero, the golden girl, the true forever love of my life. I had doubted I could stay in a relationship with her as a Normal, because she would be too different from me and we would no longer be able to share our amazing communication. But she crashed the idea. And she finally erased this misconception that I had—and probably most Extra types also had—that we were somehow more suited than any of the Normals to carry the world forward. My takeaway was that the pure ones never needed Extras in the first place, and it was the flawed messes like Adam and myself who would never make it without them. Melinda certainly had her share of flaws and her Extra did an amazing job of helping her to expand her vision and incorporate them into herself so that she could become the sort of stable, centered being we all need so much. But going forward without one, I figured she would only need an occasional boost from Adam or me. However, as is usual with such large matters, it shaped up in a way much different than what I thought.

I went to Melinda's apartment for dinner the next night, we cooked our usual pasta, and we spent time alone for the first time since we were abducted by the Hope people. We kept mostly silent through the meal, then went into the living room and sat on the couch. I apologized over and over for any doubts I'd had about who we still were and who we could be together. It didn't take much. We fell all over each other and spent the next hours going to all those places we couldn't before. It was such a peak experience that I told her we could never do it again because we would become addicted to the sensations and never be able to think about anything else. I wasn't serious—well, maybe a little—and she agreed, and our response was to go at it again until we crossed over into some blessed wonderland.

A while later, I told Melinda about my trip back to the scene of the Hope Community hell and my interactions with all the captive Extras. I told her about Garrett Kastner's Extra and she stayed silent as I described it in great detail.

When I finished, she asked, "Do you approve?"

"Uh, what do you mean? I thought maybe you were done with it all. Do *you* approve?"

"Well, Jade. Since we're now a real human couple in almost every way possible, when it comes to such momentous decisions, what I do next requires joint approval."

"So, you're not done with it."

"Oh hell, no."

"The thing is, that's a wild one. But I guess if anybody can handle it, it would be you."

"Oh, don't worry about it. It's been snooping around here for days and we've already established how this new and exciting relationship will work."

The next day, Melinda and I and our parents packed into a car and drove to the Land Trust in Anderson. This was the first time we had been back since the attack and we walked slowly and carefully through the destruction. Shortly after, Adam and his parents arrived, followed by Garrett's mother, Cynthia. Adam's mother, Ingrid, had never been there and he stayed closed to her and kept her in check as she inevitably reacted to the horror of the burned buildings. At one point, we all held hands, closed our eyes, and a few of us spoke words of peace and forgiveness.

We moved on through the woods, taking comfort in the vibrant colors of the changing leaves, the chirp of the different birds and—once we were away from the charred wood—the smell of the earth. We came to the stone plaza, stood in a circle, and held hands. Josephine went into the center with Melinda and put her arms around her from behind. They said the words, made the sounds, and the sky above them lit and hummed with the magic of an uncountable number of light bands. The entire group from the Hope underground had come. They glittered and danced for a minute and then spread apart so that the one we were waiting for could shine through.

I glanced over at Ingrid, wondering if she could see any of this. Her eyes looked like they were going to pop out and she swayed back and forth. Adam held her hand.

Melinda's chosen Extra flitted about and then came to the circle. It wove in and out of each of us because it was connected in some way to all of us. First Cynthia, whose son had once been the container for this energy, and it lovingly and gently touched her hands. Then to Ingrid, who had raised this same boy and suffered the same heartache when he died. And finally, to Adam. When it backed away and rose up over Melinda and Josephine, I thought it might sever in two. But it didn't, it knew it didn't need to. It knew its new host was the perfect host, possibly the only one who could contain it. It had quite a flair for drama and it slowly passed right through Josephine, causing her to shudder and laugh, and then coiled up inside Melinda where its visible light gradually faded as it integrated itself into her being.

Melinda raised her hands over her head and gave a loud whoop and we all joined in. Whoops had never been done at one of these ceremonies and I believe we all approved.

A few days later, Adam, Melinda and I drove up to Ithaca to hear some music at an outdoor area in the downtown called the Commons. The three of us pushed into the center of a multi-aged crowd and danced and sang and rejoiced with the masses. When the band took a break, we began a slow walk along the edges of the Commons, looking into store windows and searching for some quick food. Adam stopped and stared at something. At first, Melinda and I didn't see it and then it— him, an ancient man—slid into focus. He sat on a dirty ripped towel on the concrete, his back against the wall, his skinny legs in ripped pants sticking out in front of him, his boney hand, held palm up, asking for money, and he broke my heart. I reached in my pocket for cash—a twenty, a hundred, I would have given him anything. Adam stopped me, bent down, and kissed the man on top of his head. The man stuck up his thumb, grinned so wide I thought his face would break, and said, "Good going, Adam." Then he faded away.

Acknowledgments

So much gratitude to parents, siblings and their partners, children, friends, and my wife, Virginia. I would also like to thank the kind members of the Between the Lines Publishing team for their support and encouragement.

Dan Yokum's work history has mostly centered around the visual arts: as a glass artist, a high school art teacher, and a graphic designer. However, he has always loved to write, and as a graphic designer, he often created and edited text for print and the web. Writing fiction is also in his blood, dating back to grade school, and over the last few years, he has transitioned to doing it full time. He grew up in and has recently moved back to a small college town in northern New York near the Canadian border, about an hour from Montreal. He spends his free time hiking, traveling, reading, listening to or playing music, and contemplating the nature of reality.